CW01066547

AGAINST ALL
THE ODDS

Lil Niven

*This book is dedicated to my husband Pete
and daughters Loraine, Elizabeth and Heather
whose encouragement has been invaluable.*

CHAPTER ONE

The Betrothal

"You WILL marry Lord de Luc my girl," bellowed Lord Thomas Marchemont of Holyfield Hall, as he thumped the table with his fist to emphasize the point. He was in no mood to brook any argument from the young woman sitting to his left at the small dining table.

His son Geoffrey was on his right and his wife Margaret sat opposite him. It was to Joan, his eighteen-year-old daughter, whom he spoke. She did not flinch even though the force of the blow almost upended his goblet. She stared at her father in utter disbelief that he could have made such an unexpected statement. When she found her voice again her hazel eyes, normally so soft and gentle, narrowed to a pair of cold, icy flints. "I would not marry that depraved old whore-monger if my life depended on it," she said very slowly and deliberately, never taking her eyes from her father's face.

Just moments before her father had told her that he was in the process of negotiating the marriage between her and Lord de Luc, one of the richest and most despised men at the Court of Queen Elizabeth. Joan, a lady-in-waiting to the queen, spent most of her time at court and knew first hand exactly the type of man de Luc was and the appalling reputation he had acquired since arriving in London a few months previously. Despite his disgraceful behaviour, his considerable wealth, coupled with an amazing sword skill which defied his advancing years, meant that few were prepared to challenge him. Those that were either brave or foolish enough to do so did rarely lived to tell the tale.

Regardless of her outward bravado, Joan had to fight back the tears threatening to overwhelm her. No! She would not cry in front of her mother and father, and especially not in front of her obnoxious brother. She would never give Geoffrey the satisfaction of seeing her weep again. When Joan was a little girl, he would tease her until she cried, laugh at her tears, and then tease her even more.

What on earth has possessed her father to betroth her to Lord de Luc of all people? Marriage to such a man was unthinkable. She would never marry him under any circumstances, regardless of her father's wishes to the contrary, and the fact that daughters were expected to defer to their parent's choice of spouse. Although she felt utterly betrayed by her father, she knew that as a dutiful daughter she would be expected to obey him. She would rather to be promised to the poorest, most destitute man in the kingdom than to the man her father had chosen to be her future husband. Why him? Her father was as far from de Luc's social circle as anyone could be. She'd never even seen them speak to each other on the few occasions they were at court at the same time. There were also many other men equal to her rank who would be eligible to ask for her hand. None of this made any sense at all.

Lord Marchemont and his family were in their small, private dining room which they preferred to the great hall when they weren't entertaining guests, more often than not these days. It was more intimate and much warmer in there too. The heat from the fire kept the room cosy even in the coldest of weather. The remnants of their meal had been cleared away and a fresh pitcher of wine had been left beside Lord Thomas by the last of the servants, before he withdrew leaving the family to their privacy. Thomas and his wife, Lady Margaret, sat facing each other in richly carved chairs. Their twenty-one-year-old son Geoffrey was sprawled on a bench with his back resting against the table, his long legs stretched out in front of him, ankles crossed.

Geoffrey was tall and surprisingly muscular considering his indolent lifestyle. His straight dark hair was almost shoulder length, and his equally dark beard was cut in the shorter fashion which was favoured by the young men of the court. He had a swarthy complexion and intensely dark brown eyes, which together gave him an alluring enigmatic presence he used to full effect to seduce any woman who reacted favourably to his outrageous flirting. However, Geoffrey's mood could change in the wink of an eye from being friendly, flirtatious and fun loving, to ruthless, brutal and sadistic if he didn't get what he wanted, something his conquests learned to their cost when the playful dalliance quickly turned into something more sinister.

Joan sat on the bench opposite her brother, clasping her hands together in her lap to stop them from shaking, and glared at Geoffrey's back. She was a little above average height for a woman and her small breasts and narrow hips gave her an almost boyish figure. Her rich, chestnut hair that tumbled in curls over her ivory skinned shoulders was the perfect frame for her elfin features. She had soft, hazel eyes which quite often twinkled with mischief and had a ready smile that lit up her pretty face whenever she was amused. Joan favoured her mother in looks whereas Geoffrey was more like his father had been as a young man.

She knew that her brother would be somehow connected to the disastrous tidings their father had presented, concerning her betrothal as Geoffrey had turned his back on her as soon as talk of the impending marriage began. Her thinking was correct. Unbeknownst to her she had suddenly become the answer to all his problems. How fortunate he was to have such a pretty sister, who had caught the attention of the extremely rich Lord de Luc. When the man had accosted him at the court and intimated that he wanted Joan, Geoffrey had assumed that he intended to seduce her and then discard her just as he had with all the other women and girls once he's tired of them. However, he was wrong. For some reason the old fool actually wanted to marry her.

Geoffrey wasted no time in impressing on his father the difference it would make to his present woeful circumstances if he could come to some agreement with de Luc. He couldn't keep the smile off his face. The result had been beyond his wildest dreams. All their financial difficulties gone at a stroke, and all Joan had to do was marry the old cretin. She wouldn't like it of course, but what the hell? She was still a young woman, and the old boy wasn't going to last forever, was he? Now it was just up to his father to force his stiff-necked sister to accept de Luc's offer.

Before Joan was able to give any more thought to what part Geoffrey had played in her present predicament, her attention was sharply brought back to Lord Thomas. "You will obey me in this!" he roared, his eyes bulging and his face turning crimson with rage.

She stared at her father, completely

thunderstruck. She had never seen her father so angry, so resolute. He'd lost patience with her before many times when she had crossed him trying to drive her argument home, but this outburst was something very different. What was compelling him to be so adamant?

The walls seemed to close in on her and she gripped the edge of the table to steady herself. She began to tremble. She couldn't breathe. Dear God, what was happening to her? She desperately tried to fight down the panic now slowly choking her. For the first time in her life her father frightened her. Her mind was in turmoil, her thoughts racing. Nothing made sense. How could her own father even consider such a man as Lord de Luc, knowing the kind of man he was, and how on earth could she change his mind? She silently prayed that God would provide the right words, but no words came. She couldn't think straight, she couldn't think at all.

Lord Thomas was looking at his daughter with his head slightly tilted to one side; when he raised an eyebrow, she knew he was waiting for her reply. She took a few deep breaths and tried to compose herself. "I will NOT marry that old profligate!" she replied with a confidence she certainly didn't feel.

Her father's furious expression made her fear he was about to strike her. She shrank back and pushed the bench a little from the table, but when her father made no move towards her, she quickly recovered herself. "He must be nearly three times my age!" she pleaded with him. "He's a predator who stalks women, married or otherwise. He finds his victims at the brothel or at the court, he doesn't care which as long as his carnal needs are met. This is the man that you want me to marry, Father. Even the queen's own ladies aren't safe. He molested me, Father, when he found me in a dimly lit corridor between the Great Hall and the queen's own apartments. What kind of life would I have married to him?"

However, instead of being outraged at the treatment his daughter had received, her father just continued to rave at her as if he hadn't heard a single word she'd said. Once again, he hammered the table with his fist. "You will do your duty as my daughter and do as I bid, or I will have you whipped until you do submit!" he shouted, shaking with such rage that his wife feared he would bring on a fit of apoplexy.

"As you will," said Joan quietly, "but it will be to the death, not submission, for I would rather die than wed that man."

Thomas turned his attention to his wife, who until now had been sitting silently in her chair listening to his tirade against Joan. "Woman, look what you've given me for a daughter!" he shouted, spittle dribbling from the corners of his mouth. "Defiance, lack of parental respect, wilfulness and complete disobedience! You have been most remiss in her upbringing, most remiss indeed."

Margaret looked up from her needlework, wondering just how she'd been remiss when she had been allowed so little involvement in the raising of her children. Tears pricking her eyes, she shook her head slowly and continued with her sewing. She had borne witness to these fiery confrontations between Joan and her father many times before, but usually once her daughter had dug her heels in, she got her own way. This time though it seemed certain that she would lose the battle and her father prevail.

While her father was berating her mother, Joan had a sudden thought. "Father, what do you propose to offer as a dowry? Geoffrey has gambled away or caused you to spend a large proportion of our fortune. Surely you can't afford what that horrible old man must be demanding out of what little you have left!" In desperation she clung to the hope that her father's inability to pay a large dowry would save her from a fate worse than death.

"That's the whole point, Joan. He is so besotted with you that he has promised to cover all of Geoffrey's gambling debts and pay off all my creditors if I will allow you to become his bride. He's a very rich man and can afford to buy you anything you could ever wish for. You would want for nothing!" said Thomas, triumphantly.

Joan looked at him in horror. Her heart was pounding in her breast, her hands began to shake again, and she felt a strong physical pain in the pit of her stomach. She jumped up from the table. "What! You have sold me to that ogre in order to pay your debts and keep my worthless brother out of prison. What kind of a hellish prison would you be condemning me to? Father, please don't do this. Do you care nothing for me at all? Please don't sentence me to a living hell with that debauched demon. There must be another way," she sobbed, as her shoulders slumped in despair.

Geoffrey finally turned and faced her. "Surely you wouldn't want to see your darling brother languishing in a cold, damp rat infested cell, would you sister dear?" he drawled, pulling a wry face.

The anger inside Joan erupted like the lava in a volcano, as she directed her full fury towards Geoffrey. "I certainly know who the biggest rat would be," she shouted. "And yes, I would if it would force you to take responsibility for your own actions instead of expecting others to do it for you, but there's little chance of that happening is there? You're just an arrogant, good-for-nothing wastrel and you will never be any different. You're a disgrace!"

Thomas and Margaret looked on, waiting to see what Geoffrey's response would be as both siblings had volatile tempers when riled and their frequent arguments were usually extremely fierce. Surprisingly, his reply was mild, but his sarcastic smile only made Joan irater. "I'm sure you don't mean all that, Joan," he said. "After all I am your brother."

"Don't speak to me, Geoffrey," she retorted. "I don't want to listen to any more of your lies or excuses."

Joan looked towards her mother, who quickly turned her attention back to the needlework on her lap. Margaret had guessed what her daughter was about to say but there was nothing she could say or do to make matters any different. "Surely you don't agree with what Father has done and what he expects me to do, do you, Mother?" Joan asked, in the vain hope she could enlist her mother as an ally against her father.

Margaret raised her head and looked into the tearful eyes of her daughter. She had never seen Joan so distressed and vulnerable before, and her heart ached for her. "I have no say in the matter my dear, just as my own mother had no say in the choice of whom I would marry," she answered. "It was my father's decision alone and was his will that I wed."

Margaret had been brought up to believe that her sole role in life was to be obedient to her parents, to marry for the benefit and advancement of her family and to be subservient to her husband. She now reflected on how much easier it would be for Joan if she had been raised in the same way, but her spirit had always been too strong to be broken and tamed as easily as Margaret's had. Might that be the very thing that had attracted Lord de Luc? Unfortunately, the poor girl was now suffering the consequences of being allowed to have her head too often.

"Did you hear that girl?" Thomas shouted, showing no signs of relenting. "It was her father's will, and this is mine. You will marry Lord de Luc and be grateful to have such a match!"

Joan realised that she was completely alone and with no idea of how to get out of this unholy predicament. She was still mentally searching for a solution when Geoffrey spoke again. "What exactly went on between you and that man in the passageway, Joan? It must have been something pretty spectacular for him to be willing to pay a king's ransom to get you into his bed," he sniggered. as he refilled his goblet.

"How dare you insinuate that I did anything to encourage that creature, Geoffrey!" she shouted back, her eyes blazing.

"Oh, come on, Joan, really. What does it matter who you marry? One man's much the same as another in the dark I should imagine. Just close your eyes and pretend he's someone else," Geoffrey laughed. He picked up his goblet and mockingly saluted her. "All a man wants is sons. Once you've produced them your duty's done and then you can do what you like with whomever you choose as long as you don't let the old man catch you." He winked at his father, who smiled back at him.

"Oh, shut up, Geoffrey!" Jane yelled, inwardly shuddering at the mental image of what she would have to go through to conceive these sons. She knew her brother didn't care a fig about what happened to her, just as long as he could carry on his rakish life unhindered. She also knew that in no time he would be up to his neck in debt again. What then? Would he and their father expect de Luc to still keep paying or maybe hope that he would soon die thus allowing them possession of his fortune, while they looked for another rich old man to marry her off to? "The only man I will marry will be the man I can love and respect above all other men!" she stated defiantly, and, sitting down again, took a drink from her untouched goblet.

"My God, you'll have a long wait then, won't you," smirked her brother.

Joan threw her remaining wine into Geoffrey's smug face and swept from the room, ignoring her father's command to stay.

Geoffrey leapt to his feet, dabbing at his precious doublet with his lace kerchief. "Damn the woman!" he cursed and picked up his hat and cloak. "Father, you need to bring her under control quickly. She needs a sound beating and I am just the man to do it if you can't" He then stormed out of the parlour, slamming the door behind him.

"For God's sake woman, go and talk some sense into the girl," snapped Thomas. "If she doesn't marry Lord de Luc, we're all done for."

Margaret gathered her needlework, rose from her chair and without a word followed her children, quietly closing the door behind her. On her way to Joan's room, she heard Geoffrey's horse leaving the courtyard at speed. No doubt the boy was on his way to meet some of his disreputable friends.

When Margaret reached Joan's door, she could hear her daughter sobbing. She knocked on the door gently and although she got no response, she opened the door and went inside.

Her daughter was lying on her bed, crying into her pillow. Even in her wretched state, Joan was a very beautiful young woman. Though not dressed as richly or immaculately as Geoffrey, her clothes as a queen's lady were still of the highest quality; Joan kept her expenditure on her attire to a bare minimum, fully aware of her father's financial difficulties. Had Thomas any idea of how much his daughter cared? How could he be so cruel?

She sat on the side of Joan's bed and took her daughter's hand. "Oh, my poor child! I don't know what I can say to make it better."

Joan slowly turned over and sat up. She looked at her mother for a few seconds with wet eyes and tear-stained cheeks before she threw her arms around her. They stayed in that position for the next few minutes, each sobbing into the other's shoulder.

"My dear, dear Joan, you have no idea just how many times I have wanted to put my arms around you and hug you like any normal mother, but I wasn't allowed to," Margaret said. Both of her babies had been put into the charge of nannies and nursemaids almost immediately after their birth. The only times they were all together as a complete family, was on High Days and Holy Days, and even then, only for a few hours. Thomas didn't like her to spend time with anyone else but him and demanded her full attention.

The biggest regret of Margaret's life was not having been permitted to demonstrate to her children, just how much she loved them. Whenever she had suggested spending time with the children, she had been told in no uncertain terms that her place was at Thomas's side, and that her children were being well looked after without any interference from her by the people employed to do so. Her husband had been strict and overbearing from the moment she had become his wife and she had never been able to find the courage to stand up to him. She was soon made aware of his quick temper and had been frightened of what the consequences would be if she should ever cross him.

So, Margaret played no part in the children's upbringing. Thomas alone had chosen their tutors and when they weren't being taught in the school room or studying, they were attended to by a governess and the servants. When Joan reached the age when a daughter would normally confide with her mother, she shared all her hopes, aspirations and fears with her governess, because she believed her mother wasn't interested.

Joan now pulled away from her mother and held her hands. "Mother, I can't marry Lord de Luc even though I know that if I refuse, terrible things might happen to Father and Geoffrey. But I just can't. I was never so terrified in my whole life as I was when that vile man caught me in the corridor." Her voice became thick with emotion as she relived the horrifying encounter. "He grabbed hold of my wrist as he passed me going in the opposite direction, spun me around until his ugly face was only inches away from my own and then he tried to kiss me. I was so shocked, Mother, I haven't even met a man yet that I would even allow to kiss me, but this evil man was attempting to force himself on me. I couldn't believe what was happening. He is so arrogant that he believes that he can even accost a queen's lady without fear of retribution."

As Joan began to sob again, Margaret squeezed her daughter's hand gently and waited for her to compose herself. Joan soon carried on, "His stinking breath was so overpowering that I almost wretched as he drooled though his rotten teeth. He gripped me so tightly that I could hardly breathe and his free hand was all over my body. When I tried to call for help, he planted his filthy mouth on top of mine. My flesh crawled and I felt so dirty, Mother."

Margaret put her arm around Joan's shoulders and squeezed her hand again.

"I tried to fight him off, but he was too strong," Joan told her. "The more I struggled the closer he held me. He only let me go when a servant appeared and then he crept off into the shadows before he could be recognised. I am positive that if he hadn't been disturbed, that despicable man would have raped me! How could I ever marry a man like that! Life with him would be a living nightmare."

"I know, my darling girl," her mother said. When Joan began to weep again, she pulled Joan closer to her breast.

Meanwhile, alone in the parlour, Thomas turned his chair towards the fire and refilled his goblet. He stared into the flames and cast his mind back to when his son has been born and to how proud he had been. His son had been baptised Geoffrey after his maternal great grandsire and not Thomas after his own father, which was the custom. This was in honour of the role Geoffrey St John had played in Thomas's life. St John's ancestors had crossed the sea with Duke William in 1066 and he had been rewarded with rich lands and many manors in England when William was crowned King. Thomas's grandfather had taken a keen interest in him from the earliest years and had visited the manor house whenever his duties allowed. When the time came for Thomas to begin his training to become a knight, his grandfather arranged for one of his friends in the peerage to take him on as his squire. After his knighthood was conferred, his grandfather gifted him a sword made by one of the finest craftsmen in England. It was one of his few remaining treasured possessions.

Although Geoffrey had been given St John's name, his character bore no resemblance to that of his revered and well-loved great-grandfather. He had been born after a surprisingly easy labour, a strong baby with a thatch of dark hair like his father. When Thomas stood beside the crib and his son gripped his finger in his tiny fist, he would look down at the child and try to imagine Geoffrey as a man. He saw a strong, honourable and brave knight; also, a clever, well-educated man with a sharp business acumen. A man more than capable of running the vast estate when his father handed over the reins to him.

However, as the boy grew, it soon became apparent that Geoffrey was not going to be the son that his father had dreamed of. He never had any interest in learning anything in the schoolroom. He considered it a complete waste of time and used every excuse he could think of to explain his absence from his lessons. His tutors despaired. Even the threat of the direst punishment had failed to deter his habitual truancy. Instead of studying with Joan, he had spent the time he should have been using on his education creating mischief and mayhem with his friends in the villages and hamlets on his father's huge estate. He was a lazy, deceitful gambling rake, who was willing to do anything no matter how low and dishonourable to get his own way. He treated the servants shamefully, flying in to rages and lashing out over the slightest infringement. When he was just fifteen years old, he compromised on of the youngest kitchen maids who had been sent to the stables to look for any stray eggs that the hens may have laid there. When the girl was later found to be pregnant, she was sent away in disgrace. Geoffrey, of course, denied all knowledge of the affair.

He had learned how to ride at a young age as had Joan and he had been trained how to use a variety of weapons, as all young men of his rank would be expected to do. He had become very proficient in their use but had shown little appetite to put the skill to good use. The only interest he had ever shown in his father's estate, was how much he could get out of it and with how little effort. He had begun to gamble with his friends when still a young man, and even those wagers had cost his father considerable amounts of money.

Thomas knew he should have put a stop to his son's expensive pastime then and there, but he indulged him in the hope that when he grew out of adolescence, he would become more responsible with his wagering. This was not to be the case. When Geoffrey came to court his gambling became a real problem. Despite all his father's threats to cut him off and leave him to fend for himself, the situation just got worse. Soon Thomas had found himself having to pay huge gambling debts to keep his son out of prison.

The boy was also a womaniser. More than once his father had been forced to pay large amounts of compensation to irate parents whose daughters had been molested or worse. The situation had become so grim that Thomas was now having to sell off large tracts of his land to raise the cash to make good Geoffrey's promissory notes. Even though he knew the most sensible thing would be to disown his son and cast him off, his stubborn pride wouldn't allow him to do that. However, misguided his thinking, Geoffrey was his only son and heir and he was the only person able to carry forward the proud Marchemont name and prevent it from disappearing into obscurity.

He had just finished topping up his goblet when his wife entered the room quietly. She had sat with Joan until she had fallen asleep, exhausted by the ordeal she had recently undergone with her father. Margaret had turned her own chair towards the fire beside Thomas and sat down, refusing his offer of a drink.

"Well, did you manage to impress upon her why this betrothal is imperative?" he demanded. Having witnessed Joan's impassioned outburst at his announcement, he already knew what his wife's answer would be.

"She is adamant that she will never marry that man and has threatened to kill herself rather than to be forced to wed him. Husband, I believe she means every word. You know as well as I how strong willed she is," replied Margaret.

"But did you not explain to her that if she refuses, we will all be ruined? Holyfield and what's left of the estate would have to be sold and even that would only cover part of the debts we owed. Geoffrey and I would be thrown into the debtors' prison, and you would be out on the street with nothing! Joan wouldn't fare much better as I doubt her majesty would want a bankrupt's daughter serving her! She has no choice! She must marry him!"

Margaret stared at the man who had completely dominated her life for over twenty years and took a deep breath. "What about Joan? What kind of existence would her life be with that man? You are a man, and you know full well what kind of man he is! Are you really willing to give our beautiful daughter to a wretch like that knowing what he will do to her? How can you be so cruel and heartless?"

"Don't you dare lecture me woman! I must do what is best for all of us and I have made my decision. I will not change my mind!" answered Thomas angrily.

"Then you must live with that burden on your conscience for the rest of your life! I will never forgive you and neither will Joan and nor will her sacrifice make one bit of difference to the behaviour of our ingrate of a son!" retorted Margaret.

Thomas was stunned. His demure and obedient wife had never argued with him once during their entire married life. She glared at him, hatred and disgust filling her eyes. It shook him to the core. Without even excusing herself or waiting to be dismissed, she left him alone with his thoughts once more.

Thomas turned towards the fire. What an unholy mess he had made of everything. Instead of allowing his unruly son to run wild and unabated he should have acted at the very beginning to bring Geoffrey back under his control before he was entirely out of hand. Now it was far too late. His son had completely ruined him. He was backed into a corner with only one way out. His wife hated him, and his daughter? He dared not even try to imagine what his daughter must think of him at the moment.

Joan had been born three years after her brother and the birth couldn't have been more different. It followed a very painful and protracted labour which had almost cost Margaret her life. There were no more pregnancies after Joan. As Thomas watched his daughter develop, he had lost count of the number of times he wished that she had been his son. She was everything Geoffrey was not: strong willed, courageous, well educated, decisive, honest and although kind-hearted, she didn't suffer fools lightly.

Joan was a headstrong girl who did not bow to convention easily. She rode astride like a man and wore breeches when riding. She rode out with a groom as her maid could not keep up on her docile mare. She could ride any horse as well as any man and liked nothing better than to be charging through the countryside at breakneck speed. She had the perfect partner in the Arabian courser Thomas had bought her for when she finished her education. When he queried why she had named the mare Caesar, she said it was because the horse had the heart of a stallion. She beat her brother every time they raced against each other, at which Geoffrey often flew into a temper and tried to hit her with his riding whip.

Joan had been educated with Geoffrey at home. It was unusual for a girl to be instructed in anything other than the genteel pastimes of a lady, but Thomas had hoped that sibling rivalry would encourage her brother to apply himself to his studies. She could read, write, and speak

French fluently, as well as a little Spanish. She translated Latin and Greek effortlessly and had a good grasp of arithmetic and rhetoric. She excelled in everything she did, and in addition to her academic accomplishments she could sing, dance, and play the lute. Her needlework was also of the highest quality.

Towards the end of her formal education, one of her tutors introduced her to Protestantism. Joan had known of its existence but coming from a Catholic family she had been shielded from it. Although not a staunch Catholic himself, Thomas still disapproved of his daughter's disaffection, but had decided to let her go her own way until it became more certain which of the two religions would triumph in the ongoing battle. But what did all that matter now? She was to be married, become Lord de Luc's property and be bound to his will. How could he have allowed it to come to this?

Thomas turned his chair towards the table again and as he did, so he caught sight of the portraits of his ancestors, which were hanging around the walls of the parlour. Proud men all of them, who had brought honour and riches to the name of Marchemont. God, what would they think of him? What would his mother think of what he had allowed to happen to the vast estate that she had nurtured and built up to be the largest in the county? What would she say about him selling, yes selling, his own daughter, her granddaughter, to try to rectify things?

He already knew the answer—disgust and shame that a Marchmont could have allowed himself to get into such a position and then sink so low to get out of it!

Thomas sighed deeply before he drained his goblet and refilled it with what was left in the pitcher. His eyes alighted on the small portrait hanging above the mantle and smiled. The face of a young King Henry VIII, before he turned into the monster he became in his later years, looked back at him. Thomas had tried to emulate the young king's prowess on the jousting field, as soon as he had learned to handle his weapons. Henry's skill was legendary, and he was determined to match it. After receiving his knighthood, he went back to Devon to learn all he could from his mother in order to run his estate when the time came, rather than to attend Henry's court.

After Henry died, Thomas joined Edward VI's court and quickly made a name for himself on the jousting field. It was at a joust sponsored by the young king that he had beaten all the challengers and had received as his reward a hefty purse and the small picture which he treasured. Edward knew how much Thomas admired Henry's mastery of the art of jousting and had given him the picture from his own collection. Maybe he had become too complacent after Edward's great joust because his next one was his last. He met his nemesis and sustained injuries so severe that he was forced to retire from all physical pursuits. He had been blinded in one eye and left with a permanent limp and a twisted knee, which prevented him from riding at any more than a very gentle gait.

Thomas married Margaret when he was twenty-eight years old. She was a quiet, shy and very plain sixteen-year-old. Her only redeeming feature was her mop of chestnut curls that fell around her small face. However, she brought with her as part of her dowry a huge tract of land that lay adjacent to her estate, and that was much more important to him than what his bride looked like. By the time he was thirty Thomas was very rich in fortune and property.

But then circumstances brought about a big change to his life. His mother died, the Protestant Elizabeth was on the throne, and it was becoming difficult for Catholics to flourish at her court. It was also now that Margaret announced that she was with child. He decided it would be safer for them to retire to his estate in Devon, where he continued to run his estate as successfully as his mother had. As he thought back, he was brought face to face with how large and successful his estate was then, compared with the pathetic remnants he was left with now. How different things could have been. How could two offspring born to the same parents be so opposite? Why couldn't Geoffrey be more like

Joan? Why couldn't Joan have been the son? Dear God life was so unfair! Now he was being forced to sacrifice his most precious possession of all, his beautiful young daughter, to save his name, his worthless son, and what was left of his estate. There was no alternative, and it was tearing him apart. He had no choice but to allow Lord de Luc to marry Joan or he would lose everything.

"Damn Geoffrey! Damn him to hell!" he cursed and gulped down his remaining wine.

CHAPTER TWO

The Summons

Richard, only child of Sir Edmund Lovell and his wife Eleanor, was in his office on the quayside in the sheltered harbour of Topsham, a few miles downriver from Exeter. He was a tall, fair-haired, athletically built young man with an easy smile and kind blue eyes. His hair was short, and he sported a short beard and moustache. He was dressed in a plain shirt under a leather doublet, breeches and a pair of muddy riding boots. His sodden cloak was draped over one stool and his wet hat was perched on another.

He was the sole surviving child of his parents' marriage. Their first-born son, a sickly child, had died at a few weeks old just days after being baptised as Edmund. Two years later Eleanor was hesitant about her second son being named Edmund as well in case she lost him too, even though he was a strong, healthy infant. His parents therefore named him Richard for no other reason than they liked it. A third son was stillborn one year later after which Eleanor never fell pregnant again. This meant that Richard was very precious to his parents. Yet despite that he had not been spoiled as a child.

Until he was seven years old Richard lived with his parents at their manor on his father's estate, a gift to Edmund from the queen herself. It was barely a day's ride from Exeter and about an hour on horseback from Topsham. Richard was taught the basics of reading and writing by the same local clergyman who, some years earlier, had taught his father. However, it had not been all work and no play for the young Richard. His father bought him his first pony when Richard was just three years old; Richard never forgot that day, he was so excited. His father led him and his pony round and round the courtyard until Richard could stay upright in his saddle without being held. He was born to ride and was soon proficient enough to be allowed to ride out, weather permitting, with the head groom across his father's estate. As he grew older, he was able to ride bigger and stronger horses. It became one of his greatest enjoyments in life and never more so than on those rare occasions when his father was at home, and they rode out together.

It was during this time that Richard developed his lifelong love of the outdoors. At the age of seven he graduated to the grammar school in Exeter where he continued his studies until he was fourteen years old. The school was financed by the local guilds and although his father was a prominent member of the wool merchant's guild it didn't guarantee Richard any special privileges. He lived at his father's town house during this time and was looked after by his father's servants and his steward, John, who acted as Richard's father figure when Edmund was away, which was frequently. There was always work for Edmund to do at the manor or at the docks, keeping him away for weeks at a time. But his business for the guild usually took place in Exeter, and that was when Edmund was able to spend time with his son; they both enjoyed it immensely. Edmund would have liked to have spent more time with Richard during this crucial period of his childhood, but the success of the business demanded Edmund's full attention for it to continue.

Richard had been a diligent pupil and worked hard at his lessons. Although he wasn't brilliant academically, he was popular with the masters as well as his fellow students, especially Will Perceval. A year older than Richard, Will had taken Richard under his wing during those first few difficult weeks when Richard needed to adjust to life away from the security of the manor and his mother. He had an insatiable appetite for learning, was a star pupil and well qualified for graduation to Cambridge when the time came. The boys remained close friends throughout their school years and when Will left to go to university to read law they vowed to keep in touch. However, as with most promises of this kind it wasn't kept and it would be quite some time into the future before the two friends met again, under the most unexpected of circumstances.

When Richard reached the age of fourteen his formal education was complete, and he left the grammar school with a good grounding in the basic subjects. He had left the manor as a little boy and returned as a young man. Throughout his time away he had only seen his mother for short periods during what few holidays he was allowed, so Eleanor was delighted to have him back. He was already taller than his father and very fit and strong, thanks to his regular horse-riding routine. Now his most important education was about to begin and there was no better teacher than his father.

Edmund's sheep farming and shipping businesses had both grown steadily while his son was away at school, thanks to his keen business sense and attention to detail, and were now too big for him to handle alone. He had many men working for him but now he needed someone beside him at the helm to share the burden and that someone was going to be his son. Richard was eager to learn everything his father could teach him, and he did so quickly and diligently. Edmund steered him towards the shipping side, in line with Richard's interests, which allowed Edmund to concentrate on his wool trade.

Richard proved himself to be a very competent businessman under his father's supervision. By the time he reached eighteen his father was satisfied that Richard was capable of running part of the business by himself. Edmund gave Richard full control of all the shipping while he continued to oversee the sheep farming and the running of the estate. The fleeces from their large flocks were exported to the continent and cloth, dried fruit, wine and other commodities were brought back on the return trip. It served as a very successful, money-making business.

Because Richard spent a lot of his time on or around the docks, he was taught how to handle his sword very effectively by one of the best master swordsmen in the country, Master Guilliano. It was wise to be able to defend yourself adequately and for people to be aware of the fact. Drunken sailors could be very unpredictable and violent, and the dock area and the taverns were rife with them; the results of some of the drunken brawls were hauled out of the river regularly. Richard knew every one of the sailors who worked on his ships but that left a great many he didn't and a good proportion of them had less than desirable characters.

On the day in question Richard was reviewing the plans for an ocean-going ship with local shipbuilder, Ralph Long. Ralph was one of the best shipwrights in the business and Richard and his father had been delighted when the man agreed to take charge of the building of their first large ship. He hadn't come cheap, but the standard of his work meant the extra was money well spent. Ralph wasn't a very tall man but was as strong as an ox. He had a mop of black hair and a beard and moustache to match which gave him the look of a wild man. Far from being a savage, he was a very intelligent and astute man who commanded respect from everyone who worked under him as well as those who employed him. He demanded that all his workers put in a fair day's work for their pay and those caught slacking discovered to their cost what penalty they faced for defaulting. Well paid work was hard to find so most kept to their task.

Richard used shallow-drafted ships to ferry cargo to and from the continent because they were easier to sail up and down the river and could be used close to shore when necessary. However, his father could see the prospect of making good profits by trading with the colonies which were now emerging in the New World. There would be a great demand for goods from England and he was sure there would be plenty to fill the hold for the return voyage. After much discussion, and the weighing up of all the pros and cons along with some complex financial calculations, Richard and his father had decided it was worth the risk to commission the building of an ocean-going ship.

It was a huge undertaking and involved a large investment, not all of which was their own. Because of the amount of capital involved, every detail of the fabrication was closely scrutinized. Sir Edmund wanted the ship ready for its maiden voyage before the onset of the winter storms. During his meeting with Ralph Long, Richard was pleased to see that the project was progressing according to plan, without incurring any extra costs. Barring any unforeseen incidents, the ship would be completed on time.

An urgent knocking on the door disturbed their meeting. "Come in!" shouted Richard, still leaning over the plans laid out on the table in front of him.

The door swung open and in strode a man splattered with mud from head to foot. The rain dripping from the brim of his hat was running down his dirty face, leaving clean streaks in their wake, and the water pouring from his saturated cloak soon created a puddle on the floor. "I'm looking for Richard Lovell," he panted, looking at each man in turn.

"I am he," answered Richard, straightening.

"I have an urgent message for you from London sir," said the man. He walked across the room towards Richard, leaving small puddles in his wake, and handed him a letter from the leather pouch he'd retrieved from inside his cloak. Richard stared at the rain-soaked young man as he took the letter from him; he was almost dead on his feet. Who would have sent someone traveling all the way from London to Topsham in such haste and in such dreadful weather conditions just to deliver a letter to him? There had been weeks of almost continual rain and many routes were impassable and those that weren't very difficult to travel.

"My horse and I need to rest before we return to London, sir," said the messenger, trying to wipe some of the mud from his face with the back of his hand. "Can you recommend a decent tavern?"

Richard was staring at the seal on the back of the letter. He had seen that seal before on correspondence his father had received from London.

"A tavern please sir?" the rider asked again, his drenched cloak still dripping water onto the floor.

"A tavern?" repeated Richard absently and dragged his eyes away from the letter. "Oh yes, a tavern," he said giving his full attention to the man at last. "There's a reputable one called The Bush at the end of the street. Tell them I sent you and you'll be well looked after." Richard waved the letter in the air. "What about the reply?"

"My orders were to deliver the letter and that was all, sir," said the messenger. He was already looking forward to a good, hot meal and a decent bed before he had to begin his miserable return journey to London in the same frightful conditions, he'd ridden through to get here. He consoled himself with the thought that his journey home would be a lot more leisurely than the one he'd just completed. He saluted and was gone as quickly as he'd arrived.

Ralph had been watching the event with interest and was waiting for Richard to open the letter, but Richard had no intention of sharing its contents. He returned to the plans on the table, folded them carefully and handed them back to Ralph. "I think we're finished here," he said. He then walked across the room and opened the door. "I'll come to the yard tomorrow."

At this dismissal Ralph reluctantly wrapped the papers in a waterproof pouch. He would have loved to know what was in that letter, but Richard stood at the door waiting for him, so Ralph left the office, holding the pouch above his head as he ran the short distance to the shipyard through the pouring rain.

Richard closed the door and examined the seal on his letter again, "Why on earth would Sir Francis Walsingham, the queen's spymaster, be writing to me," he thought. He knew his father had dealings with Walsingham and with Sir William Cecil, the queen's secretary, when he needed new passports or licenses for his continental trade, but he himself had never met either of the men. However, this letter was clearly addressed to 'Richard' Lovell. Richard turned the letter over once more and then broke the seal.

He quickly scanned the contents. "Dear God! What is this all this about?" he said and re-read the short note again. *It is imperative that you come to see me immediately. You must tell no one you are coming to London and your journey must be undertaken with the utmost secrecy. I cannot over stress the urgency of this command.* The word "command" was underlined, and the letter was signed by Walsingham himself.

To refuse to go would be commercial suicide, given that many of his father's business ventures were dependent on official co-operation from the palace—never more so than now when he was about to begin his trans-ocean trading. But what was so important that Sir Francis Walsingham required his presence in London so urgently and so secretly? Richard had never even been to London in his life or had any dealings with Walsingham and how could he just drop everything and leave for London when he was up to his neck with his work here? There must be some terrible mistake.

But almost as quickly as he had the thought, Richard dismissed it. He knew that a man in Walsingham's position didn't make that kind of mistake. Richard also knew, despite his misgivings, that he had no alternative but to comply with Walsingham's instructions and go to London without delay. He carefully put the letter into the pocket of his jerkin, donned his wet hat and cloak and left the office locking the door behind him.

Richard walked the few hundred yards to The Bush, deep in thought. It was still raining but he hardly noticed. He wished his father was in Topsham so that he could seek his advice and ask him if he could throw any light on the reason for Walsingham's missive, but Edmund had left his manor several days ago to attend an important guild meeting in Exeter. Richard could send his father a message or even go himself, but then Walsingham had insisted on speed and complete secrecy. If he followed his father, how long would it take in this weather to get there and back? Would the extra time make much difference? How the hell would he know when he didn't have any idea what the emergency was!

Richard couldn't make any sense of it at all. Everything had happened so out of the blue that his usual calm, measured approach to sudden unforeseen situations seemed to have temporarily deserted him. He was completely mystified. Why did Walsingham want *him* to go to London? Why him and not his father? The whole situation was ridiculous! Richard thought again about ignoring the summons but quickly ousted the idea. Who knew what the repercussions might be if he disobeyed such an important a man as Sir Francis Walsingham?

By the time Richard reached the tavern he

realised he had no alternative but to comply. He ran up the stairs to the room he kept for when he was in Topsham, packed a few clothes and other essentials into his saddlebags, made sure he had enough money in his purse for the journey, and left by the back door. He headed across the deserted courtyard to the stables where he kept his stallion, Diablo. Within an hour of receiving Walsingham's summons and without a word of explanation to anyone, Richard was in the saddle and on his way to London.

It was still pouring with rain as he made his way along the road leading out of the village. The water that ran down the hill towards the river over the already saturated ground had turned the narrow street into little more than a bog. No one saw him leave Topsham as the streets were almost empty, and those who were about were far more intent on getting out of the rain than taking note of who was riding by.

Once he had left the village behind and reached the open country, Richard focused his mind on the mystery of Walsingham's directive. It must be something connected with the business and if that was the case surely it should be his father who received Walsingham's letter, not him. What else could it be? Richard wrapped his cloak around himself even more tightly and pulled his hat down further. Would this damn rain never stop? Diablo was an intelligent, sure-footed steed and was making remarkably good progress through the quagmire that the roads had become after the incessant rain of the previous weeks but even Diablo was unable to go any faster than a trot. It was going to be a long and difficult journey to reach London at all, let alone as quickly as Walsingham had demanded.

Horse and rider picked their way carefully through the many small streams running across the roads from fields ploughed and planted with seed, ready for the next harvest. There had been a poor harvest last year because of the unusually wet autumn and many of the poorest people had starved to death over the winter months. The Catholics were proclaiming it as 'the wrath of God' because England had broken away from the Pope and the True Church, but Richard did not subscribe to that reasoning as there had been many other failed harvests in years gone by before the reign of Henry VIII. What wasn't in doubt was that another bad harvest would cause untold suffering to a population already ravaged with hunger and disease.

As they progressed Richard relaxed a little and began to think back over recent events for anything that might shed any light onto why Walsingham had sent for him. Some months earlier he had been riding through a large forest on a huge tract of land his father had purchased adjacent to their estate, when he heard raised voices followed by vulgar laughter. Edging a little closer to the sound, he'd peered through the trees and seen Geoffrey Marchemont and his two disgusting friends, Anthony Dryden and Robert Fiske. They were accosting a pretty girl working in the field with some other peasants. Geoffrey was leaning from his horse trying to steal a kiss; when the lass refused, he jumped from his horse, grabbed her by the waist, pulled her towards him and kissed he roughly. A man working a little further up the field from the girl suddenly ran towards Geoffrey, brandishing his pitchfork. "Let her go!" he shouted.

"Really," sneered Geoffrey. He turned to face the man. "And who the hell might you be?"

"She's, my wife. Leave her be!" yelled the young man.

Geoffrey menacingly drew his dagger. "And if I don't?"

Undeterred, the young husband kept advancing. Fearing their friend was about to get skewered, Geoffrey's two companions jumped from their horses, took hold of the man and forced him to drop his pitchfork just before he reached Geoffrey and the terrified girl. The rest of the field workers looked on in horror as Geoffrey laughed and began dragging the screaming girl towards the bushes.

This wasn't the first time Geoffrey had appeared in the fields and helped himself to a pretty girl. Men had been maimed before now by him or one of his friends for trying to protect their womenfolk. When one peasant threatened to go to Lord Thomas for redress, his cottage was mysteriously burnt to the ground.

The girl's frantic husband desperately tried to free himself from his captors. "Don't fret so," Geoffrey shouted over his shoulder. "You'll get your turn, but you'll have to wait until my friends and I are done with her first."

The two men holding the girl's husband laughed along with Geoffrey as they gripped the struggling man even tighter.

By now Richard had seen and heard enough. He touched his mount's flanks gently with his spurs and Diablo responded immediately. They bounded out of the trees behind Anthony and Robert who were now having to fight very hard indeed to restrain the demented young husband who could see what was about to happen to his wife and desperate to prevent it. A startled Geoffrey spun round to face Richard while still maintaining his grip on the struggling girl. "What the hell are you doing on Marchemont property?" he demanded.

"This is not Marchemont property anymore. Your father has sold it to mine and therefore it is you and your friends who are the trespassers, not me," said Richard.

Geoffrey was furious. "My father had no right to sell this land. It's part of my inheritance. Why would he sell it to your father? This is part of a lord's estate and certainly not for the likes of you and yours. You're peasants!" he roared. In an effort to emphasize his superior rank and to wrong foot Richard, he demanded to know how a "peasant" like him came to be riding such a magnificent black stallion. "The only way you could be in possession of such a fine horse is to have stolen it," Geoffrey said. He glanced across at his two friends, who readily agreed.

Geoffrey had recognized the horse immediately as the one he had lost in a race some weeks ago. He'd been drunk when he made the bet and was far from sober for the race. At the off he had cruelly dug his spurs into his horse who then leapt forward with such force that Geoffrey had fallen off. He had been a laughingstock but even that humiliation hadn't galled him as much as seeing his prized mount in Richard's hands.

By chance Edmund had been witness to the fiasco and, after Geoffrey stormed away cursing his rotten luck, Edmund had approached the winner of the horse and persuaded him to sell the handsome beast. Sir Edmund then gave the horse to his son as a gift.

"I'll have you hanged as a horse thief," Geoffrey now threatened.

"Knowing the kind of man you are my father suspected that this situation might arise at some point and gave me the bill of sale which I keep here," said Richard, tapping his pocket.

Before Geoffrey could react, the girl, who was still trying to wriggle free from his grasp, bit the back of his hand. He spun her around to face him and struck her hard. As her legs crumpled under her, Geoffrey gripped her waist again and continued to drag her into the undergrowth. The girl's spouse renewed his efforts to break free from his captors as Richard leapt from his horse and drew his sword.

When Geoffrey realized that Richard was coming at him with sword drawn, he released the girl. She sank to the ground, sobbing loudly, while Geoffrey drew his own sword and turned to face his adversary. Marchemont's friends hurried over to join Geoffrey, drawing their own swords as they did so.

The girl's husband lifted her to her feet and embraced her tenderly, thankful that she was relatively unharmed and unmolested. Once Richard was satisfied that the man and his wife were safely reunited, he returned his attention to Geoffrey. "Leave this place now and take these men with you," he said, pointing to Anthony and Robert with the tip of his sword.

"And if I refuse, you will do precisely what?" taunted Geoffrey. He knew that the odds were overwhelmingly in his favour. But before Richard could reply, the rest of the peasants, who had been following what was happening closely, now left the field and formed a half circle around the three antagonists brandishing their tools. Here was a man who was prepared to stand against young Marchmont and his friends and they weren't about to let him be murdered in front of them.

"I think you should take your horses and leave before there's any more trouble," said Richard his sword still pointing at Geoffrey. The girl's husband had retrieved his pitchfork and was now standing menacingly beside Richard, his fork raised towards Geoffrey.

Geoffrey pointedly surveyed each peasant's face in turn. "You'll all pay dearly for threatening the son of a peer of the realm. I'll see you all hanged and be damned to Hell!" he promised.

They held their ground and continued to wave their pitchforks and scythes.

Geoffrey realised that the odds had now shifted in Richard's favour and being a coward, slid his sword back into its scabbard. His friends, disappointed that they had been deprived of their sport, did likewise, gathered their horses and remounted. When Geoffrey had climbed into the saddle he leaned down towards Richard, still holding his sword, and in a voice that only Richard could hear whispered, "The next time we meet I will make sure you are alone, no witnesses, and we will finish this."

Richard said nothing but met the malevolent look in Geoffrey's eyes with an unwavering stare. Geoffrey looked away, spurred his horse on, blew a kiss towards the girl and galloped off.

Richard watched the three men disappear over the field before sheathing his sword. After reassuring the peasants that Geoffrey had no authority on Sir Edmund's land and therefore no grounds on which to claim any kind of retribution against them, he remounted Diablo. The field workers thanked him once again for his intervention and with a wave Richard returned to his task of surveying his father's new acquisition.

Surely his encounter with Geoffrey Marchemont couldn't be the reason he was now being ordered to London. He had done nothing wrong—Marchemont was the guilty one. No, surely Sir Francis had more important things to attend to than to interest himself in such trivia. It must be something else. But what? Could it be to do with something that had happened even further back? Something concerning his father perhaps? But if it was something to do with his father, why was it him that had been summoned?

As Richard continued on his way, by now thoroughly soaked to the skin, he began to think over some of the things his father had told him when he was younger. When Richard's grandfather had died, Edmund, being the eldest son, had taken his father's place as the head of the family. He'd done so on one of the larger farms still being worked on the estate, adjacent to that of the Marchemonts, and continued to care for his mother until she died peacefully in her sleep not long after his father. His younger sister, Anne, had fallen in love with a visiting farmer's son who had come to discuss buying some of Edmund ewes and one of his rams. After more visits the boy asked for permission to marry Anne and the two moved into the lad's home with his parents. His younger brother, Gilbert, was already almost as proficient in sheep farming as Edmund and left to take on a rented farm in Yorkshire. Edmund had been courting Eleanor for a while by this time and once his family left his farm to begin their own lives, he finally asked her to marry him.

Many landowners had recognized the profitability of sheep farming and the owner of Edmund's father's farm was no exception. Farmland was increasingly being turned over to grazing for sheep. Many peasants had been turned out of their homes and left to fend for themselves as best they could as they were no longer required to work the land. It only took one or two shepherds to care for hundreds of sheep. Edmund's father, too old himself to adapt to the new ways but eager to keep his farm, had seen the way that sheep farming was developing. He sent Edmund to learn as much as he could from the shepherds and breeders on the most profitable farms in the district. By the time Edmund took over the farm from his father he was already proficient in spotting the best ewes for breeding and introducing good new stock into the flocks to ensure the best quality fleeces.

It was while he was visiting another farmer in

Hertfordshire, with a view to buying two of his best rams, that Edmund met the then Princess Elizabeth.

She had been commanded by her half-sister, Queen Mary, to come to London without delay. The princess was at Ashridge, Hertfordshire and was so disturbed when she received the royal summons that she sent a message claiming that she was too ill to travel. She understood only too well that if she went to London her life would be in grave danger. Mary was a staunch Catholic determined to return England to the Roman Catholic faith under the control of the Pope. Elizabeth had been brought up as a Protestant, the new faith which had been championed by her half-brother, the late King Edward VI and it was the only faith she knew. Many people at Mary's court regarded Elizabeth as a threat to the queen after a protestant plot to depose Mary in favour of her had failed. Simon Renard, the Spanish ambassador to the Court, was trying to persuade Mary to have her half-sister executed as a traitor as he believed Elizabeth was involved in the plot. When the two doctors the queen had sent to examine Elizabeth judged that she was fit to travel the young princess had no choice but to obey. The doctors returned to London to give their verdict to the queen and the Princess Elizabeth truly believed that she was preparing for what would be her final journey.

Elizabeth was far from well, probably brought

on by fear, when she began her journey attended by just one lady as the queen had decreed. She travelled in the queen's own litter, which had been sent for Elizabeth's use, so determined was Mary to get her sister to London, whatever the state of her health. She was escorted by a dozen soldiers and three members of the queen's Privy Council. Within a day of setting out the princess became so ill that those traveling with her feared that she was dying, and a messenger was sent on ahead to the nearest dwelling to announce the arrival of the Princess Elizabeth.

By chance this was the farm that Edmund was visiting. He and the farmer met the party as they arrived at the farmhouse. Edmund was profoundly shocked and moved to see how pale and frightened the young princess was. Without any thought of the penalty for a peasant who dared to lay his hands on a royal personage, he stepped forward and before anyone could protest or intervene, he lifted Elizabeth out of the litter and carried her inside to the only chair in the room, placed beside the fire in readiness.

The councillors scurried in behind like three mother hens who had lost their chick. They had been completely taken by surprise and weren't sure know how to react to this young farmer who had taken command of the situation whilst they were still deciding how best to transport the princess into the house. Edmund gently sat her in the chair before making way for the princess's lady and the farmer's wife, who had filled a bowl with soup from the pot which was warming above the fire. Elizabeth's hands were trembling so badly that she was unable to hold the bowl herself. Her lady took the bowl from the wife and ate two spoonful's herself to prove to the queen's men that the soup was not poisoned, so frightened were they that something might happen to the princess before they delivered her to London.

Once they were satisfied that the soup was not tainted, they allowed the lady to give the soup to the princess. Elizabeth's companion fed her one small spoonful at a time until she could eat no more. She was still shivering when she had finished, so Edmund fetched his own cloak and laid it over her like a blanket. Their eyes met briefly; Elizabeth's had the look of a frightened animal. He'd seen that look before in deer being hunted for their lives by the hounds and it angered him that such a young girl should be subjected to such terror.

While Edmund had gone outside to bring more wood for the fire the Privy Councillors had perched their rather corpulent bodies on the small benches which sat at either side of the table in the middle of the room. The farmer produced three small tankards into which he poured some of his own rather poor ale and his wife filled three more bowls with soup from the pot at the fire and placed them on the table in front of the men with a plate of fresh bread and cheese. Although it was not the kind of fare these fine gentlemen were used to having served to them, they ate and drank heartily enough after being on the road all day. The lady was also given a bowl of soup which she ate while sitting on a stool at Elizabeth's feet.

Eventually the heat from the fire and the few mouthfuls of soup began to take effect and Elizabeth finally stopped shivering. A little colour had returned to her cheeks, but she was still very weak. However, when the last of the cheese and a second tankard of the farmer's ale had been consumed the queen's men decided that the princess was well enough recovered to continue her journey.

Edmund, who had replenished the fire with fresh logs, was leaning against the door as there was nowhere to sit. He was appalled when he heard their plan and walked across the room towards Elizabeth, where he remonstrated with the three men. "This young woman is in no fit state to travel to the next farm, let alone to London," he said, momentarily forgetting that "this young woman" was a princess of the royal blood. "She can't even stand unaided. It would be madness to force her to carry on while she is so unwell."

Under normal circumstances Edmund would never have dared to contradict the servants of the queen, but he was incensed at the thought of the young princess being dragged through the countryside on a litter over rough roads while she was so ill. The queen's men were sympathetic towards Elizabeth's plight, but they were terrified of what Mary would do if they delayed. Her orders had been explicit: "Bring the girl to London immediately and without any excuses!"

Edmund continued to press his argument home. "You do realise that if you persist with your plan to continue your journey now, without allowing the Princess Elizabeth time to rest, there is every likelihood that when you arrive at the palace you will be delivering a corpse! What would her majesty have to say then?"

He glared defiantly at the three councillors. The lady nodded in agreement, but the farmer and his wife were staring at Edmund open-mouthed. What on earth was he thinking? These were the queen's men, not a bunch of peasants in a field! If Edmund didn't stop berating them, they were all likely to be arrested and carted off to London with the princess!

But Edmund stood his ground. The Privy councillors huddled in the corner of the room and held a brief discussion. One said that if the girl died on the way it would save the queen having to order her execution and it would be considered as God's will. Another disagreed saying that if she died before reaching London her protestant supporters would accuse them of murdering her and that would ignite the tinderbox that was just waiting for a spark and what the queen was desperately trying to avoid. They were on the horns of a dilemma. Carry on to London and risk the girl's death, or delay and risk the queen's wrath.

They decided that they would stay at the farmhouse overnight and leave at first light. Elizabeth was taken and put to bed immediately by her lady and the farmer's wife before the men had time to change their minds. The cot in which the princess was lain was the farmer's and his wife's and couldn't have been more different from the bed she was used to sleeping in at Ashridge. She was supported on a thin mattress which had been supplemented by furs from the litter and she was covered with two equally thin blankets, which were the best the farmer and his wife had to offer, another fur from the litter and Edmund's cloak which she still had with her.

The lady settled herself into the chair. It was Edmund who had fetched it from the fireside and placed beside the cot. The farmer and his wife were completely in awe of the great personages who had taken over their home and seemed incapable of performing any tasks unless prompted to do so.

The soldiers carried their own meagre rations with them and were bedded down for the night with the horses in the barn. They spent a considerably more comfortable night lying in the straw than their superiors did in the house wrapped in their cloaks and sitting on the benches, resting their heads on the table. The queen's men rose early the next day after precious little sleep, with aching backs and short tempers, hoping that they wouldn't have to endure any more such nights before they reached London.

Princess Elizabeth was well rested but still weak and wan. Her lady persuaded her to take some gruel and a little milk from the farmer's wife as she sat by the warm fire while the gentlemen had a little bread and cheese and a tankard of ale. When they had finished, they were eager to get on their way again even though the sun had barely crept above the horizon. The soldiers were already assembled outside, and the litter had been prepared. Elizabeth was still unable to walk unaided and so when she was ready Edmund was allowed to carry her to the waiting litter. As he gently lowered her into it, she quietly thanked him and promised that should she be spared, she would not forget his kindness towards her.

Elizabeth reached London safely and was not executed as she had feared but was eventually allowed to return to the country. Although she was once again placed under house arrest, she did manage to have discreet inquiries made about who Edmund was and where he came from. When the protestant Elizabeth became queen, following the death of the childless Mary, things became difficult for those Catholics who had supported her half-sister's very unpopular religious policies. The peer who owned Edmund's farm was one of the casualties of the initial upheaval. Although it wasn't the largest of estates it was profitable, and it was now that a grateful queen made good her promise to Edmund. He was summoned to court where she bestowed a knighthood on him and granted him the manor house and the estate on which his farm stood.

Sir Edmund moved into the manor house with his wife and son and immediately set to work laying the foundations of the very successful business he had today. He had bought extra land and more sheep with the profits he made from selling first class fleeces. Then he bought the mill on the side of the river where the fleeces were washed and prepared for export. As his business grew Elizabeth saw to it that he had no problem in obtaining the relevant export and import licences he needed when he bought three shallow-drafted ships of his own capable of sailing up and down the river and across to the continent.

Everything Richard's father did or had ever done was completely legal and above board. Edmund was a sharp businessman, but he was an honest one. He always complied with the law and kept strict records of everything he brought into the country as well as what was sent out. No, there didn't seem to be any reason why Walsingham's cryptic message would concern his father but what had it got to do with him?

Richard knew that the only way he was going to find the answer was to go to London and confront the queen's man himself.

CHAPTER THREE

The Arrival

Richard arrived in London after days of difficult riding and long detours where the swollen rivers had washed away several bridges and the gentle fords had become raging torrents. He'd spent seven miserable nights sleeping in uncomfortable beds after eating unpalatable meals. The landlord's excuse was always that they were unable to get fresh food because of the weather. Richard was in no position to complain and needed to keep up his strength so just ate what he was given in the various taverns along the way, however distasteful. He would set off again the next morning wearing cold, damp clothes as everything he carried in his saddlebags was still wet from the previous day's soaking. This was insane! He should be at home in Topsham, warm and dry, having slept in his own snug bed and eaten a hearty breakfast instead of straddling his exhausted mount looking like a drowned rat even before setting off. He had questioned the wisdom of even starting out on this journey in these conditions many times since he left home and more than once seriously contemplated turning back. He didn't like being forced to do something he didn't want to, especially when he didn't know why. He really regretted not leaving a note for his father. If he was honest with himself, he would have to admit that Walsingham's message had not only unnerved him but frightened him a little too. He had no idea what he would be getting into and wasn't at all sure he wanted to. He had arrived. No turning back!

Not long after he got his first glimpse of London the rain finally stopped the sky cleared and the sun began to shine. What little heat was in the sun began to warm his wet clothes and steam was rising from the shoulders of his cloak as he reached the city gate. He was only slightly less miserable in the sunshine than he had been in the incessant rain he'd encountered throughout his whole journey. Everything he possessed was as sodden as the clothes on his back. He had not been dry since the minute he left Topsham. Now here he was in London at last, cold, wet, tired and hungry.

Having finally reached his destination he was impatient to meet the cause of his wretched pilgrimage and demand an explanation. He had no idea how to find Walsingham other than his office was somewhere in the palace. He didn't even how to get to the palace. He threw a couple of pennies to a beggar who was sitting by the gate and asked for directions. The filthy, ragged man grabbed at the pennies which had landed in the mud beside him with gnarled hands and gave Richard some garbled directions with much waving of his arms. Richard wasn't much the wiser but carried on along the main thoroughfare.

He hadn't travelled very far when he came across a man selling meat pies. As soon as he got a whiff of their meaty aroma his stomach growled. He quickly caught up with the man and bought one of his pies. Richard hadn't realized just how hungry he was until after he had wolfed down the pie in a couple of bites. He was almost tempted to return to the pie man and buy more but he was more anxious to get to Walsingham than to satisfy his appetite.

He began to pick his way carefully through all the filth and rubbish that was lying in the street. The ground underfoot was covered with a mixture of mud, offal, animal and human waste and heaps of garbage that had been left by the many hawkers and pedlars who were doing business there. The stench was almost overpowering. He was thankful to have such a surefooted mount as more than once he deftly steered Diablo out of the path of waste, both liquid and solid, which was thrown carelessly from the windows above without any thought for the people passing below. Eventually Richard was forced to hold his kerchief to his nose. How could people live with this stink and all the tons of waste being trodden underfoot by both people and horses?

Sellers and tradesmen were standing at their stalls all shouting out their wares, each one louder than their neighbour. Their half-naked children were shrieking and yelling as they played amid all the filth and chased each other in and out the stands and tables where their parents were plying their trade. They received a good clip round the ear too if they were caught causing damage to any of the goods on display. The bellowing, squealing and squawking of the animals and birds which were waiting to be slaughtered behind the fowlers and the butcher's establishments was deafening. Diablo suddenly reared when he was startled by a pack of scavenging dogs that had run out of an alley and into the street almost under his hooves, but Richard skilfully brought him back under his control again. Nevertheless, he was still cursed and scolded by some of the many people milling about the market stalls who had been forced to jump out of the way of Diablo's flying hooves.

There were more horsemen trying to weave their way through the crowds of pedestrians as well as carriages and carts forcing the folk to clear a path or risk being run down. As Richard came to a junction in the road, he noticed that the heavily laden cart that had turned off into the narrower street just in front of him had lost one of its wheels which caused it to tilt and spill a good part of its precarious load all over the road. The very busy little street was now completely blocked. Things quickly became ugly when other carters, impatient to get by, threatened to set about the unfortunate driver who was trying to calm his frightened old nag. Shortly after some of the drivers had begun to throw the scattered load in all directions in an effort to clear the way, two soldiers and a constable arrived using their pikes to force their way through the crowd of noisy spectators and looters. They put a stop to the looting which had begun immediately after the goods had fallen from the cart and prevented any further escalation of the ugly situation by press-ganging three of the most troublesome carters into replacing the rogue wheel and reloading what was left the dislodged goods back onto the vehicle. After a lot of grumbling and cursing from the drivers and heckling from the crowd of onlookers the job was completed, the street cleared, and order restored.

"My God! I thought Exeter was bad enough, but this is much worse. These people are crazy," thought Richard after he'd watched the incident unfold. He had never seen so much humanity all in one place at the same time even on a market day in Exeter and he found the press of so many people a little alarming.

Once the backlog of people and vehicles

waiting to enter the narrower street had cleared, he urged his mount forward but no sooner had he began to advance than he had to pull him up sharply to avoid a barrel that was careering down the street unattended and threatening to mow down anyone who was not nimble enough to get out of its path. The people scattered in all directions, knocking over stalls, falling over one another and landing in the filthy quagmire, both rich and poor alike. The pickpockets were soon at work in the mayhem that followed as people tried to find their feet again. It was pandemonium and Richard was forced to dismount when Diablo began to get pushed violently by the panicking mob. The barrel passed safely and smashed itself to pieces against the wall of a house disgorging its contents of fine wine. Richard continued on his way watching with some amusement as people rushed to scoop up the wine out of the mud with their hands.

He meandered his way through the crowd whilst keeping a tight hold on the reins, his purse and his saddle bags which now hung over his arm. Before he had proceeded a dozen more yards, he heard the hue and cry and turned to see a man careering towards him clutching a loaf of bread in one hand and knocking folk out of his path with the other. He was being pursued by three or four men all shouting and brandishing staves. Richard stepped aside to allow the thief to pass. His priority was to see Walsingham and not to get involved in any local disputes; plus, he reckoned that a man who would risk getting himself hanged for stealing bread must be desperate. Perhaps he had a family on the brink of starvation. Richard pressed on after the men following in the wake of the thief had run by him scattering everyone in their path. He secretly hoped that the poor man would escape with his precious bread.

Living in Topsham he had never given London much thought but even in his wildest dreams he could never had imagined it to be anything like this. The experience had made him even more determined to get to Walsingham, sort this mess out and get home again as quickly as possible. He had seen the palace from a distance, but it had taken far longer to reach than he had anticipated. He had not expected his journey through the streets to be so fraught with incident or such a great swell of people.

Richard was relieved when the last few hundred yards to the palace proved to be relatively straightforward. There were less people wandering about the street but a considerable increase in the number of soldiers. Unfortunately, however, gaining entrance to the place turned out to be almost as difficult as his journey had been to reach it. He was stopped at the gate by one of the palace guards who demanded to know what business he had to be there. Richard explained that he was here to see Sir Francis Walsingham in answer to his letter in which he had asked him to come to London. The guard then wanted to see the letter. Richard was about to take the letter from his pocket when he remembered that his visit was to be kept secret. Was the guard an exception to Walsingham's instructions? Richard had no way of knowing. Better play safe.

"I didn't bring the letter with me. I left it behind," Richard lied, averting his eyes from the soldier's face for fear he would see the deceit reflected in them.

The soldier looked him up and down carefully. "That's a fine excuse if ever I heard one. Sir Francis has a great many enemies who would dearly like to see him dead. How do I know you're not an assassin sent to kill him?"

"Dear God! Do I look like an assassin?" Richard said crossly.

"You look more like a vagrant to me, filthy and dishevelled," replied the soldier.

"Oh hell, why didn't I stop somewhere to clean myself up before attempting to see Sir Francis?" thought Richard. It was too late now. "If I was an assassin, do you think I'd ask to be let in through the gate?" he said, beginning to lose patience with the man. "Why can't you send a message to Sir Francis and tell him I'm here?

"What, and get dragged in front of the captain for wasting Walsingham's time if you turn out to be just another peasant complaining about being turned out of his hovel by his lord! I've been caught out that way before and I've no intention of getting another earful," he said, looking over towards the guardhouse.

"You can't keep me standing out here all day. I've travelled a long way to reach London and I want to see Sir Francis Walsingham. I'm not moving until I do!" said Richard.

"If you don't keep a civil tongue in your head, I'll have you thrown into a cell where you can cool your heels for a while," the guard angrily answered.

Richard realised he had better change tack quickly or there was a danger he'd never get to Walsingham. "Look, is there nothing at all you can do?" he asked, in a more conciliatory tone. "I did receive a summons from Sir Francis, and I have been traveling for many days as you can see by the state of my clothes." He opened his arms to reveal a still damp and very muddy cloak.

"I'll send a message to his clerk but that's all. If he's in his office, maybe he'll come and vouch for you but if there's no response you will leave immediately or face arrest."

The guard gave Richard's name to another soldier who was standing a little further away and sent him off to Walsingham's office. Richard watched the man walk across the courtyard and noticed that there was a guard stationed at every door leading into the building. Small groups of soldiers were also scattered about the area, some standing talking while others sat where they could play cards or throw dice though all were in easy reach of their weapons. Richard wondered if giving his name to the clerk would be of any use since if his visit was so secret Sir Francis probably wouldn't have told his clerk anything about it. What would he do if the reply was negative? It would be no use trying to make a dash for one of the doors; he'd be caught before he'd gone five yards, arrested, and thrown into prison to be forgotten about for no one would come looking for him since nobody knew he was here. What a ridiculous position to be in! How could he have been so stupid not to have left a note for his father. There was no prospect at all of the guard on the gate letting him enter without any verification from Walsingham's office. Then what?

It was beginning to look as if his dash across the most difficult terrain he'd ever encountered in the most inhospitable weather conditions had all been in vain. Richard paced up and down in front of the gate under the watchful gaze of the guard and after what seemed an eternity the messenger returned with a young man at his side.

The young man strode towards him, hand outstretched. "Richard! You've arrived."

"Will Perceval, what are you doing here?" Richard said, shaking his hand.

"I'm Sir Francis Walsingham's clerk and I've come to escort you to his office," Will replied. "Let him through, he's expected," he said to the guard.

The guard stepped aside and allowed Richard to enter. Will and Richard made their way between two groups of soldiers to the stables with Diablo.

"Do you know why Walsingham has sent for me?" asked Richard, delighted to see his old friend again.

"I've no idea," said Will. "I didn't even know you were coming."

"But when you spoke to the guard you seemed to be expecting me?"

"If I hadn't let him think that he wouldn't have let you in. There's a rumour of an imminent assassination attempt on the queen and security is very tight, so it was fortunate that I was in Walsingham's office when the soldier came in. I didn't think there could be two Richard Lovells, which is why I came back with him" said Will, smiling at Richard.

They reached the stables, and with Will's help Richard found a stall for his horse and a groom willing to look after him for a couple of pennies. Satisfied that Diablo was in safe hands, Richard followed Will towards the palace. Before they entered Richard tried knock some of the drying mud from his cloak with his hat.

"You look as if you've been doing some hard

traveling, Richard," said Will.

"I've just endured my longest, most arduous and most miserable journey thanks to Sir Francis. I received a letter from him asking (or should I say commanding) that I come here immediately."

Will laughed. "Sir Francis never 'requests' and it's a very brave or very foolish man who ignores his summons."

"I gathered that. That's why I'm here in this state," said Richard, pointing to his muddy cloak and dirty boots.

"So I see!" Will chuckled. "You'd better come to my room where you can wash and change into some dry clothes and then we can go and get something to eat."

"Thanks, but I want to see Walsingham first," replied Richard, impatient to know why he had been summoned here so urgently.

"Sir Francis isn't here," said Will. "He left London three days ago in a great hurry."

"What!" Richard bellowed. "I've just about broken my neck to get here through the most bloody awful conditions because of the urgency of his letter and he's not even here when I arrive! Where the Hell is he and more to the point when will he be back?" He was absolutely furious. He had hoped to see Walsingham immediately, get this business (whatever it was) out of the way and leave for home again after a good meal and a decent night's sleep.

"I've no idea when he'll return," said Will, taken aback by his friend's outburst. "Richard, stop shouting or we're going to attract the attention of the palace guards and that's not the best thing to do at the moment. Everyone's on high alert and very jumpy," he added, nervously watching for any reaction from the soldiers nearest to them.

"But I can't stay here waiting for Walsingham. I need to get back to my business in Topsham," said Richard, his voice still raised. He knew how important it was for the ship to be finished on time and how much his father was depending on him to see that it was done. Now he was going to be stuck here until God knows when, waiting to see a man he didn't know for Heaven knows what reason. "Is there anyone who does know when he'll be back?"

"I'll take you to Thomas Phelipps, Walsingham's secretary. He should be back in the office by now. He might be able to tell you more than I but Sir Francis can be very secretive and he doesn't always confide even in his secretary," said Will.

At the entrance the guard on the door stepped aside when he recognised Will, but not before he'd had a good look at the dirty, dishevelled man accompanying the young clerk. Richard followed Will through a warren of dark corridors each with many rooms leading from them. All the twists and turns reminded him of the story of the Minotaur's labyrinth from the mythology lessons he and Will learned at the grammar school all those years ago. He was grateful to have Will as his guide. Even if he had somehow managed to get into the palace Richard would never have found his way to Walsingham's office unaided. He had never been in such a big building in his life before and was totally confused by all the dimly lit passageways that seemed to lead off in all directions before they finally reached their destination.

When they entered the office, they found Phelipps sitting at his desk, bent over some paperwork he quickly covered when the door opened. The room had one small window which allowed very little light or fresh air into the dismal office. Richard's eyes quickly became adjusted to the dinginess of the room and soon picked out the shelves of books and scrolls that covered every wall and the pile upon pile of papers and letters that littered the floor. Three desks, one small and two somewhat larger ones, also covered in papers, together with their accompanying stools, were squeezed into what little available floor space remained. Each had a single candle perched beside its inkwell but only the one on Phelipps' desk was lit and it was hardly producing enough light to read by.

Will introduced Richard and explained that he had been sent for by Sir Francis. A small, unkempt but scholarly looking man peered at

Richard over the rim of his spectacles which were sitting rather precariously on the end of his nose. He was balding but still had a band of thick hair running from the top of his ears to the back of his neck which coupled with his copious beard gave the impression that he was wearing a permanent muffler.

"Ah yes! Sir Francis is expecting you and left word that when you arrived you were to be lodged with Will until he returns," said Phelipps. He repositioned his spectacles on the top of his nose; they made his eyes appear owl-like as he blinked at the two young men.

"Really! And when might that be, may I ask? said Richard angrily. "I have urgent business at home, and I don't have time for this delay. If he hasn't returned by the day after tomorrow, I shall leave."

"Sir Francis's instructions are that you remain here until he returns, and you are to tell no one why you are here."

"Well, that won't be difficult will it, since I've no idea myself why I'm here," said Richard.

Phelipps glanced at Richard for a moment and then turned his attention back to the papers on his desk.

"I'm not going to tolerate being treated this way," Richard told him, in danger of losing his temper again. "I am a merchant trader, no threat either to the kingdom or the queen. I've broken no laws and yet I've been ordered here with no explanation why and now I've been commanded to stay until Walsingham decides to show himself! I think I'll just return home and stop wasting my time!"

"Your orders are to stay here until Sir Francis returns," Phelipps answered.

"Orders!" Richard shouted. "I'm a merchant not a soldier and I shall not be 'ordered'!"

"No matter, you are to remain here until Sir Francis returns."

"Damn Sir Francis!" yelled Richard.

Will was astonished at his friend. He'd never heard anyone shout at Phelipps before, except Walsingham.

"When is he expected to return?" demanded Richard.

"Who knows?" answered Phelipps with a shrug. He pointed to the door, indicating that the interview was at an end.

"Now look here, that's not good enough!" Richard began to cross the room towards Phelipps, but Will took Richard's arm and bundled him out of the office.

Richard wrenched his arm out of Will's grasp. "What the hell are you doing?"

"Not wise, Richard. Phelipps might not look much but he is a very important man in Walsingham's organization. In fact, second only to Sir Francis himself. It wouldn't do to cross him," said Will, trying to calm Richard's ruffled feathers.

"I don't give a damn who he is," snapped Richard. "I'll not be treated like this by anyone, let alone a quill wielding clerk."

"He's much more than a quill wielding clerk. Much more. He is the best cipherer and codebreaker in the country, maybe in the world," said Will. "I'm sorry Richard, but I don't think there's anything you can do other than hope Sir Francis isn't away for too much longer."

"How long is he usually away for?" asked Richard hopefully.

"Hard to tell really. Sometimes a couple of days, sometimes two or three weeks."

"Oh my God!" groaned Richard. "I hope it's not weeks."

Will led him along yet more corridors until they reached his room. "It's nothing grand but it serves its purpose," he said apologetically when he caught Richard's expression. The accommodation was sparse and barely adequate. It had an even smaller window than the one in Walsingham's office, two pallets, a small chest for Will's clothes, a small table upon which sat a candle, and a few rushes were strewn about the floor. Richard was thinking he'd seen better rooms in the poorest of inns and was hoping his stay would be shorter rather than longer in this most draughty of places.

"Well at least I'll have someone I know sharing my room this time," Will said cheerfully. "I'm almost afraid of turning my back on some of the creatures Walsingham foists on me."

"You mean you're forced to share your room with strangers?" asked Richard, raising his eyebrows.

"Oh yes, frequently, and if I dare to complain I'm reminded very sharply that the room belongs to Walsingham and that I'm privileged to have the use of it!" said Will, a little shamefaced.

"But who are these people?" asked Richard, appalled that his friend seemed to have no rights at all.

"Who knows! Some stay hidden for weeks while others are only here for a night," Will replied. "All I'm told is they are important to Walsingham's spy network and not to ask any questions," replied Will.

"God knows why I'm here as I've nothing to do with his spies or his network."

"Never mind all that now, let's get you respectable again and we can go and eat," his friend answered.

It was fortunate that Will was about the same size as Richard because all Richard's clothes were still damp and in dire need of being cleaned after such a journey. While Will cleaned off the mud that was spattered all over his boots, Richard washed the muck off his hands and face in the bowl of water that Will had fetched for him, trimmed his unkempt beard and combed his hair. Then he put on his first dry clothes since he had left home, albeit clothes more suited to a clerk than a merchant. But it was a welcome change nevertheless from the wet clothes he'd lived in for a week.

Once ready the two of them set off for a nearby tavern where good hot food and reasonable ale were served. "My God, that was good, Will!" said Richard, as he finished the last mouthful of pie. "The food at a couple of the inns I stayed in on the way here was little better than pigswill, the excuse being that because of the weather they hadn't been able to get fresh supplies, although I got the feeling it was more likely that because I was a stranger I wouldn't complain as much as the locals." He leaned his back against the wall and stretched out his long legs, beginning to relax at last. He was warm and dry for the first time in days, eaten the best meal he'd had since he'd left home and was enjoying Will's company.

Will shouted to the landlord for more ale, before he asked Richard, "Did you complain?"

"No. I was far too weary to argue and far too hungry to go without," said Richard, remembering just what a wretched journey it had been.

"Richard, have you really no idea why Sir Francis has sent for you?"

"None whatsoever. In fact, I was hoping that you could tell me."

"No chance of that I'm afraid, he plays his cards very close to his chest and I'm certainly not in his confidence," Will said. "I'm just a general dogsbody sent hither and thither to deliver notes, to collect notes, to eavesdrop on conversations without being seen and relay information back to Walsingham, to sit at my desk for hours on end copying copious amounts of papers and in between times trying to decipher what Walsingham and Phelipps are talking about. I swear they've got a language all of their own!"

"What about Phelipps? Would he know why I'm here?" asked Richard hopefully.

"Even if he did, you'd get no information from him. He's as tight-lipped as Sir Francis. No, Richard, I'm afraid you're going to have to wait for Walsingham to return and then ask him yourself," replied Will.

The landlord appeared with two more tankards of ale and the two young men fell into an easy conversation reminiscing over old times. They chatted about their time at school together and caught up with what they had each been doing with their lives since they last saw each other.

"How did you end up here?" Richard asked Will. "I thought you were going to become a lawyer when you got your degree Cambridge."

Will was the son of a very prosperous glove maker who catered to the nobility. He used the most exquisite and expensive materials available and charged the prices to match. His workmanship was second to none and he was the first option of many of the lords and ladies at Court even though he lived in Exeter. He was the craftsman of choice and especially so if the gloves were to be presented to the queen as a gift. A person's standing at the Court could be won or lost depending on how Her Majesty received the offering. Perceval had provided private tutors for his son until he was old enough to attend the grammar school. Will had been a constant source of encouragement to Richard and had helped him to overcome many of the difficulties he'd encountered with his lessons while at school and he'd never forgotten his kindness.

"After I left the university," Will said, "my father wanted me to gain some knowledge of the circle he hoped I would be practicing in before I went on to Gray's Inn. I arrived home to discover that he'd acquired this post for me with Walsingham after he had produced a pair of exceptional gloves for Her Majesty on Sir Francis's behalf. The queen had been so overjoyed with them that she had praised Walsingham in front of the whole court while showing off her new gloves. He was delighted, since Her Majesty always seems to scold him more than praise him. She sometimes gets frustrated with the many precautions he takes to protect her person especially if they prevent her from doing something she wants to do that might risk her safety. Although she usually takes his advice eventually, she berates him dreadfully.

When my father approached him about finding work for me in the palace Sir Francis offered me this position. I must admit that I haven't done much legal work since I arrived here, in fact I haven't done any but I have certainly learned a lot about life at court and most of it isn't very pleasant. It appears to be a very agreeable place on the surface but the undercurrents are vicious. Some who come to court never see home again."

"Why? Do they abandon their families in favour of life at court?" asked Richard. He couldn't understand why anyone would want to leave their family to stay at a court that, according to Will, was undesirable.

"Not exactly," said Will. "Some end up being tortured in the Tower before being executed, others are sent to prison where the lucky ones go on to the gallows, the rest are left to rot until they die."

"Dear God in heaven! What are they guilty of?"

"I'm sure a lot of them are guilty of nothing more than being in the way of a rival who wishes to usurp their place. Palms are greased, false accusations made, plots hatched against them and they are dispatched," said Will.

"But how can that be if they are innocent?" Richard returned. He'd been brought up to believe the law of the land was there to protect the innocent.

"The queen's hold on the throne is permanently under threat from parties wishing to replace her with the Catholic Mary, Queen of Scotland. The prospect of that happening fills the Council with terror and if there's the slightest hint, no matter how tenuous, that a person is involved in a plot against Her Majesty then that person soon disappears one way or another."

"Even if the accusations are false?" asked Richard, shocked.

"Even if they are false," replied Will. "These are dark times, Richard, and we must all be careful that what we say cannot be misconstrued and that we are not found in the company of anyone suspected of being a threat to the Crown," he added. "Richard, don't trust anyone while you're here. Complete your business with Walsingham as soon as you can and go back to Exeter. This place is a hotbed of conspiracy, and no one is immune from being dragged into the underworld of the plotters or the evil doers who would like to see our country tear itself apart making it vulnerable to invasion from France or Spain."

Richard was quite taken aback by Will's description of court life. Whenever he had thought of the queen's court (which wasn't very often) he'd imagined it as being a harmonious place peopled by the great and good and ruled over by a gracious monarch.

When Will saw the disappointment in Richards' face he stood up and slapped him on his back. "Come on, I'll take you to the Great

Hall and introduce you to some of my friends. You'll be safe enough with them, they've nothing to gain by stabbing you in the back," laughed Will. "And you never know, you might even see the queen herself! The court is usually dead at this time of the year but because of some very tangible evidence (according to Walsingham) of a Catholic plot against the queen's life she decided to take his advice that she would be much safer in London than traveling about the countryside even though there is still the threat of the plague here."

CHAPTER FOUR

The Confrontation

When Richard and Will entered the Great Hall, it was alive with the buzz of dozens of conversations. People stood in small groups, talking together, and some of the discourse was loud and animated while others were quieter and more intimate. Others were seated playing cards or throwing dice under the huge pillars that ran the full length of the Hall on both sides. One or two folks were playing chess, while being observed and advised by interested onlookers.

Richard had never seen such a large and so beautifully decorated room in his life. The many windows were long and high, and the sunlight must have flooded the whole space during the day. One of the huge stone fireplaces contained the best part of a tree trunk burning in it. The ceiling was most beautifully and intricately decorated with plaster, the workmanship beyond belief. Richard stared open-mouthed at the many rich tapestries hanging on the walls, the numerous examples of ornately carved oak panelling, the portraits painted by the finest artists. He found it hard to believe that all these people seemed to be totally unaffected by all this grandeur.

There was a multitude of sumptuously dressed folk with their servants attending on them. The lords and ladies in attendance were dripping with the most magnificent jewellery, from their hats to their shoes; the diamonds and precious stones sparkled like spangles in the flickering candlelight. So much wealth displayed in just this one room. What a contrast to the poor people and all the beggars he'd encountered on the way to the palace.

There was so much going on and so much to see. Richard didn't know where to look next—his eyes darted from one marvel to the next. It was too much to take in at once, and all this opulence in the same building as Walsingham's dingy office and Will's woeful lodgings! Why had his father not told him about this place and all of its wonders? Whenever Edmund had returned from London after a meeting with Walsingham or Cecil he talked only of their business dealings and never once mentioned the Great Hall.

Then it occurred to him that his father might never have even been in the Great Hall. It was more than likely that his meetings had taken place in an office or one of the many other rooms in this huge building, some of which he had passed on his way to Walsingham's office. But surely his father would have been knighted in the Great Hall. Maybe he had been too nervous to notice what a magical place it was? However, Richard knew his father had no great love for London and so would have headed for home as soon as his business had been completed, whatever that business might be. He suddenly realized that Will was watching him with a silly grin on his face.

"It has that effect on all newcomers," Will laughed. "Come, my friends are over there."

He guided Richard over to a small group of men standing in the corner. Almost as soon as the introductions had been made, they were all talking and laughing together as if they'd known each other for years. Will's companions were about the same age as him. James and Walter were the sons of knights, Edward, the ward of another and John worked for Sir William Cecil doing more or less the same as Will did for Walsingham. When one of the young men asked what had brought him to London, Richard replied that he was a merchant and had business with Walsingham. This was accepted without question as merchants and the like were always calling on Walsingham or Cecil for official paperwork such as licenses and passports. A very close eye was kept on all imports and exports and so decisions made by these two important men could ultimately decide the success or failure of a business. This was why Richard had answered Walsingham's summons when bidden even though he desperately wanted to ignore it. His father's ventures depended heavily on Sir Francis's co-operation, and he dared not risk losing it.

Their conversation had just returned to what life was like living in the palace when they were rudely interrupted. "What have we here then?" sneered Geoffrey Marchemont, as he staggered drunkenly across the room towards him with his friends Anthony and Robert in tow.

Richard spun around to face him.

"Well, if it isn't that upstart Lovell!" Geoffrey slurred. "I hardly recognised you all dressed up like a quill-pusher. Are you trying to disguise the fact that you're nothing more than a peasant and have no right to be here? This is no place for the likes of you, peasant! How dare you presume to enter the queen's court! Get back to your sheep where you belong. You certainly smell like one." He sniffed around Richard and pinched his nose.

"Aye, we can smell him from here," sniggered Anthony.

Many of the people within earshot started to laugh while others just stared, waiting to see what the stranger's reaction would be. Richard reddened with embarrassment and could feel his anger rising.

"Come on, Marchemont, you're drunk," said Walter, taking him by the arm. "Just take yourself off and stop causing trouble."

Geoffrey shook him off angrily without his eyes leaving Richard's face. "Maybe you need a little something to persuade you to leave, like the point of my dagger perhaps," said Geoffrey, and his mood suddenly changed from that drunken joker to one of sheer hatred. He spat on the floor in front of Richard and drew his dagger from the sheath attached to his belt.

Everyone within the range of the drunken youth's blade moved backwards so quickly that some even fell over each other. Richard's hand was just starting to reach for the hilt of his eating knife when a clear, commanding voice rang out across the Hall, "I'll have no bloodshed at my court!"

Everyone around them immediately bowed or curtsied very low to their sovereign lady, Elizabeth. Geoffrey and Richard dropped to their knees beside each other, Geoffrey still holding the naked blade in his hand.

The queen stood over the two kneeling men. At the best of times she had the temper to match her red hair, but she was further on edge because of the assassination threat. To see a drawn blade in her own Great Hall filled her with fury. "Do you know the penalty for brandishing a knife in my presence?" she demanded.

She waited a few moments for the enormity of her words to sink in. The whole room held its breath.

"Well! Answer me!" the queen demanded

crossly.

Both men remained silent.

She glared down at Richard. His hands were noticeably empty. "Who is it who dares to disturb the peace of my court?" she asked him.

"Richard Lovell, your majesty, son of Sir Edmund Lovell," he replied, never taking his eyes off her feet.

"Let me see your face, boy," commanded the queen.

Richard raised his eyes and gazed up into the face of his dread sovereign who, because he had allowed that damned Marchmont goad him, now held his life in her hands. When Elizabeth looked at him, she saw the features she had seen in his father all those years ago and she mellowed instantly. "Ah, Sir Edmund. He is a true and loyal subject. I know him well, and you are his young son now grown," she said, smiling. "If you are of the same nature as your father, I know you would not attempt to draw your blade unless you were extremely provoked to do so."

She transferred her gaze to Geoffrey and after glaring at him for a few seconds held out her gloved hand to Richard. "Welcome to my court, Richard."

He kissed her hand, very relieved that he wasn't on his way to the Tower, and then he reverted his eyes to the floor once more. Will and his friends also breathed a sigh of relief as the queen rarely, if ever, forgave such an infringement and they too had been waiting for the guards to rush across the Hall and arrest Richard and Geoffrey.

Elizabeth's mood changed again as she stared down at Geoffrey. "And you, who are you?" she demanded, scowling at him.

"Geoffrey, your majesty, son of Lord Marchemont of Holyfield Hall," he stammered, still holding his dagger in his right hand and trembling with fear. He was in awe of Elizabeth's fiery temper and knew very well what the consequences could be. The penalty for drawing a blade in the queen's presence was the amputation of the perpetrator's right hand.

"Really," she said. Her eyes travelled around the room until they rested on Lord Thomas, who, mortified by what his idiotic son had done, was trying to make himself as inconspicuous as possible beside one of the great pillars. "What a great pity your father neglected to teach you some manners before he brought you to my court" she said scathingly, glaring at Lord Marchemont over the heads of the two kneeling miscreants. Before Lord Thomas could offer any kind of an apology for his drunken son's disgraceful behaviour the queen, followed by her ladies, walked gracefully on towards her throne which stood on the dais at the head of the hall, acknowledging her subjects, nodding her head to one side and then the other as she went.

Geoffrey was still kneeling, but his recent

terror had now turned into a smouldering anger. He was incandescent with rage. Before he could rise however, one of the queen's ladies came to Richard, already on his feet.

"Richard, her majesty wishes to speak with you. Will you follow me please?" she said.

Richard looked into the eyes of the most beautiful woman he had ever seen and stood rooted to the spot. His heart skipped a beat as he began to tingle from head to foot. He felt himself being drawn into those two, clear, warm, hazel eyes like a bee to a flower. "This must be one of God's angels come from Heaven," he thought, still unable to draw his eyes away from her lovely face.

"This way sir, please, the queen is waiting," said the vision.

Richard pulled himself together. This angel wasn't a messenger from Paradise but from the queen and, so he obediently walked behind her to the dais. However, he already knew that he would follow this woman to the ends of the earth and more if she wished it.

Geoffrey rose from his knees, his vengeful eyes boring into Richard's back. Not only had he received a severe public rebuke from the queen but she had invited Richard, that peasant, a country bumpkin, a nobody, to go to talk with her while he, the son of a lord, had been left kneeling in the rushes on the stone floor.

"I will make you both pay dearly for this

insult, I promise," Geoffrey muttered under his breath. He got to his feet and stormed out of the Hall followed by his two friends.

Richard was allowed to sit on the step below the throne. This was a great honour indeed, and bestowed only on a few. Her majesty inquired about his father's health and was most interested to hear about his latest venture; perhaps there may be a chance for her to profit too from Sir Edmund's trade with the colonies. She was always looking for new ways to increase her coffers without having to lay out too much herself. They chatted for several minutes before Elizabeth ended the conversation by calling for her favourite, Robert Dudley, the Earl of Leicester, to begin the dancing. The minstrels up in the gallery began to play the music for the volta as Dudley had requested and he escorted Her Majesty down the steps to lead the dance.

Richard bowed deeply to Elizabeth and then found himself searching for those hypnotic eyes that had so completely bewitched him. When he did find them, they were staring back at him, although they averted themselves immediately when they met Richard's gaze. He reluctantly dragged himself away when a courtier came to the angel and escorted her onto the floor to dance. As he made his way back to Will and the others Richard was imagining how wonderful it would be if it were he who was her partner.

Richard manoeuvred his way around the

couples who had joined the queen and Leicester and on the centre of the floor. Will and his friends were desperate to discover what had happened between Richard and Geoffrey to cause such hatred and also what it was that his father had done to be so favoured by the queen. Richard on the other hand was even more desperate to discover who the beautiful young woman was. The questions began on both sides immediately Richard reached them. For the first few seconds everyone was talking and no one listening. When Richard raised his hand the others paused long enough for him to demand to know the name of lovely young girl was who had escorted him to the queen.

"You mean you don't know?" asked Will, surprised "She's Geoffrey Marchemont's sister, Joan."

Richard was stunned. He knew Geoffrey of course, and he knew Geoffrey had a sister, but he'd never had the opportunity to meet her since their families moved in very different circles. How could such an angel be sister to such a devil? It was almost incomprehensible that they could be siblings.

"No use setting your cap at that one," said James. "Apart from being out of your class she's just become betrothed to that old creep Lord de Luc."

Richard's heart sank. "Who's he?"

"He should be here somewhere. He rarely

strays far from Court, unless to a brothel, but he usually finds what he's looking for here," said Will, casting his eyes around the Hall. "Ah, there he is, standing in the corner."

Will pointed towards two men engaged in a very heated conversation beside one of the many huge pillars that supported the roof of the Great Hall. The young man was waving his arms about and clearly remonstrating with the older man who had an expression of sheer contempt on his face.

"He doesn't look that old," said Richard, nodding towards the younger of the pair.

"No, not him. He's the husband of the woman de Luc has been seducing for the last two months," said James.

"Dear God in heaven, you surely can't mean the other one, he's a decrepit old man!" said Richard, his eyes widening in disbelief.

"Don't let his looks fool you," Will said. "He's as strong as an ox, very handy with his sword and as rich as Croesus, the latter being the only reason he's been able to get his claws into Joan. It's no secret that Geoffrey and his father are deep in debt. It's also no secret that the only way out for them is to let Lord de Luc marry her and then he will pay off all their debts."

"It's the talk of the whole court, I can tell you," said John.

"Almost all the decent folk here are disgusted with what Lord Marchemont has done," James added. "Joan is a very popular and well-liked young woman with plenty of admirers in the junior nobility."

"Surely the bride's father pays the dowry to the groom, not the other way round," Richard remarked.

"Apparently de Luc is determined to have her whatever the cost," Walter put in. "It's a very unorthodox arrangement but nevertheless it is a legal betrothal."

"But that's monstrous!" said Richard. "Dear God, she's little more than a child compared to him."

He stared at the shadowy figure of the man who was destined to marry his beautiful Joan. Lord de Luc was a tall, wiry man despite his advancing years. He displayed the beginnings of a slight stoop and was thin faced with a hooked nose; his eyes were close set and his moustache and beard failed to conceal a pair of fleshy lips. Although he was indoors, de Luc was still wearing his dark cloak and hood and looked for all the world like an oversized vulture. He seemed to sense that he was being observed and he glanced across the room towards Richard. For a second their eyes met and Richard shuddered with revulsion at the sight of such an evil looking creature and quickly turned back to Will and his friends.

"That can't be allowed to happen," said Richard angrily. "There must be something that can be done to prevent it."

The young men standing with him were astonished by his sudden outburst. Just who was this friend of Will's? He'd only recently arrived in London and knew neither Joan or Lord de Luc and yet he was reacting like a jilted suitor.

"What on earth's the matter with you, Richard?" Walter said. "These things happen, even where you come from, I'm sure. Women often marry much older men if that's what their father wishes. They must do as they're told."

"As it should be," muttered Edward.

"But she's such a beautiful young girl and he's an old man!" said Richard.

"So what?" Will returned. "Why are you so incensed? She's just another girl and the goings on of the elite are no concern of ours and if we try to make them so we will soon be lacking bed and board, if not our heads. It's just her hard luck that she was born a Marchemont!"

"Come on now, we'll soon be thinking that you've taken a fancy to her yourself," joked John. When he caught sight of the look on Richard's face he exclaimed, "My God, you have, haven't you!"

All the friends stared at Richard as if he'd grown an extra head, and then began to laugh.

"For heaven's sake Richard, what's wrong with you?" Will said. "You're only going to be here until Walsingham gets back and then you'll be going home to Topsham. This is none of your concern and you'd be a fool to try and make it so! This is no time to get yourself involved with a woman, especially that one. Just because the queen asked to speak to you doesn't put you in the same class as her. She wouldn't even give you a second glance."

"Not only that but de Luc wouldn't take too kindly to you sniffing about what he already regards as his property," said Walter, who couldn't understand how Richard could have formed any kind of attachment at all to Joan since he had only set eyes on her for the first time less than an hour ago. The man must be losing his sanity.

"You don't understand, any of you," started Richard, but before he could say anything further that would make him look an even bigger idiot Will spoke again. "Oh, come on, Richard, just forget it will you? It's nothing to do with us and it's getting late, I've a lot of work to do tomorrow and I need a decent sleep before I tackle it. Let's go."

Will bade his friends goodnight, while shrugging his shoulders and shaking his head, as he directed a reluctant Richard towards the door. As they made their way back to Will's room again through a maze of passageways Richard's mind was in a turmoil.

"How could anyone in their right mind expect a beautiful young woman like Joan to marry such a horrible old man as de Luc? What was worse it was her own father who was insisting that she did just that." In his head he knew that he should forget all that was happening at Court, focus on seeing Walsingham, then getting himself back home as soon as possible to resume his busy life in Topsham. However, his heart was telling him something entirely different.

What had happened to him when he looked into that young girl's eyes? Whatever had occurred, he felt it had been reciprocated by Joan. He knew nothing of being in love personally but from what he had perceived in some of his acquaintances was that they had met someone they liked, spent time with them, gradually fallen in love and then married. But if this wasn't love that he had experienced when had observed the expression in Joan's eyes then what was it? His heart already knew that come hell or high water this was the woman he was going to marry no matter what the obstacles were.

His head was telling him he was being a stupid fool as a man in his position had no chance of making a jot of difference to what had already been ordained! He knew nothing about Joan other than she was a queen's lady and also Geoffrey's sister. What little he knew about Lord de Luc was what Will and his friends had told him and yet he had already made up his mind that, no matter what, he would never allow his beloved to marry that man. Within a matter of hours of reaching London his life had been turned upside down when he had fallen hopelessly in love with a girl he had only just met. He had no idea how it had happened or what he was going to do to make everything right.

They reached their room and Will lit the candle which sat on the small table. He discovered a note that had been left on his bed while they were out and took it over to the light to read it. "It's from Phelipps," he said. "Walsingham's back and wants to see you at first light."

"What! Oh, not now, surely. Why did he have to return so soon?" complained Richard.

Will was at a complete loss. He couldn't understand his friend's complete change of attitude at all since it was only earlier that he was in a temper because Sir Francis wasn't here and now he was just as displeased because he was. This unpredictable man wasn't the strong, decisive Richard he had known at school.

"I don't know why your stance has changed so quickly from what it was earlier," said a rather confused Will. "From the time we were at school together I thought I knew you but that doesn't seem to be the case anymore. We'd best get some sleep now as we've both got an early start tomorrow." Will knew from bitter experience that Walsingham didn't take too kindly to being kept waiting.

As Richard climbed into his cot, he cursed Sir

Francis for the second time in as many days. It took him many hours to settle off to sleep. He couldn't keep his mind off Joan and what lay in store for her if he couldn't find a way to prevent it. He couldn't understand how he could be so affected by a woman he had seen for only a few short minutes, but he knew that from now on he would do everything in his power and more to rescue her from the terrible fate that awaited her or die trying!

The following morning Richard was standing in front of Walsingham's desk before the sun had cleared the horizon, feeling a bit like a naughty schoolboy summoned by one of his masters. Will had been sent away on an errand and Phelipps was absent. The man sitting opposite Richard was dressed all in black, had a full head of hair, a thick black beard and the most piercing amber eyes that Richard had ever seen. They seemed to be looking deep into his soul and he didn't like the unnerving feeling it gave him. It was almost like looking back into the eyes of a cat that was ready to pounce.

"Good morning, Richard. I trust you are well rested," said Sir Francis in a deep voice, as he stood up and offered Richard his hand.

Richard found himself staring directly into those penetrating eyes again and felt even more uneasy. Walsingham was as tall as Richard, and although not as well built he had a strong handshake. "Good morning, Sir Francis. Yes, I am rested, thank you, but impatient to know why I have been summoned here with such urgency. There must be some mistake. My father deals with any business matters relating to London. I just deal with shipping and in that respect I don't really have the time to be away from home. My father is relying on me to see that his latest project is completed on time and I can't do that from London, sir," said Richard. The words had tumbled out of his mouth like water over a waterfall. Why was he so affected by this man's presence?

"Patience, Richard. I'm fully aware of your father's business but what I require of you is far more important than your father's ship," said Walsingham.

He sat down again and offered Richard a stool, but remaining on his feet, Richard asked, "What is it that is so much more important than my father's ship that I had to ride through the wettest weather in living memory for days on end to get here?"

"The safety of this realm and the life of your sovereign," said Walsingham quietly.

"How does that have anything to do with me?" Richard shot back. "I'm a wool merchant's son, not a soldier and certainly not a spy, which is what your work is about."

"It's not a spy or a soldier I need but a man I can trust with a ship capable of crossing to France and getting in close to the shore. I think you're that man, Richard," said Sir Francis, looking him straight in the eye.

"How can you be so sure of that?" Richard returned, trying to avoid those eyes. "How can you presume to know me that well when you've never even met me before and why on earth would I want to go sailing off to France? If I don't get sunk by the Spanish, pirates or God knows who else I'll probably drown anyway. I'm not a sailor!"

"You're right, I don't know you but I do know your father," Walsingham said. "I believe you are a lot like him and his loyalty to Her Majesty is unquestionable."

"How can you believe you know what kind of man I am when you have only just met me? I love and respect my father, yes, and I try my best to emulate him but I'm not him!"

"Are you telling me you that have no allegiance to your Queen and care nothing for your country?" asked Walsingham, a menacing quality to his voice now.

"Of course I do, but surely you have more qualified men to do whatever it is you want doing," Richard answered. "I'm not skilled in spying or fighting or even sailing for that matter. I run a shipping office, for God's sake! I don't sail ships!"

"I do indeed have men more suited to carry out this mission, but they are being closely watched and I cannot risk failure under any circumstance. The life of our sovereign lady is at stake," replied Walsingham, quiet and controlled again.

"But I've never done anything covert before. Surely there must be someone, somewhere more suited to the task than I," pleaded Richard.

"At this moment you are the most suited and my only hope. I'm no happier about it than you but that's the way it is!"

Richard stared down at Walsingham but admitted defeat. He hadn't missed the veiled threat of being accused of treason and knew that Walsingham wouldn't hesitate to carry it out if he didn't comply with his wishes. Resigning himself to his fate he sat on the stool. "Just what is it that you want me to do?" he asked, with a grudging acceptance.

"I have an agent in France who has a package which he must deliver to me personally," said Sir Francis. "This should have been done two weeks ago but the boat that was going to rendezvous with him disappeared without a trace. I need to get another one out there as soon as possible but without raising any suspicions. You are the ideal man, Richard, and because your boats are in and out of Topsham all the time no one will question its departure. You must get home again as quickly as you can and employ a crew that you can trust with your life, because that is exactly what you will be doing. I will give you your instructions before you leave and, Richard, you must be in France within ten days at the most."

"Ten days! It could take me that long just to get home," Richard protested. "Have you any idea of the weather conditions I had to ride through just to get here and who knows what the roads will be like on the way back. There's no way I could find a suitable crew at such short notice let alone ready the ship to sail to France. You're asking the impossible Walsingham."

"Then you will just have to do the impossible. You must be there in ten days," repeated Sir Francis.

"Look, Walsingham, you just don't understand. Apart from what I've already explained there are many other things that could delay our departure, not least the weather," said Richard.

"Then you must pray for fair winds as Her Majesty's life depends on your safe return with your passenger and the intelligence he brings with him," said Walsingham. "Collect your belongings and I will meet you at the stables in half an hour."

Completely exasperated, Richard replied, "For God's sake, man, it's not possible in that time scale. It can't be done!"

"Ten days, Richard, ten days," said Walsingham. He opened the door and ushered Richard out.

Richard took himself back to Will's room,

where he almost collided with his friend in the doorway.

"Watch out! You're in a hell of a hurry, aren't you?" said Will, rubbing the elbow he'd hit off the door post.

"I'm glad you're here," said Richard. "I didn't want to leave without saying goodbye."

"Why, where are you going? Is it something to do with Walsingham? What did he say to you? asked Will, the questions tumbling out one after the other in quick succession.

"I'm going home. That man is a lunatic and the sooner I'm away from here the better," Richard answered, wondering how he had let himself be talked into this madness and by what miracle he would be in France in ten days.

"Are you coming back?" Will asked, desperate for Richard to confide in him. "What did Sir Francis want with you?"

"I don't know and I can't say," said Richard. "Now I really must get ready to leave."

Will was somewhat put out that Richard hadn't been more forthcoming but nevertheless he said his goodbyes and wished Richard well. It took just a few minutes for Richard to pack his saddlebags and to head for the stables. As he was striding across the yard, he met Joan coming in the opposite direction. Their eyes met and his heart jumped.

"Joan, what are you doing here at this hour?" asked Richard, forgetting all protocol and keeping his eyes fixed on hers.

Joan's heart hammered inside her breast. "I've just returned from my morning ride. I ride out every morning before I'm required to attend the queen."

"Alone?" queried Richard.

"No. I ride out with one of the grooms," she said. "Are you going riding?"

At that moment Walsingham shouted Richard's name from inside the stables.

"No, I'm leaving the palace this morning," Richard told her.

"So soon?" asked Joan. "But you've only just arrived!" Dear God, what could she say to prevent him leaving? Why did she want to prevent him leaving? What had happened to her when her eyes had met his? Was it only yesterday when an emotion she had never known before suddenly launched itself from deep within her and exploded as the buds of spring burst into summer? Ever since she'd taken him to the queen, she hadn't stopped thinking about him. She only knew his name. Where did he come from? Why had he come and why was he leaving? He was going away before she had the opportunity to find the answers to all her questions and more.

Richard saw the confusion in her eyes and noticed that she was trembling. He impulsively reached for one of her hands. When he touched her, his whole body reacted in a way he'd never experienced before. He was euphoric. He could see from the expression on Joan's face that she had been affected in the same way. At that moment their two souls merged as they held hands and looked deep into each other's eyes, seeing their love mirrored from one to the other. How could this have happened. It felt so right, so perfect.

The spell was broken by Walsingham shouting for Richard's attention again. "Curse that man," thought Richard, but to Joan said, "I really must go now," and reluctantly retrieved his hand from hers. "I will come back just as soon as I can."

"But, Richard, that might be too late," said Joan, tears in her eyes.

Richard knew only too well why it might be too late and wanted to wrap her in his arms and kiss the tears away—but Walsingham, beginning to lose patience, was demanding his presence in the stable immediately. He raised her hands to his lips and kissed each one gently before he was forced to walk away from the woman who held his heart in her hands. The woman who he loved more dearly than his life and who, if he didn't get back in time, would be condemned to be chained forever to a man she hated. He was being torn in two and he knew that if he looked back, he would run to her and embrace her tightly, never to leave her again.

It was with a heavy heart that he marched into

the stable, cursing Walsingham to hell under his breath. He had never felt so wretched.

"These are your charts and instructions," said Walsingham, handing Richard a large pouch. "Guard them with your life. Under no account must you let them out of your sight," he added in a tone which intimated to Richard that attempts might be made to steal the pouch from him and that as a consequence, his life could now be in danger.

A groom brought Richard's horse already saddled and ready for the journey. As Walsingham watched Richard secure the pouch in his saddlebags, he reminded him again that no one, not even his father, must know of his mission. "Remember this whole realm and your queen are depending on you, Richard. Don't let them down, or me," said Sir Francis, putting his hand on Richard's shoulder.

Richard mounted and with one last look at Joan's forlorn face he gently touched his horse's flanks with his spurs and galloped out of the yard. As he passed through the palace gate, he began to ponder just what it was he had got involved with. He already felt out of his depth. He wasn't used to all this secrecy and deceit nor was he the kind of man who gambled his life and those of others on risky, hazardous adventures; he wasn't cut out for this kind of thing. Not for the first time did he ask himself why on earth had he allowed himself to be put in this position by Walsingham.

When he had wakened in the morning, he had been just a wool merchant's son. Now a few short hours later he was a man carrying fate of his sovereign and his country on his shoulders. It didn't seem possible that this transformation could have happened so quickly. However, he had given his word and now he must see his mission through.

Joan watched him leave the courtyard and continued to look after him long after he was out of sight. She returned to her duties, heartbroken, her tears still damp on her cheeks.

CHAPTER FIVE

The Preparations

Richard arrived in Topsham after four days of hard riding. He knew he would never have done the journey so quickly without Diablo's remarkable stamina. Richard himself had rested for only a few hours each night, arriving at the inns late in the evening and leaving immediately after an early breakfast. Every time he had slept, he'd used the pouch containing Walsingham's instructions as his pillow, always making sure the door to his room was firmly locked.

It was much easier to travel the roads now after several warm, dry days although some of the rivers were still higher than they would normally be at this time of year because they were still being fed by all the excess water coming from the hills and many of the fords could still only be crossed by brave horses with competent riders. Richard was able to avoid most of the detours he'd been forced to take on his way to London for which he was extremely grateful as time was of the essence. He'd managed to save even more time by avoiding some of the deeply rutted roads and riding cross-country wherever possible. Conditions were still far from perfect but thanks to his mount's resilience and sure-footedness combined with his skill as a horseman Richard had reached his destination safely and in reasonable time.

Not long after he had left London, he realised he had no idea when the marriage between Joan and Lord de Luc was due to take place. Perhaps it wouldn't matter how quickly he returned—he might still be too late. He had to believe that he would get back in time to save Joan or he would go insane, and he knew he was going to need all his wits about him to accomplish the mission he'd been given.

Throughout his journey he kept going over in his mind everything that Walsingham had said to him in London. The more he thought, the more apprehensive he became. He had severe doubts about the possibility of putting together a good crew at such short notice and was even less sure about being able to reach France within Walsingham's ten-day deadline. The man just couldn't be reasoned with and was adamant about the ten-day rendezvous. Four of those days had already been spent just getting home and the pace and conditions of that journey had tested the endurance of both horse and rider to the limit At least Diablo would have a good rest before his next outing. For Richard there was no such luxury. It was going to be well-nigh impossible to keep to Walsingham's schedule but he would do his damnedest to keep his word.

When he hadn't been thinking about the task set by Walsingham his mind had been firmly fixed on Joan. He was besotted with her. Never in his wildest dreams could he have imagined falling in love so quickly and completely with such a beautiful woman, and the most wonderful thing was that she appeared to be in love with him too. At this particular time in his life the last thing he was thinking of was becoming involved romantically with a woman. He knew what Will and the others had said was true. She was far above him in status and class and under normal circumstances he could never have hoped to win her love. But the situation they were both in at the moment was anything but normal. When he had touched her hand and looked into her eyes, he knew his love for her was mutual, but he also knew that if he couldn't change the future that awaited her that love would be lost to him forever. He was determined that he would never let that happen.

Walsingham had dragged them apart before they'd even had a proper chance to speak to each other. Almost all they knew about each other was their names and that they were in love. It was totally bizarre. Once again, he silently cursed Walsingham and the infernal mission he had been charged with, temporarily forgetting that if the man hadn't summoned him to London he would never have met Joan. How he wished that instead of sailing off to France he was still in London with her, searching for a way to rescue her from Lord de Luc's evil clutches. God grant that this business of Walsingham's would be completed successfully and as soon as possible!

He had eaten sparingly on his way from London, not wanting to take any more time than was absolutely necessary to refresh himself and now he was very hungry as well as completely exhausted. Nevertheless, as soon as he'd stabled his horse at The Bush, leaving explicit instructions as to how Diablo was to be cared for after his arduous journey, and still carrying his saddle bags containing Walsingham's precious pouch, he immediately set off in search of one of his captains. He was so tired he could hardly put one foot in front of the other. However, he was in luck and found his best man at the first tavern he tried.

His captain, Tom Ashe, was sitting with four other sailors in the corner by the empty fireplace, drinking ale and obviously in high spirits. They were laughing and singing together very loudly and very out of tune. Richard shouted to the landlord above the din of the busy tavern and ordered seven tankards of ale to be brought over to the table in the corner.

When Richard reached the table, the men were all laughing raucously at a joke that one of them had just finished telling and it was plain to see that they had been drinking heavily for some time. His man had tried to stand when he saw Richard approaching but he was so unsteady on his feet that he fell back onto the bench, much to the amusement of his comrades who dissolved into hoots of drunken laughter. There were shouts of gratitude when the landlord placed the tankards of ale on the table. The sailors seized one a piece rowdily, thanking Richard for his generosity and spilling a good proportion of their ale while clumsily trying to toast him. Richard lifted one of the remaining two vessels and downed it in almost one swallow before drinking his second more slowly, slaking the thirst that had been growing since breakfast. Refusing the offer of more ale from the drunken seafarers he turned his attention to his captain.

"Tom, I'm glad I've found you," began Richard, who was mightily relieved at not having to search all taverns of the town, looking for someone who he could trust and rely on. Captain Tom Ashe had worked from the very beginning of their continental trading, first for Sir Edmund and then for Richard. He was honest and reliable and a first-class sailor who had sailed their ships backwards and forwards to France and the Netherlands many times and in all kinds of weather and in all that time he had never lost a crew member or a cargo. "Can you stand, Tom?" Richard asked him. "I need to talk to you privately. Are you fit to walk outside?"

"Aye, sir," said the captain. He got unsteadily to his feet whilst holding on to the table until he found his balance. Even in his drunken state Tom was puzzled by Richard's sudden arrival at the tavern, the state of his travelling clothes and the level of anxiety he was displaying. "What's amiss Master Lovell?" Tom slurred rather apprehensively. This was completely out of character for his young, usually calm and measured employer. He knew that his latest cargo was all present and correct as he had personally overseen the unloading of his ship with the excise man earlier in the day so presumably Master Lovell's agitation was nothing to do with that.

"I'd rather talk outside," said Richard, reluctant to speak in such a public place. They made their excuses to the sailors who shouted a noisy farewell and immediately broke into song again.

Richard ushered Tom into the yard behind the tavern. He drew a bucket of water from the animal trough and gave it to the captain who emptied it over his head and returned the bucket to Richard. After he had shaken his head a few times and dried his face on his hat Tom sobered up quickly. He was eager to hear why Master Lovell had come looking for him. Richard made sure that there was no one within earshot before he began to speak. "Tom, I need you and the best crew you can muster to accompany me on a voyage. They must be men we can trust as well as the best of sailors."

"Aye sir, I can do that," said the captain, now completely lucid again. "When are we sailing and where to?"

"We sail on this evening's tide and you'll be given your destination when we're at sea," answered Richard.

The expression on his captain's face was one of utter shock. "Oh no, Master Lovell, sir, we could never be ready to sail so soon. We only docked this morning and you saw the state of the crew in the tavern. You must know too, sir, that you'll never get a crew to sign on unless they know where they're going."

Richard did know and it was the one thing that worried him most about this venture because if he couldn't secure a crew the whole thing would fail before it even started. "Look Tom, I can't explain now but believe me it is imperative that we find a crew and leave tonight and in complete secrecy. I would never normally ask you to undertake a voyage under these circumstances, but these are not normal times," said Richard, who was conscious that precious time was passing by.

Tom was more than a little intrigued. Here was a man who kept both his feet on the ground, knew his business inside out, and dealt with everyone openly and fairly. So why did he want to ship out of Topsham so soon and so secretly? This was completely out of the ordinary.

"Tom, I can't pretend there won't be any risk involved or that the voyage won't be a dangerous one, but I can tell you that it will be the most important one we'll ever make," continued Richard.

By now Tom was beginning to feel quite unnerved. Combined with his unkempt state and the way he was clutching his saddlebags, although he had no horse with him, Richard gave Tom the impression that he was slightly deranged. Richard was obviously afraid of something or somebody as he was continually casting his eyes about the shadows like a hunted man. Something wasn't right.

"Sir, you don't look well. Perhaps I should take you to your lodgings." Tom suggested as he tried to take Richard's arm.

"There's nothing wrong with me, Tom," said Richard testily, and shook himself free from Tom's grip. "Look, I know this is unorthodox and completely out of character, but I really can't tell you our destination until we've cast off but what I will tell is that our mission is crucial and concerns the security of this realm and everyone in it. You'll just have to trust me for the moment," said Richard. "I'm begging you Tom, find me a crew and quickly or we'll miss the tide. Promise them whatever you have to get them to sign on."

Tom didn't know what to think. How had

Master Lovell, who had never ventured any further than Devon, as far as he knew, got himself involved in matters of national security? Tom knew Richard to be a straight and honest man and as such he was sure that this voyage, whatever its purpose and destination, would be lawful, even if unconventional, but as for finding a crew with as much faith in Richard as he had, well that was going to be another matter!

"Tom, please, we're wasting time," pleaded Richard.

"I'll do my best sir, but it won't be easy and if I do find any sailors willing to go, they'll be looking for something on account," said the captain.

"Of course," said Richard and he reached into his purse and handed Tom some coins. "Make sure they're on board before you give them any money or you'll never get them out of the tavern," warned Richard, "and tell them there'll be more when the job is completed. Come, we must hurry. I'll meet you on the quay when it's time to sail and remember to recruit your men quietly, this is a secret voyage."

Tom would have liked to have learned more but he knew Richard had told him all he was going to before they were at sea, and besides, Richard had already turned away and was heading in the direction of The Bush. Richard was well known and well respected by the sea-going fraternity in Topsham and Tom knew he was going to have to rely heavily on that reputation to persuade a competent crew to join them and even then, it was going to be difficult to get any decent seaman to sign on blind.

When Richard arrived at The Bush he went straight up to his rooms, threw off his cloak and unpacked his saddlebags. He spread the charts on his cot and read Walsingham's instructions again. They were to leave Topsham as quietly as possible and sail to the Cap Gris Nez on the coast of France where they were to wait offshore opposite the small cove under the site of King Henry's old fort built on the cliff top. At dusk they are to sail in close to the shore and wait for a signal light from the beach which would tell them that their passenger was on his way to be picked up. They in turn were to show a light to guide him to the boat. Had Walsingham any idea of the danger he was putting him, his crew and his ship in? They were going to be sailing at night without light, which was hazardous enough in itself, and then during the day when they would be prey to Spaniards or pirates, they were to sit offshore, defenceless, and finally they were to navigate their way into an unfamiliar cove by failing light. Then, if by some miracle they survived would their passenger be there, and would they get him and his information back to London safely and in time?

"Dear God, I must have been mad to have allowed myself to get forced into this position," thought Richard. He carefully folded the papers and returned them to the pouch, which he then secured inside his tunic.

He washed and tidied himself up a little before went down into the busy tavern and secured himself a hot meal and a tankard of ale. He'd had nothing to eat since early morning and he tucked into his stew and fresh bread with relish. He soon cleared his plate and as he sat cradling his tankard in his hands his thoughts bounced backwards and forwards from Walsingham's mission to Joan. Would he return in time to prevent Joan's marriage to Lord de Luc, and even if he did just how did he intend to prevent an entirely lawful wedding? Kidnap Joan and run away to the continent? No, that would mean they would be fugitives for the rest of their lives and never be able to return home which would break his parents' hearts. Challenge de Luc to a duel? He couldn't do that either as he might be killed himself or end up on the end of a rope on the gallows for killing de Luc. Either way his father would be left without an heir and Joan without the man who loved her with all his heart. There must be a way to save the girl who now held his heart in her hands.

These thoughts now filled his every waking hour, and he was determined to find a way but first he must succeed in Walsingham's rescue mission before he could embark on his own. Damn Walsingham, for the umpteenth time!

When he'd drained his tankard, Richard

returned to his room to try to snatch a few hours' sleep before he was due to meet Tom at the ship. He closed his eyes and saw Joan's lovely face. Soon he was dreaming that she was wrapped in his arms and about to yield her body to him but then the beautiful image was shattered and replaced by one of a triumphant de Luc snatching Joan from his embrace and carrying her away. Richard sat bolt upright in a cold sweat.

"There must be a way to wrest Joan from him and I WILL find it!" he promised himself. He lay down again and after much tossing and turning he eventually drifted off again into a restless sleep.

Richard arrived at the wharf just after the sun had gone down to find his captain and crew were already aboard and preparing the ship for their voyage. It was a fine evening with a stiff breeze, which would send them swiftly on their journey, and not another soul to be seen on the wharf. As Richard threw his gear onto the deck and jumped down after it, Tom walked across the deck to meet him and he didn't look happy.

"I'm sorry sir, but this was the best I could get and I was lucky to get them," he said. "They are good sailors but they include a few very rough diamonds I'm afraid. In fact, one or two of them have been suspected of piracy in the past. They also didn't come cheap, Master Richard. I had to promise them a considerable amount to persuade them to sign on for the trip. It's only because of your reputation that they were willing to trust your word, but I would hate to think what would happen if for some reason that word wasn't kept."

"Thank you, Tom. I'm sure you've done your best and I appreciate that. I won't forget what you've done for me today," said Richard.

The sailors had seen Richard come aboard and had acknowledged him with a nod of the head before they resumed their duties.

"My God, a motley crew indeed!" thought Richard, as he looked from one to the other of the sailors on the deck. It was the minimum crew required to handle the ship and among them there were one or two who he would never like to turn his back on but beggars can't be choosers and he had no choice but to take what he could get and hope for the best. "Are we ready to put to sea, Captain?" he asked.

"Aye, sir, we are," replied Tom.

"Then let's cast off, put our trust in God and hope we can get this venture concluded as quickly as possible," said Richard.

"And what exactly is the venture Master Richard, sir?" asked Tom, raising one eyebrow.

"Patience, Tom, patience. You'll know soon enough now," replied Richard, taking one last glance up and down the quayside. He was relieved to see that there was no one but themselves on the dock. The captain quietly gave the order to cast off and without showing any lights they silently slipped out of the harbour into the gathering gloom. Richard knew that what he was about to embark on wouldn't be an easy voyage, even with the most experienced of crews, let alone one botched together at the last minute and likely never having sailed together before. Little did he know just how near impossible it would turn out to be.

At the same time as Richard was leaving for France, Joan was in the Great Hall at the palace looking for Will. She had not stopped thinking about Richard since they had said their farewells in the stable yard. Why had he left so suddenly and where had he gone? She was sure from the look she'd seen in his eyes when they parted that he felt the same for her as she did for him. How could fate be so cruel as to part them almost as soon as they had met? The Hall was crowded but as Her Majesty was not present Joan was able to stand on the dais beside the throne to see above the heads of the throng. She spotted Will talking to John on the far side of the room and she made her way towards them through the mass of folk who were too busy with their own agendas to even notice her as she beat a path across the Hall.

"You're Richard Lovell's friends, aren't you?" Joan asked the two young men.

"Yes, we are, Mistress Joan. I'm Will and this is John," answered Will, motioning to the man standing beside him. It wasn't every day that a queen's lady deliberately sought out a couple of humble clerks and both men were intrigued and rather flattered.

"Do you know where he is?" asked Joan hopefully.

"I'm sorry, no I don't. I haven't seen or heard anything of him since he left for Topsham a few days ago on some kind of mission for Walsingham," replied Will.

"When will he return to Court? I must see him soon before it's too late," said Joan.

"Too late for what, my lady?"

"Oh, never mind. I'll need to find Walsingham," she said impatiently.

"You'll be wasting your time," Will told her. "He's the most secretive, tight-lipped man I've ever met. You'll get blood from a stone before you'll get any information out of Sir Francis and he doesn't like being interrogated, Mistress Joan. It might be better if you just wait until Richard returns."

"I should have known you would be of no help," Joan said, and ignoring Will's advice, she stormed off to find Walsingham, roughly pushing her way through the swarm of people as she went.

"I wish I knew what the hell was going on," Will complained to John. "First Richard appears from nowhere, summoned by Walsingham. Then he's dispatched to heaven knows where at a moment's notice and leaves as if all the demons in hell were chasing him. Now Joan Marchemont, the sister of the man who wants to kill him, is desperate to find him for some reason and I'd love to know why."

"Richard started to act strangely after he'd met her if you remember," said John. "Do you think that she's involved in Walsingham's plan too?"

"I doubt it! The only woman he seems to have any time for is the queen herself. But then what do I know? Nothing, as usual. All I ever get is 'Will, go here, Will, go there, Will, do this, Will, do that' but I'm never allowed to become properly involved in anything that's important," complained Will. "The only person Walsingham confides in is Phelipps and he's every bit as secretive as Sir Francis."

"I have the same problem with Cecil," said John. "Here, Will, you don't suppose there's something going on between your old friend and Joan, even after such a short time, do you?"

"I very much doubt it! They're worlds apart and she's betrothed to another man. Let's forget about them and go and eat before it's too late," said Will.

Joan was so intent on reaching Walsingham's office that she didn't notice Lord de Luc coming down the corridor in the opposite direction until it was too late. De Luc blocked her way. "Well, my dear, this is an unexpected treat," he said.

Joan froze, feeling like a small animal trapped

by the mesmerising gaze of a snake just before it struck. There was no escape. Her mouth was suddenly dry and her flesh began to creep at the thought of him touching her.

"Come, my love, it's time we got to know each other a little better," de Luc said. He cupped her chin in his hand while the other gripped her tightly around her waist, and brought his mouth down hard on hers, but Joan kept her teeth firmly clenched and resisted the pressure of his tongue trying to force its way between her lips. She tried in vain to free herself from his iron grip and was in danger of fainting when he finally stopped kissing her. She lifted her hand to strike him but he was too quick for her and caught her wrist.

"My my, quite the little vixen aren't we? I'm going to enjoy taming you my dear," de Luc sneered. "I think it's time I started to put pressure on your father's creditors to demand their payment from him. Then he will be forced to honour our little agreement sooner rather than later."

"I would kill myself before I would allow you to take me as your wife," vowed Joan, still struggling.

"Oh, my precious," de Luc said, grinning, "I most certainly will take you for my bride and then take you to my bed where I will teach you how to please me. We will do well together, you and I. I much prefer it when my ladies put up a fight, but I inevitably have my way!"

"Get your hands off me!" screamed Joan, and finally managed to wriggle free.

"Oh wonderful," said de Luc, "you've no idea how much I'm looking forward to getting you all to myself. Now I must leave you, my love, and go in search of certain creditors."

He was still laughing loudly when he reached the door at the end of the corridor. Trembling, Joan leant against the wall for a few seconds to catch her breath; she then fled as fast as her legs would carry her for fear that de Luc would return. She kept running until she reached Walsingham's office, where she rushed headlong through the door unannounced. A startled Walsingham and Phelipps both rose from their stools as a very distressed and dishevelled Joan almost fell to the floor. "Oh, Sir Francis, thank God you're here!" she gasped.

"My Lady, please calm yourself," said Walsingham. He helped her back to his seat and motioned to Phelipps to pour her a goblet of wine. After she took a few sips of the wine he asked apprehensively, "Mistress Joan, what brings you here in such haste? Is something wrong with Her Majesty?"

"No, of course not!" she snapped. "Sir Francis, you must tell me the whereabouts of Richard Lovell. I believe he is away on some business of yours, but I must speak with him before it's too late. Tell me where he is so that I may go to him," pleaded Joan, beginning to lose her composure and starting to cry.

"I'm afraid where he is you cannot go, mistress," said Walsingham quietly.

"But you don't understand. If I don't find him soon my life will be ended. When is he coming back? I don't have much time left," Joan sobbed. The encounter with de Luc had completely unnerved her and she desperately needed Walsingham to reveal where Richard was. She believed that if only she could get to him, he would make everything right. He would protect her against Lord de Luc and somehow prevent him from marrying her. She didn't know how but she knew that he would, somehow. "Please, Sir Francis, tell me where I can find him," she pleaded.

Walsingham was out of his depth. He was used to dealing with traitors and assassins and the like but certainly not with distraught women. "I'm also impatient to see Richard too, my dear young lady, and I'm expecting him to arrive sometime in the next week." He went down on one knee beside her stool and held her hand. "I promise you that as soon as he gets back, and we have concluded our business I will send him to you immediately Now you must return to the queen before she misses you. You know that she doesn't like her ladies to be out of her sight for too long."

Joan tried to protest, but with a nod from Walsingham, Phelipps gently ushered her out of the tiny office. She had no option but to hope that if Richard did return within the week, he would still be in time to rescue her from de Luc.

"Well, I wonder what that little outburst was all about," Phelipps said.

"I believe that Mistress Joan is about to be sacrificed by Lord Marchemont to that ogre Lord de Luc in return for having his debts paid and that she, unfortunately, has fallen in love with our young Richard," Sir Francis answered.

"Holy Mother of God!" Phelipps exclaimed. "The poor child. How could any father allow his daughter to be subjected to such depravity?" Normally he had little concern for the unsuitability of any marriages. It was how things were done; women married whoever their father chose for them. But de Luc was an exception. He was evil personified.

"How indeed," said Walsingham. He picked up his quill and began scratching on a piece of parchment.

CHAPTER SIX

The Voyage

Despite all of Richard's misgivings his ship reached its designated position off the French coast by mid-afternoon on the appointed day, thanks to the strong following wind they had picked up when they left the English coast. When they had reached the sea after leaving Topsham Richard had revealed their destination and unveiled their mission as promised. It didn't go down well. Some of the crew wanted to return to port immediately while others labelled it a suicide mission that would see them all ending up in at the bottom of the sea.

Tom and Richard had a hard time persuading them to stick with it and see the mission through. It was only after much arguing and the offer of even more coin that the crew agreed to carry on. Richard had no idea where he would get all this extra money he was promising but that was a worry for another day. Although the crew had worked almost non-stop since the new deal had been reached, he wasn't at all sure that he trusted any of them to keep their word.

They managed to steer clear of any other shipping during the day, but it had been much more risky sailing at night when they couldn't use any lights. The helmsman had steered a course using the stars when he could see them while the rest of the sailors took it in turns to listen for tell-tale signs that there were other vessels close by. They did this in complete silence to prevent any noise alerting any nearby vessel to their presence.

So far, they had avoided any unwarranted attention, and everything was going to plan, much to Richard's relief. The crew were happy too as it seemed that they were going to earn a lot of money for little effort. When they had lowered the sails and dropped anchor the captain posted two lookouts and stood the rest of the crew down until dusk. They tucked into some of the few rations they had brought with them and then found somewhere on deck to curl up to catch some sleep before it was time for them to manoeuvre the ship into the cove and closer to the shore. Richard, although not a sailor, had been working alongside the crew doing whatever he could to help, despite still recovering from his dash from London, and was just as tired as they. When he had eaten, he pulled his cloak tight around his shoulders, leaned back against the main mast where he had been sitting, and closed his eyes.

He should have known that his good luck wouldn't hold. In less than half an hour there was a cry from one of the lookouts. "Sail astern, Captain!" he shouted.

Richard, startled out of his sleep, leapt to his feet and was soon standing at Tom's side.

"Where away?" asked the captain, as he raised his telescope to his eye.

"Off toward starboard," answered the sailor.

"Dear God!" Tom exclaimed. "It's a Spanish galleon in full sail!"

He handed the glass to Richard, who took a look. "Even if we could raise the sails quick enough, we could never outrun her," Richard said. "She's far too fast."

Tom took the glass back from him. "Do you think they're looking for us, Master Richard?"

"I don't know. I don't think we were seen leaving port and we haven't noticed any vessel following us," Richard replied. "But we're a cargo ship and if they think we're carrying something valuable they won't pass up the opportunity to help themselves."

"If they board us, we could put up little resistance, sir. We only have a couple of side-arms and whatever the crew has. Certainly nothing to match what the Spaniards will have," said Tom.

"Damn!" Richard cursed. "Could we get in closer to the shore before they reach us? If we could do that they wouldn't be able to follow us without running themselves aground."

"We wouldn't have time to raise the anchor let alone set the sails. She's coming too fast," Tom said.

The crew was now fully awake, hanging over the ship's rail and watching the galleon closing in at great speed. "My God, she's heading straight for us. She's for ramming us, sir!" shouted one of the sailors.

"Hell's teeth! Isn't there anything we can do to get out of her path?" Richard yelled at Tom. Surely his mission wasn't going to be scuppered by a damned Spaniard.

"We can try, Master Richard," said the captain. When some of the crew prepared to jump ship before they were run down by the huge galleon, Tom drew his pistol and ordered the sailors to stand fast, threatening to shoot the first one to go over the side. They reluctantly returned to the deck and began to haul up the anchor and raise the sails as fast as they could.

The captain took the wheel himself, keeping his pistol within easy reach while Richard lent a hand to get the main sail up. Although the men put their all into hoisting the sails it seemed to take forever for them to lift and the galleon was still bearing down on them. Richard stole a glance at the Spaniard. They weren't going to make it in time. The ship was travelling towards them at a terrific rate of knots, and they were directly in its path.

The sailors kept to the task as none wanted to receive a bullet in their head. Richard could see the sheer terror in their eyes as they heaved on the ropes. "You can't let me die now!" he silently screamed at God. "Not now! I need to get back to Joan!" He pulled on the rope with a strength he didn't know he possessed but the effort was testing his heart and lungs to their limit. He felt his pumping heart was about to explode and his lungs were almost ready to burst.

"Heave, damn you!" the captain yelled. "Put your backs into it before we're sliced in half!"

The sailors were swearing profusely and cursing everyone from their captain to their god. They were all at their limit and almost at the state of collapse when suddenly the sails caught the wind and the captain spun the wheel to steer the ship out of the Spaniard's path. It was a close-run thing; the galleon passed with very little water between them. Richard wondered if they'd even been noticed by the other ship's crew. The swell from the near miss hit them broadside with enough force to knock most of the crew off their feet. The ship rocked violently from side to side before settling.

"My God, Tom, we're bobbing about like a damn cork in a barrel," choked Richard, his hands on his knees. His hands were bleeding from hoisting the sail and he had a nasty cut on his forehead where he had hit it on the ship's rail when he had lost his footing. The crewmen who had fallen when the ship lurched were also finding their feet again, rubbing bruised heads and limbs and cursing the Spaniards to hell or worse.

"I'm sorry sir, but we only had time to load half the amount of ballast needed to compensate for the lack of cargo by the time I'd found a crew and got them back to the ship," Tom replied. "We were lucky to get that much done. The lads nearly broke their backs heaving it all on board."

"Well, let's hope we don't have need of the other half before we reach home," said Richard.

Just then there was another shout from the look-out. "Sail astern to starboard!"

"Holy Mother, not another," said Richard, mopping the blood from his brow with his kerchief.

"She's not a Spaniard, sir, she's a privateer and she's on the same course as the galleon!" shouted the lookout.

Richard could now see the oncoming ship himself. "What the hell's going on, Tom?" he asked.

"Damned if I know, Master Richard."

It was one of the dubious sailors who offered the most likely explanation, no doubt having served on a privateer himself. Richard had heard many gruesome stories about One-Eyed Jack and he was of the opinion that most of them were probably based in truth. He was a nasty piece of work, not the kind of man you would turn your back on, and Richard would have preferred not to have had him aboard. Now laughing, Jack said, "I'd bet my last penny that the Spaniard's carrying a rich cargo and that these lads are going to relieve them of it and good luck to them."

"Aye, and let's hope they send the murdering scum to a watery grave," said one of the others.

"Well that explains why they weren't interested in us!" Richard returned. "I don't think that they even saw us."

Meanwhile the second vessel was coming towards them as if the devil himself was chasing her. It almost seemed to skim across the tops of the waves. Tom had managed to reposition Richard's ship, so the privateer shot past them with plenty of room to spare. As she passed by, Richard's crew shouted and waved their encouragement and a few of the men on the other ship acknowledged them, but most were busy making ready for the battle that was to follow when they overhauled the galleon. Richard guessed that more than one member of his crew would have preferred to have been aboard the privateer rather than sitting on his ship, but he had no time to think about that now or the near miss they'd just survived because the sun was beginning to disappear below the horizon. They must set a course to bring them in closer to the shore before it got too dark for them to see anything at all. He didn't want to end up stranded on a sandbank or dashed against any jagged rocks.

They sailed in as close as they dared and dropped anchor. Now they just had to sit tight, tend to their abrasions, and wait for the signal.

After about half an hour Richard thought he saw a flash of light on the top of the cliff but couldn't be sure, it was so brief. He was still staring through the gloom when Tom tapped him on the shoulder and pointed to the shore. Someone was swinging a lantern.

"Hopefully that will be our man, Captain," Richard said. "Show a light and lower the longboat and we'll go to meet him."

The captain gave the order and the sailors jumped to. The boat was lowered quickly by practised hands and Richard along with four others set off into the near darkness. Richard sat in the stern while the sailors began to make short work of rowing the distance between the ship and the shore, guided by the lantern. They were only about a hundred yards from the shore, heading towards where the lantern was signalling when Richard saw the flash.

Everyone heard the shot that followed. There was a dull thud followed by a scream and then both man and lantern disappeared under the waves. Richard quickly lit the boat's lantern and the horrified sailors picked up their oars again and rowed swiftly towards the spot where the man had disappeared. When they neared the place Richard held the lantern high above his head, waving it backwards and forwards in an arc, until he saw the body floating face down on top of the waves with its life's blood ebbing away into the sea.

Richard jumped into the water, now only at chest height, and turned the man over. By some miracle he was still alive, but only just. Richard shouted for help and one of the sailors jumped into the sea beside him; between them they took the man's weight and prepared to lift him into the boat.

"Leave me and save yourselves," gasped the man. "I'm done for, there's nothing you can do for me now." He turned his head toward Richard. "Are you Walsingham's man?"

"Yes, I'm Richard Lovell sent by Sir Francis to bring you to England," replied Richard.

"I'll never see England again," whispered Walsingham's agent. He painfully took a leather pouch out of his jerkin and handed it to Richard. "Take this, guard it with your life and give it only to Walsingham," he spluttered. Blood trickled from the corner of his mouth.

"Master Richard, we've got company, sir," said one of the sailors still in the boat.

Richard looked towards the shore. He saw the light and then heard the splash as two people ran into the water and started to head for them. The light from the lantern that had helped them to locate the wounded agent had also led the assassins directly to them.

"We need to get back to the ship now before they reach us," said the sailor.

"I can't just leave him," Richard protested, still cradling the wounded man's head.

"Go, leave me. I'm a dead man. Go now and get the package safely to London," wheezed the man.

Choking on his own blood, he breathed his last. Richard released him and watched him slowly drift away on the current.

"Sir, we must leave now. These men are coming fast," said another of the sailors.

The seaman who had assisted Richard in the water was quickly hauled back into the boat but as they took hold of Richard another shot rang out. Richard felt a searing pain in his left shoulder and fell backwards into the sea again. Two of the men jumped into the water and were attempting to lift Richard up over the side when the assassins reached them and tried to wrench him from the sailors' grasp. One-Eyed Jack, who was still in the boat, produced a cudgel from his belt and brought it down so hard onto the head of one of the assailants that it split the man's skull. His legs crumpled beneath him and he disappeared under the waves without another sound.

His companion was still struggling to pull Richard away from his rescuers when the sailor previously with Richard in the water leapt back off the boat, pulled his dagger from his belt, and forced it between the other killer's ribs. The assassin let out a scream. His lifeless arms released their hold on Richard and his body drifted off in the same direction as Walsingham's messenger.

The four sailors managed between them to get Richard back into the boat and began to row for all they were worth towards the light showing on their ship. Tom and the others had heard the two shots and the screams and were extremely anxious for the longboat to return. When Tom saw Richard lying in the bottom of the boat, he thought he was dead; he felt immense relief when he heard him moan as the sailors lifted him onto the deck of the ship.

The boat was raised and secured, the captain gave the order to get under way while Richard was carried carefully to Tom's cabin and sat on the bed. While Tom did his best to stem the blood which was oozing out between Richard's fingers, Jack related what had happened, although elaborating somewhat on his part in rescuing Richard.

The bullet had ripped a hole through Richard's shoulder and had shattered some of the bone. Apart from not being a doctor, Tom had nothing medical with which to clean his wound or instruments to remove the splintered bone; he padded the hole as best he could with what clean rags he could find and formed a sling out of his own shirt, Richard moaning and swearing through the whole process. Tom wondered who it was that had killed their intended passenger and then tried to kill Richard. How had they known the time and place for the rendezvous? After all, Master Richard had insisted on absolute secrecy and no one on board knew where they were headed until they were underway. Also, who was their intended passenger and why was he so important? Finally, if Richard died how could he explain it to Sir Edmund? So many unanswered questions.

When Tom had finished, Richard tried to stand up, but he had no strength in his legs. Tom persuaded him to lie down and rest and then went back on deck. Richard wanted to argue but knew in his present state he would be no help to anyone. He lay back and closed his eyes.

They were sailing at night again but there was just a gentle swell and no sign nor sound of any other ship. Unless the wind changed, they should reach port on time, but Tom was worried about Richard. If the wound wasn't treated properly and soon, it would become infected and then his chances of pulling through would be virtually nil. God grant that they get him home quickly and safely.

About three hours into the voyage the wind dropped. This was the last thing Tom needed. Time was of the essence, both for the success of their mission but even more importantly now for Richard's survival. A short time later they saw the first lightning on the horizon lighting up the storm clouds which were gathering above them. Before long they were being buffeted by huge waves whipped up by a fierce wind. If these conditions were to worsen the lack of proper ballast would probably lead to the ship's demise and the loss of all their lives. The wind had turned one hundred and eighty degrees and now instead of helping them towards England the storm was blowing them back to France.

The severe rolling of the ship had wakened Richard. He dragged himself off the bunk but as he tried to stand his head began to swim. He managed to steady himself and staggered out of the cabin onto the deck gripping his shoulder. He was very weak from the loss of blood and almost immediately he was flung into the mainmast by the force of the wind. He screamed out in pain as his shoulder felt the full impact of the collision with the mast. Somehow, he managed to hook his free arm around the mast which prevented him from being swept off the deck and into the sea. Anything that was unsecured was being hurled about the deck or launched over the rail into the churning cauldron of the sea. Richard might have been master of his father's shipping business, but he was certainly no sailor. He began to retch violently and soon parted with what remained of the meagre meal he'd eaten earlier. Every heave sent a searing pain through his shoulder.

Soon there was nothing left to bring up and the pain in his shoulder became unbearable. Some of the sailors had roped themselves to the ship's rail as they tried to reduce the sails before the wind ripped them from the mast. A torrent of sea spray whipped across the deck, stinging the hands and faces of everyone exposed to it. Others were thrown about the ship like bits of flotsam as they tried to gain purchase on the deck and were hanging on to anything secure that they could reach. The ship was being pitched and tossed in the tempest just like a child's toy ship thrown into the river rapids.

Through the chaos Tom noticed Richard clinging on to the mast. He made his way to him by pulling himself along the rail. The noise of the wind, almost deafening by this time, was too strong to stand against so Tom crawled the rest of the way to the mast, hoping he wouldn't be hit by any flying debris. He had to shout directly into Richard's ear to make himself heard. "Good God, Master Richard, you shouldn't be out here in your condition. Let me help you back to the cabin!"

"No, Tom. If I'm going to die, I'd rather see it coming!" shouted Richard, with what little strength he had left. He hung on tightly to the mast with one hand while the other tried to protect his shoulder which had started to bleed again. "Are we making any progress?"

"I don't like the way this is developing, Master

Richard! I really don't. It's most unusual to get a storm like this at this time of year. We're finding it almost impossible to keep her heading into the wind even with two of us at the wheel. We may have to turn and run with it just to stay afloat if conditions get any worse!"

The wind was now roaring around the ship like a howling banshee and it was getting hard to hear anything else above it.

"No captain, I forbid it!" Richard yelled, fighting to be heard above the screeching of the gale, and struggling to cling to the mast. He was weakening very quickly. "We must go on to London. We must continue with our mission!"

"Look, I'll try, sir, but the crew's already talking about turning back and putting into a French port to wait out the storm. They're frightened, sir, and so should you be!" Tom bellowed. "It's one of the worst storms I've ever sailed through if not the worst and this ship is less than stable even for mild conditions at the moment let alone a damn near hurricane."

The sailors had already taken most of the sails down although some had been badly ripped and it now required three men to wrestle with the wheel to hold the ship on course.

Richard's legs finally gave up the fight and he slowly slipped down the mast. He rested on the deck with his back against the big lump of oak. Tom used a piece of spare rope to tie round Richard's waist and lashed him to the mast since he no longer had the strength to hold on unaided.

"Please, Tom, I beg you, don't let them turn back. We must carry on to England or everything will be lost!" shouted Richard, using the last of his strength.

"Master Richard, sir, if we continue to sail into the teeth of this storm everything will be lost. The crew, the ship and yourself. You would be no use to Walsingham or anyone else then! We can't take the risk and besides, if the crew want to go back to France, they would have no trouble at all over-powering us and taking matters into their own hands. You know the kind of men they are!"

Richard was drifting in and out of consciousness at this point and Tom could hardly understand what he was trying to say, only that he kept pleading for them to carry on to London. Eventually Richard's mind descended into delirium. Images of Joan, de Luc, Walsingham, the ship and the storm chased each other around his fevered brain. At one time Joan was on the ship with him, kissing and embracing him, and he really believed he could feel her holding him tight. In the next instance de Luc was floating away off the ship into the tumultuous sky with Joan in his grasp. Richard tried to follow but he was bound to the ship.

Walsingham stood over him and berated him for failing in his mission. He accused him of being weak and spineless for not trying hard enough to complete his task. He was threatening to ruin Sir Edmund and his business because of his traitorous son. As Richard made a grab for Walsingham's throat the apparition disappeared.

Richard regained consciousness briefly to see Tom and One-Eyed Jack staggering towards him. They hung on to the ship's rail as the huge waves crashed over the deck. "I'm sorry, Master Richard," yelled the captain, "but we must turn back. We've done our best, but we can't hold her on this course any longer and if we take one of these waves broadside it will sink us. Even if we had enough ballast in the hold, we still couldn't beat this storm."

"The captain's right," Jack growled. "This is absolute madness. Master Richard, we're fighting a hurricane not just some stray squall! If we don't turn back now, we'll all end up dead and nothing you could pay me would be enough for me to risk that," growled Jack

"No, Captain, no," said Richard as loudly as he could, while trying to escape the mast and get to his feet. "If we don't deliver Walsingham's information on time, we will be sentencing our beloved queen to death and throwing our country into a bloody civil war. We must go on."

Another huge wave broke over the bow and the force of it knocked Richard hard against the bottom of the mast. He screamed out in pain. "Captain, please, I beg you, all of you, to keep going," he pleaded, before he lost consciousness again.

This time there were no images, just a huge black abyss. When he came round again, he tried to focus through the sea water that was still being thrown over the ship like a waterfall. It was stinging his eyes and dripping down his face. The deck was still heaving up and down as if it wanted to be free of them all. He managed to clear the water out of his stinging eyes with the back of his free hand just long enough to see Tom and three other crew members, including Jack, having a very animated conversation whilst holding on to each other and one of the masts to prevent themselves from being washed overboard. At times, because of the lack of ballast and the ferocity of the storm, the deck was pitched at seventy degrees or more and every wave threatened to smash them to pieces.

Richard was trying desperately to keep his eyes open and remain conscious but he was wet, cold, very weak and his shoulder was bleeding again. The force of the waves battering his feeble body seemed determined to relieve him of what little life he had left. Is this what it felt like to die? No, he couldn't die. He wouldn't die. He couldn't bear the thought of never seeing Joan again. Dear God, she would spend the rest of her life with that wretched man believing that he had deserted her. She would never know how he hard he had fought to get back to her, how much he loved her. She would think he had betrayed her. He would never let that happen. He would get back to her and find a way to get rid of that fiend de Luc. Then they would be wed and his life would be complete.

The last thing he saw was Tom and One-Eyed Jack hauling their way up the deck towards him, carrying a rope. It was time to make his peace with his God. "Oh, my darling Joan!" he whispered to himself. "I am so sorry. I have failed you. I love you, Joan."

CHAPTER SEVEN

The Search

When disaster struck at the shipyard, Richard was nowhere to be found. On the day after he had sailed for France the master carpenter fell from the top of the main mast and broke his neck. Later that same morning the body of one of the caulkers was pulled out of the dock with his throat cut, probably the result of a drunken brawl the night before.

For the ship to be completed on time these men would have to be replaced as soon as possible, but Ralph could only do that with Richard's permission. It would cost a tidy sum to hire tradesman with the same level of expertise as the two who were lost, especially at such short notice. Ralph knew one or two men who would fit the bill perfectly, but he also knew that they would need to be offered a sizeable incentive to entice them away from the shipyards where they were already working. If they were already being paid a decent wage, they wouldn't be too keen to pack up and leave for somewhere new. As he needed Richard's authority before he could do anything, Ralph immediately set about trying to find him. He couldn't afford to waste too much time hiring the new men if he wanted to keep the build on schedule. He'd been promised a sizeable bonus if he got the ship ready for sea on time and he wasn't about to put that at risk if he could help it.

Ralph hadn't seen Richard since the messenger had arrived from London and that must have been a couple of weeks ago now. Until the accident had happened work on the ship was proceeding exactly on schedule and he'd had no reason to speak to Master Richard. However, it was strange that he hadn't called in at the shipyard to reassure himself that all was well. Ralph had been very busy overseeing the build and he guessed his employer had been busy too.

When he arrived at Richard's office, he was surprised to find it locked. It wasn't like Richard to be out of the office at this time of the day. When Ralph questioned some of the men who were working close by it soon became apparent that Richard hadn't been seen there for some considerable time. It was equally unusual for him to be absent for such a long time. He was often seen on the wharf as his ships were coming and going regularly, loading and unloading cargo, and although his captains were capable of handling the operations themselves Richard liked to double check himself that everything was correct and that all the relevant paperwork was in order for the harbour master's office and the excise men.

Ralph's next stop was The Bush where Richard kept rooms. The landlord told him that he too was quite concerned. Richard had disappeared for many days without any warning or explanation and then suddenly reappeared out of the blue a day ago, completely exhausted and very dishevelled. He was extremely hungry, and he had demanded that the landlord produce a meal for him as quickly as possible. He devoured the large meal in the shortest time, almost as if he was afraid that someone would steal it away from him before he had chance to finish. After the landlord had served a couple of impatient travellers he returned to Richard's table, hoping to reassure himself that all was well with, but Richard had already gone up to his room.

Later in the evening after most of the drinkers had left the tavern, the landlord went up to Richard's room on the pretext of offering him a nightcap. When he received no response to his knock, he quietly opened the door, only to discover that once again Master Richard Lovell had disappeared— so quickly this time he had even forgotten to lock his door.

Both Ralph and the landlord agreed that Richard's behaviour was most unusual and very mysterious. Ralph decided that the best course of action would be to send a messenger to Sir

Edmund Lovell's manor house in the hope of finding Richard there. When the messenger was despatched, he was instructed to carry on to Sir Edmund's town house in Exeter if neither Richard nor his father could be located at the manor.

There was obviously something seriously amiss. Ralph was beginning to fear that Richard could be in some kind of trouble or even fleeing from someone who intended him harm.

Although Richard was not at the manor his father was. He returned to Topsham with the messenger, a very worried man. Edmund hadn't seen his son for several weeks but that was not unusual. Richard was kept busy in Topsham and his father was either on his estate or with the wool merchant's guild in Exeter. However, Sir Edmund was very concerned about Richard's unexplained disappearance, reappearance and then sudden disappearance again, Eleanor too was very worried about her son's whereabouts. She had been with Edmund when the messenger had arrived in some haste. She had urged her husband to return to Topsham with the man and to find Richard.

On arrival at the port, he went straight to the boatyard to find his shipwright. Ralph quickly told him everything he knew about Richard's absence and the situation in the yard. After giving his approval for the release of extra funds to secure the services of another master carpenter and a replacement for the murdered caulker Edmund left Ralph to deal with it while he went on to Richard's office, using his own key let himself in. He sat at Richard's desk and began to carefully go through Richard's papers for any clue as to where his son might have gone and why.

After scrutinising every single piece of paperwork in the office Edmund was still none the wiser. He had been disturbed a couple of times by captains who had discovered the office was occupied and had called in to hand over all the paperwork that they'd held while Richard was absent. They were also at a loss about what could have happened to Master Richard and were unable to furnish Edmund with any information.

He didn't realise how long he'd been searching until his hunger pangs reminded him that he hadn't eaten anything since arriving in Topsham much earlier in the day. He decided to have a meal at The Bush where he hoped he might gain some information about his son from the landlord. Sir Edmund returned all the papers to Richard's desk and the cupboards, relocked the office and walked the few hundred yards to the inn. After he finished his meal he questioned the landlord, who had already anticipated that Sir Edmund would be looking for information on his son's whereabouts. Unfortunately, the landlord could only repeat what he had told

Ralph earlier.

Sir Edmund went upstairs to Richard's rooms to see if he could find anything there that would shed some light onto where his son had gone to in such haste without leaving any word. The first thing to catch his eye was Richard's saddlebags lying empty on the bed; this suggested that wherever Richard was, he hadn't gone on horseback. Most of his clothes were still in his closet. As far as Edmund could tell just his personal effects and the clothes he wore when working with his men on the dock were missing which suggested that he didn't intend to be away for long.

After a quick search revealed nothing more of any relevance Sir Edmund walked across to the stables and found Diablo standing quietly in one of the stalls. He introduced himself to the groom who was sitting cleaning some tack on a bench under the hayloft.

"Aye, Sir Edmund, I recognise you, sir," said the groom.

"Can you tell me when you last saw my son, Richard?" asked Edmund.

"That would be two days ago, sir. He arrived in the yard as if Satan himself was chasing him, his mount exhausted and lathered in sweat, and Master Richard almost dead on his feet. He'd obviously been riding hard for some time but the odd thing was sir, that after grabbing his saddlebags and giving me a little extra to see to his horse he headed straight to the tavern by the wharf instead of going into The Bush which I thought was rather strange, him being so done in after his journey."

"Yes, that was rather odd," agreed Edmund. "Can you remember anything more?"

"No, nothing else, sir. That was the last I saw of him. His horse recovered quickly after some extra oats, a good rub down and a proper rest. He's a real champion and no mistake, sir, but now he's fit again he's beginning to get restless. He needs to be exercised. Do you know when Master Richard is coming back sir?"

"No, I wish I did." Edmund dropped a few coins on the bench. "Can you arrange for Diablo to be ridden out daily until my son returns?"

The groom lifted the pennies and put them into his pocket. "I can that, sir. I'll see to it myself. Diablo doesn't take too kindly to strangers on his back but we know each other well enough."

Sir Edmund left the stables intending to head for the tavern by the wharf, in an effort to retrace his son's footsteps. Just as he came out of the stable yard to join the street again, he met Ralph, walking hurriedly towards inn. "Ah, Sir Edmund, I'm glad I've found you," Ralph said. "After you had left the shipyard, I remembered something that happened about two weeks or more ago. There has been so much happening these last few days that it had completely slipped my mind."

"Something concerning my son's disappearance?" asked Edmund hopefully.

"I'm not sure, sir. When Master Richard and I were in his office discussing the progress of the build, a messenger arrived from London. The letter he brought was so urgent that he had ridden here directly from London through all the heavy rain we were having at the time. It was a miracle he ever reached Topsham when you consider the state the roads were in."

"Who was the letter from?" asked Edmund.

"I don't know, sir. I was dismissed before Master Richard opened it, but I did notice that he seemed very puzzled when he examined the seal."

"Did the messenger say anything that might indicate who the letter was from?"

"No, sir. He just asked for the recommendation of a decent tavern and Master Richard sent him to The Bush," answered Ralph.

"Thank you, Ralph. I think I'll go and have another word with the landlord," said Edmund. However, all the landlord could tell Edmund was that the messenger had stabled his tired horse for the night, had a meal, took a room and was gone again at first light as soon as he'd finished his breakfast. He'd sat alone for both of his meals and although the landlord had tried to strike up a conversation with him, he was very reluctant to answer any questions about who he was or where he'd come from.

Edmund was intrigued. "He must have had a dreadful journey as it hadn't stopped raining for days. Whatever message he brought in such conditions must have been very urgent ," he thought to himself. Who did Richard know in London when he'd never even been to London? Who would be important enough to be able send an urgent letter by special messenger from London to Topsham in conditions that no sane person would ever consider travelling in? Did the contents of this letter have anything to do with his son's disappearance? So many unanswered questions.

His next port of call was the seamen's tavern by the wharf. It was as busy as always with sailors who had just returned from the sea and had money in their pockets and those who were about to put to sea and were having one last drink, or two, before they left. The landlord and barmaids were rushed off their feet in the noisy, crowded room, which reeked of stale sweat, spilt ale and worse, as they tried to keep up with the demand for ale and food. Edmund had to wait for several minutes before the landlord served him his tankard of ale. He would have liked to have questioned the landlord about Richard, but it was almost impossible to make himself heard above the din and the landlord was far too busy to stop and listen even if he could.

Edmund weaved his way around the room, carrying his tankard with him, deftly avoiding the melee of bodies that were staggering about in the hope of recognising any of the sailors present. It had been a while since he'd had anything to do with the shipping side of the business, as it was now Richard's. He guessed that the crews now would be very different to the ones he'd employed years before. None of the faces were familiar and he was about to give up when one of the sailors who had been with Captain Ashe when Richard had arrived headed to the bar to get his tankard refilled. The old sailor came across Sir Edmund and said cheerfully, "Sir Edmund! I haven't seen you in here for a long while."

Edmund immediately recognised him as a member of the first crew he had ever employed. "Ned! I thought you'd have been sailing with the Devil by now, you old scoundrel!"

"No. sir. He hasn't managed to persuade me to join him yet but I've come very close to it more than once," Ned replied. He pulled his old, ragged shirt away from his neck, revealing a scar running across his throat.

Laughing, Edmund said, "Close indeed!"

They walked back to the bar together and Edmund ordered another two tankards of ale as soon as the landlord looked their way. In the corner of the room where it was a little quieter, they found seats on a bench that two very inebriated seamen had recently vacated. When they had both sat down Sir Edmund asked Ned if he'd seen anything of Richard recently.

"Aye, sir. I saw him a few days ago. I was here drinking with Captain Ashe and a few others. We had only docked that morning and we were enjoying the fruits of our labours, if you know what I mean." Ned winked at Edmund. "Master Richard looked as though he hadn't slept for a week. He was very rough, sir, very rough indeed and most eager to talk to Captain Ashe. He'd only been here for a few minutes before they left together by the back door."

"Do you know where they went?" asked Edmund.

"I don't know where Master Richard went, sir, but Captain Ashe was all over Topsham trying to put a crew together to sail on the evening tide and us only arriving on the morning tide too."

"Where on earth would they be they sailing to at night and with what cargo so soon after the ship had docked?"

"That's just it, Sir Edmund, Captain Ashe said he couldn't tell the crew what their destination would be, but only that Master Richard would see that they were well paid for the voyage they would be undertaking," Ned answered. "It was nigh impossible for the captain to get anyone at all to sign on let alone the type of seamen he was looking for. Men don't like to commit themselves unless they know what they are signing on for."

"Did Captain Ashe manage to put a crew together?"

"Aye, of sorts. Beggars can't be choosers, especially for an unknown destination and at such short notice. They'll have cost Master Richard a pretty penny too. I just hope he doesn't live to regret it. Captain Ashe did manage to get the bare minimum crew required to sail the ship but I heard that they included a few very shady characters who were out to make easy money and not caring how they got it. Your son will need to watch his back. Sir," warned Ned. "I wouldn't sail with them for any price!"

Edmund now had serious concerns for his son's safety. "Why has Richard gone with them? He's no sailor. He only has to look at the sea to feel queasy, never mind sail on it! Is there anything else you can tell me, Ned?"

"No, sir. They sailed on the evening tide and no one has seen or heard anything of them since."

Edmund thanked Ned and gave him the price of another couple of tankards of ale before he returned to his son's rooms in The Bush. "What in God's name was Richard doing and why?" he thought to himself. "Where was he going to get all this money he'd promised to pay these men? Why hadn't he left a note to say where he'd gone.?"

Richard seemed to have vanished into thin air.

Edmund sat on the stool beside the window and tried to piece together everything he had learned so far. His son had disappeared immediately after receiving an urgent letter from London. But from whom? Then, several days later he and his horse had reappeared again after what appears to have been a long and exhausting journey which had left both horse and rider completely exhausted. Instead of giving himself time to recover Richard had raced off to find Captain Ashe. Having found him he then asked him to put a crew together without delay, to sail on the evening tide. But to where and for what purpose? This was not like Richard at all. He was not a foolhardy man. He always thought things through logically and carefully before he would make any decisions or take any action and he certainly wouldn't go off, secretly or otherwise, without leaving word for his father. No, something must be seriously wrong to cause Richard to behave in this manner. But what?

Edmund, no longer a young man, felt weary after his journey from Exeter earlier in the day and from his exploits in Topsham. Still, he decided to visit the quayside where their ships were moored to search for any clues there which might help him to find Richard. It was almost dark as Edmund made his way along the quay. He soon came across a drunken seaman who was stumbling along the wharf some yards in front of him. Eventually the man fell down into some sacks lying against the wall of an old shack. By the time Edmund approached him he was leaning against an old barrel and trying to cover himself with some of the sacks. "Do you sleep here every night?" inquired Edmund.

"If I do, what's it got to do with you?" growled the drunk.

"Nothing at all, but I was wondering if you were here two nights ago, and if you saw anything unusual?"

"And if I did, what's it worth?" asked the sailor, looking directly into Sir Edmund's face.

"If I believe that the information is genuine, I'll make it worth your while."

"You're no doubt wanting to know about Richard Lovell's ship that slipped out of the harbour unnoticed then."

Edmund ignored the sailor's filthy, outstretched hand. "What do you know about it?"

"Well, that same ship had only been unloaded earlier in the day after it arrived from the Low Countries," the sailor answered, "and then in the early evening along comes Tom Ashe with a few men and they start loading ballast and supplies as fast as they can go. Something funny going on here I thought to myself, so I just stayed out of sight and watched them."

"Then what?" asked Edmund.

"What about a bit to show good faith first?" The informant thrust his hand out even further. Edmund threw a couple of coins to the man, who quickly tucked them into his belt before he continued, "Well, just after the sun had disappeared Master Richard himself came hurrying down the wharf and boarded the ship. Thought he'd got on board unseen he did, but he hadn't seen me tucked away in here, had he?" laughed the sailor. "Then they cast off with a crew of just seven or eight and left quietly without even showing one light. Plain stupid if you ask me sailing off into the night with such a small crew and one or two of them were queer fish."

"What do you mean, queer fish?" asked Edmund.

"One-Eyed Jack for instance," the man replied. "I wouldn't turn my back on that one, he's a bad lot."

A bad lot indeed, thought Edmund, feeling alarmed. One-Eyed Jack had lost his eye in a fight with one of Edmund's crew members years ago and then a couple of weeks later that same crewman had disappeared, never to be seen again. Just what had Richard got himself into and why hadn't he come to his father first? Edmund threw a couple more coins towards the drunk which he greedily retrieved and stuffed into his belt before heading back to The Bush. Even though he didn't really have the time to spare Edmund felt that the only way to get to the bottom of this mystery was to go to London himself, discover who had sent that letter to Richard and why. He had no idea who he would be looking for or where to find them, but he couldn't just sit and do nothing while his son might be in great danger.

He stayed overnight at The Bush and then set out for his manor house at daybreak to prepare for his journey to London, something he wasn't looking forward to at all. He was getting too long in the tooth now to be chasing all over the countryside on what could well turn out to be a wild goose chase. He would have to explain to Eleanor why he was suddenly going to London without alarming her too much. She doted on Richard and would be distraught if she thought his life was in any kind of danger.

Unbeknown to Edmund the plague had arrived in Topsham a couple of days before him at the first place it usually did—the docks. By the time he reached his estate he was already displaying the first tell-tale signs. He had begun to vomit, had a raging fever and was finding it very difficult to remain upright in his saddle or control his horse. Almost as soon as his horse had trotted into the courtyard Edmund toppled from the saddle and landed heavily on the ground. The people who were working in the yard rushed to help him but shrank back in terror when they saw the black swellings on his neck. Someone ran to fetch Eleanor while the rest crossed themselves and continued to back away from Sir Edmund.

Eleanor arrived quickly and immediately recognised the symptoms of the black death revealing themselves so clearly on her beloved Edmund. He had been perfectly fit when he'd left with the messenger very early in the morning the previous day but she knew the plague needed very little time to manifest itself. She warned all those present in the yard to keep a safe distance away from her husband. No one needed to be told twice. The yard soon emptied as everyone went back to their duties, each one praying that this terrible scourge would pass them by. The plague showed no mercy to anyone, from the highest to the lowest in the land, all were susceptible.

After a mammoth struggle, Eleanor managed to get Edmund up to his room and into bed. John, the steward had been desperate to help her, but she sent him away with a few very stern words. She gave orders that no one was to enter the room for any reason, no matter how urgent, and that all food and drink was to be put into the basket which she would lower from the window. She built up the fire but left the window open and then set to work on her husband.

By now he was delirious and thrashing about the bed. The black nodules were visible under his arm and in his groin. He was in terrible pain and kept crying out. The only words she could understand out of his ramblings were Richard, London and ship. She had no idea what any of it meant. She wondered if he had found Richard and briefly considered sending to Topsham for him to come home but she realised that by the time he reached the manor his father would be over the critical period or dead. She was very afraid it would be the latter and also, she didn't want to expose her son to the danger of the plague. Eleanor shouted to one of the servants from the window and instructed her to put all the items that she asked for into the basket which she lowered. Then she turned her attention back to her husband.

First, she stripped Edmund and then lanced the dreadful black buboes, dressing them with a poultice made of butter, onions and garlic. After this she made some potions using her own recipes. Rose, lavender, sage and bay to alleviate his headache, wormwood and mint to quell the nausea and to clear his lungs some liquorice and comfrey. Finally, she bathed him in vinegar and dressed him in a clean nightshirt. It took almost every ounce of her strength as Edmund was no lightweight and she had already had a struggle to remove his clothes before she had begun to treat him. She bathed herself in vinegar and rosewater before putting on fresh, well-perfumed clothes. Finally, she sent for more wood to be left outside the bedchamber door, so that she could keep the fire built up, and a pitcher of fresh water.

As she sat beside Edmund's bed, continually bathing his feverish forehead with cold water, she recalled all his teasing about her little room off the kitchen where she kept her herbs, potions and recipes written in her own hand.

Her mother had been a wonderful herbalist and healer and had taught her everything she knew. She had also urged her daughter to speak to all the old healers in the villages and to share her knowledge with them and in turn to learn from them. Eleanor made a point of meeting the old women at least once a year and Edmund always laughed at her and said she'd soon be called a witch, owing to the amount of potions she brewed.

She gave him some of her home-made medication at regular intervals, lanced and re-cleaned his stinking boils and replaced all the dressings and burnt the old. She thanked God for giving her such a wonderful mother and prayed that Edmund would be safely delivered from this pestilence.

Eleanor lost all track of time. Edmund tossed about in his bed and deliriously ranted on about Richard sailing away, about having to find him, about letters, about London. She tried her best to calm him while having no idea what he was talking about. From listening to his ravings she realised that something was amiss with Richard and that worried her. What on earth could have happened to Richard that had put his father into such an agitated state? She couldn't leave Edmund in his present condition to look for Richard herself. She dared not even leave the bedchamber for fear of spreading the plague since she would surely be infected herself by now and she must tend to her husband for as long as she was able. Eleanor felt torn in two. She was terrified she was going to lose her husband and terrified that she might lose her son because something had clearly taken place that had caused Edmund such terrible distress.

After three of the worst days of her life Edmund's fever broke and he drifted into a natural sleep. At last, Eleanor allowed herself to rest after nursing her husband continually and alone through the nightmare that was the plague. She lay down beside him, thanking God for answering her prayers and sparing him. She was relieved that Edmund was going to live, but as she surrendered herself at last to the sleep that had been waiting to claim her for so long, she fully expected to be a plague victim herself by the time she awoke.

CHAPTER EIGHT

The Reunion

When Richard regained consciousness, he felt as if his whole body was on fire. He had a pain in his shoulder that was almost unbearable, and he couldn't open his eyes. He began to panic. Where on earth was he and why couldn't he move? He blinked his eyes a few times and they eventually opened, albeit they stung like hell. Once he'd managed to get them focused he could see he was on a ship, or at least what was left of a ship. As he looked about him his memory returned.

They'd actually survived the tempest, but where were they headed and how long had he been unconscious? He saw that some of the crew were attempting to sail what was left of the battered ship while others were trying to do makeshift repairs with whatever material they could find. Everything that had been on the deck had been swept overboard by the wind and waves. The only available timber the sailors could use was that which had been ripped from the masts and was now gently swinging in the rigging like corpses in a gibbet. His crew were beyond exhaustion, their eyes red-rimmed from lack of sleep and the constant battering from the stinging sea water. Their movement was almost mechanical. They were like dead men walking.

He became aware that the terrible storm was over. The raging gale had been replaced by a gentle breeze and the black storm clouds by the sun which was shining in a clear blue sky. It was amazing just how quickly the weather had turned again from the ferocious to the tranquil. He couldn't believe just how close to death they had come in their small ship. It had been tossed and thrown like a piece of stick from one huge wave to the next. One instant they'd been riding the crest of a wave and the next they were at the bottom of a trough with the waves breaking over them. Their survival was nothing short of a miracle. As Richard relived the terror of being trapped on a ship in the middle of a maelstrom, he vowed to himself that he would never set foot on a vessel again.

When he tried to rise he discovered that he was held fast to the mast by a rope. The excruciating pain he felt when he moved caused him to cry out. Tom was tying off a rope a little further up the deck when he heard Richard's cry and came striding towards him. "Master Richard, you're awake at last," he said, smiling. "We were beginning to worry about you. We've been too busy trying to save the ship to attend to you properly but we're out of danger now and the vessel is just about watertight again. We have some water left in the hold but at least we're still afloat."

"What the hell am I doing tied to this mast? Get this damned rope off me!" demanded Richard, albeit in a weak voice.

"Hold fast there, sir," said the captain, as Richard grimaced with pain again. "We tied you to the mast to keep you from being washed overboard. We knew we'd be far too busy trying to keep the ship upright to be able to keep watch over you. Now hold still while I get this rope undone."

Tom's strong fingers soon made short work of the knots even though they were still wet. While Tom worked Richard was able to observe him closely. Tom looked dreadful. His clothes were torn and his hands and face were covered in cuts and bruises. "Dear God, they must have been to Hell and back while I've been completely out of it." thought Richard.

"You there, give me a hand to get Master Richard into the cabin," Tom shouted to the sailor busily repairing one of the sails that had been ripped in the storm; it wouldn't be perfect but it should catch some wind if they could haul it up what was left of one of the masts. When Tom and the sailor gently pulled Richard to his feet he yelled out in pain again and his legs gave way under him. The two men took hold of him under his arms, which caused him yet more pain, and dragged him into the cabin. Richard cursed the two of them for their roughness as they laid him on the bunk.

The sailor returned to his task, leaving Tom alone with Richard. He undid the laces on Richard's jerkin, ripped his blood oaked shirt open and gently peeled the dressing away from the angry looking wound. Richard winced but hadn't the strength to complain. Tom didn't like the look of it at all and cast about for something clean to wipe away the blood. Finding something dry to use for a new dressing wasn't going to be an easy task. After the great storm they had just lived through everything on the ship was sodden. Eventually he settled on a piece of cloth taken from Richard's own shirt and when he'd re-dressed the wound as best he could, he bound Richard's arm to his chest with a strip of sail-cloth taken from one of the ruined sails to hold everything in place. Tom was terrified that because of his lack of medical knowledge Richard would not survive until they reached their destination.

Richard was feeling much more comfortable despite still running a high temperature. The generous tot of rum that Tom had magically produced from the flagon which sat in a cradle in his locker made him feel even better. The mission and the urgency to get home came flooding back and Richard was anxious to know how much time it had cost them having to return to France and how soon could they expect to reach England.

"I've no idea what day it is," said his captain. "We lost all track of time so I don't know what time we have lost but we never went back to France, Richard. We have just entered the mouth of the river Thames and are limping upstream towards the palace with what little speed we can muster. We're in a very sorry state but we will get you there." In spite of his ordeal, Tom managed a broad smile. "I presume that's where you want to go."

"Tom, that's great news!" Richard managed. "How on earth did you manage to persuade the crew to carry on when they were so determined to return to France?"

"Well sir, I'm afraid I had to stretch the truth somewhat, may God forgive me," said Tom. He looked towards the heavens and crossed himself. "I told the lads that it was Her Majesty's own secret mission, that she knew her life depended on its success and that she also knew only her very best sailors would do for such a dangerous voyage. I told them that they'd been specially picked on behalf of the queen herself. I also told them that she had put you in charge of the mission and that you, in turn, had sent me to find them."

"My God, Tom, and they actually believed you?" asked Richard, amazed at his captain's audacity.

"Aye, sir. It wasn't that difficult. They're conceited enough to think they're the best sailors in the world and although they are a rough lot their loyalty to the queen is surprisingly unshakable. They wouldn't do it for you or me, sir, but they braved that storm from hell for Elizabeth and believe me we were nearly done for more than once. We came close to floundering more than a few times but thanks to the strength and determination of the crew we came through it, but only just. In all my years as a sailor I have never encountered a storm like that one and I never want to again. Those lads spat in the face of that hurricane. God knows how they did it but they managed to keep the ship afloat, even though it was falling to pieces around them, until the wind abated. They spent every last ounce of their strength doing it. I've never seen men fight so hard to stay alive. I think we've all been blessed by God himself, Master Richard, for this crew was granted the gift of superhuman strength to survive! No doubt when they've all rested and had time to recover from their ordeal, they'll think it well worth it if only for the bragging rights it will give them at the tavern."

"I'm sorry, Tom, but I thought the worst when I saw you and One-Eyed Jack coming at me with that rope," Richard whispered. "I thought my end had come!"

"Why no, sir. When we'd decided to meet the

storm head on, we knew that you were in no state to look out for yourself, so we thought you'd be safer tied to the mast and a good job we did too the way those waves kept crashing over the deck. When the storm had finished with us you were the only thing still on the deck other than the crew. You'd have been swept away with everything else and no mistake."

"Thank you, Tom, I should never had doubted you. I owe you my life. I won't forget what you and this crew did for me." Richard painfully reached into the pocket inside his jerkin. "The pouch has gone! Tom, the pouch isn't there!" He tried to get out of the bunk, but he didn't have the strength and fell back again.

Tom put his hand reassuringly on Richard's arm. "Calm yourself, Master Richard, calm yourself. I took the pouch as a precaution when you lost consciousness just in case anyone's curiosity got the better of them."

"Where is it now?" asked Richard, once again grateful for his captain's quick thinking.

"I put it in my boot, sir," Tom replied. He sat on the end of the bunk and removed his wet boot. "I'm more than glad to be rid of it. It's been nipping my toes something fierce."

He handed the pouch to Richard who thanked him again and returned it to his pocket. "How long until we reach the palace?" Richard asked, impatient to get this mission over and done with so that he could return to his beloved Joan. He prayed he wouldn't be too late.

"Hopefully not too long sir. We're trying to catch what little breeze there is with what sails we've managed to repair but we've lost one mast completely and another one is only half its original size. We've also lost most of the rigging too," Tom replied. He surveyed his crippled ship once again and marvelled at how, against all the odds, they had managed to keep her upright. "We're doing the best we can."

The conversation with Tom had taxed what little strength Richard had. "When we get there I must see Sir Francis Walsingham right away," he said, barely conscious. "It's imperative that you get me to him immediately. Do you understand Tom?"

"Aye sir, I understand. Now you just get some rest and I'll wake you when we dock," said the captain, and after making Richard comfortable he left the cabin to return to his duties.

Richard gave into his terrible pain and slipped into oblivion. In his fevered state Joan came to him She was crying as she told him that he was too late and that she was already married to de Luc. Her husband stood beside her, and as he led her away he began to laugh almost hysterically. Richard reached out to her but before he could touch her the vision vanished.

When they finally tied up at the moorings beside the palace, after yet more energy sapping manoeuvres negotiating the tidal currents,

Captain Ashe gave orders to the crew that no one was to leave the ship nor anyone allowed on board before he returned. When he had received an assurance that the sailors understood their orders he set off to find Walsingham. He was stopped at the gate by the palace guard and refused entry. No matter how hard Tom tried to persuade him of the urgency of the matter the guard would not let him pass.

Things were becoming heated when the Captain of the Guard appeared. He had heard the sound of the raised voices and had come from the guardhouse to investigate. Tom hurriedly repeated his story again but, unlike the sentry, the senior officer had been briefed by Walsingham about the possibility of Richard's arrival some days earlier, though more in hope than expectation after the great storm. He grasped the situation immediately and sent a message to Walsingham, then accompanied the captain back to his ship.

Tom wakened Richard gently. He was barely conscious, burning up with fever and in great pain. Tom feared for his life. Richard 's wound had needed proper medical attention many days earlier and he worried it was now too late to save him.

When Walsingham arrived with Phelipps and Will, he took everything in with one glance and sent Will back to get a stretcher. While Phelipps took the Captain of the Guard and Tom outside,

Walsingham sat on the bunk beside Richard. He was shocked to see just how ill the boy was. This wasn't part of his plan when he sent Richard to France.

"Pouch in here," said Richard, tapping his jerkin weakly with his free hand.

Walsingham removed it, taking care not to jostle Richard. He opened it, took out the paper, and quickly read it through. "Oh well done, Richard, well done indeed!" he exclaimed. "Without a doubt you have saved your sovereign's life and your countrymen a lot of unnecessary bloodshed. I am only sorry that you have been so badly hurt. We must see that your wound is treated right away. There is also a young lady of the Court who is going to be overjoyed when she hears that you have returned."

Richard smiled weakly but before he had the chance to ask about Joan, Will appeared with the stretcher and was followed into the cabin by the others who had been waiting outside. Before he was transferred to the stretcher Richard asked Walsingham if he would send a message to his father who by now must know of his disappearance and be concerned for his welfare. Sir Francis promised he would and gave orders that Richard was to be taken to Will's room and that no one else was to be admitted until he got there himself. After Richard had been taken off the ship, Walsingham turned to Captain Ashe.

"Captain, we feared you would be lost in the storm," Walsingham said. "Many ships, larger and better equipped than yours have sunk without a trace and many more are missing. Many good men lost their lives in that tempest. God knows how you managed to stay afloat, let alone get home. You must have an exceptional crew."

"That and a lot of luck, sir," Tom replied. "Now if you have no further need of me sir, I must get this ship back to Topsham. My crew are exhausted and my ship in dire need of repair. Sir Edmund will be less than pleased when he sees the state it's in and even more so when he learns how much Master Richard has promised to pay the crew for undertaking the voyage."

"Don't worry too much about Sir Edmund. I will be in touch with him shortly and will furnish him with enough facts to explain the damage to his ship. But remember, Captain, the details of this mission must still be kept secret for a while longer yet. Can you square that with the crew?" asked Walsingham.

"I can that, sir, don't worry about them." Tom answered, with a lot more confidence than he felt. To himself he thought hopefully, "Surely if I found a way to get them to sail headlong into that storm, I can find a way to get them to keep their mouths shut for a few weeks."

"Thank you again, Captain, and good luck," said Walsingham, and he left the ship to return to Richard.

Almost immediately Tom gave the order to cast off. The weary voyagers were soon heading back down river to the nearest boatyard, where they could put in for some necessary repairs to see them safe home and for the crew to get some well-earned rest. They could probably sleep for a week. They would also need to replace the sails they had lost in the storm too. It was going to prove a very expensive venture for Richard and his father. That wasn't Tom's problem, however. Soon they and their ship would be in a fit state to head for home and the handsome payment they had been promised. There would be a lot of ale flowing in the tavern that day!

On his way to Will's room Sir Francis sent for his own physician, Rodrigo Lopes, requesting him to come immediately to tend Richard's wound. It took the messenger a little while to find the doctor but when he did the man collected his bag and followed Walsingham's man to where Richard was lying in his cot. In the meanwhile, Walsingham had sent Will with a discreet note to Joan informing her of Richard's return.

Joan could hardly contain her excitement when she read the note and bade Will wait while she made her excuses to Her Majesty. She returned with him to his room and Richard, arriving just after the doctor had finished removing the bone splinters from his patient's shoulder and applied a clean dressing. Joan was horrified to see all the blood-soaked rags sitting in the bowl beside the cot. Walsingham motioned to Will to remove the offending bowl which he did quickly. By now Joan was on her knees beside Richard, kissing and caressing his hand.

"Madam, please!" said Lopes, trying to strap Richard's arm to his chest again.

Reluctantly Joan got to her feet again and stepped back. Richard had not taken his eyes from her face since she had entered the room and was praying that his mind wasn't playing tricks and that she was more than just the vision he had seen every time he had closed his eyes since he had left for France. When Lopes had finally finished his task Joan rushed back to Richard's side. Walsingham thanked his physician for his ministrations and signalled everyone else to vacate the room, leaving Richard and Joan together.

When they were alone Joan kissed first his forehead and then his lips. "Oh, my love, I thought I might have lost you forever. I was so afraid for you when I discovered that you had been sent away on one of Walsingham's missions. Far too many times before people who were working for him have disappeared without a trace and I was terrified that you had become yet another. I was right to be concerned for your safety too, wasn't I?" she said, gently touching his shoulder. "What happened to you?"

"Joan my angel, don't worry about that now. I'm here with you now and that is all that matters. I will soon get over this." He lay his free hand over hers, still resting on his shoulder. "What of de Luc?" he asked, as the full horror of what might lie in store for his beloved Joan came flooding back.

"Don't get worked up about that now. First you must rest and give your shoulder time to heal. We can talk later but now I must return to the queen." Joan bent over him and kissed him tenderly on the lips; Richard slid his free arm around her waist, weakly, and drew her to him. This must be what it is like to be in heaven, he thought, as he breathed in her soft perfume and felt her heart beating next to his own. Although Joan too would have been content to stay in his arms forever, she finally pulled herself away gently from his embrace and promising to return as soon as she could kissed him once more and slipped out of the room.

Richard had his eyes closed and was blissfully reliving their embrace when Will appeared with the medication the physician had prescribed for Richard. "Dr. Lopes says you are to take this," said Will. He handed his friend a drinking vessel.

Richard peered into the cup. "What is it?"

"He said it was something to deaden the pain and to help you sleep," Will answered, so Richard downed the contents in one swallow. He pulled a face at the taste of the liquid. "My God, Will, are you sure it's not poison?" he spluttered.

"He didn't promise it would taste good, you baby, just that it would help you sleep," laughed Will. "Now do as you're told and rest, otherwise the next time Mistress Joan comes to visit we'll need to send her away."

"Don't you dare," Richard returned, and he settled back onto the pillow and let the obnoxious potion take effect.

Richard slept until the following morning when Will brought him something to eat and drink. It was only then that Richard realised that he hadn't eaten for several days. He finished everything on the plate and the tankard of ale that came with it. Will cleared it away and returned with water to wash and shave Richard, who by now was beginning to look like a vagabond. Richard was still trying to drag the comb through his matted hair when there was a tap on the door.

Will opened the door to reveal Joan standing there in her riding habit. She swept by him with a quick 'good morning' and pulled a stool to Richard's cot and sat down. Will tactfully left the room, taking the bowl of dirty water with him.

After kissing Richard and sitting on the bed beside him, Joan said, "Let me," she said, and began slowly untangling his hair with her fingers and the comb. "I think I'll call you my

'Richard the Lionheart' for this is more like a lion's mane than a man's hair," she laughed.

Richard smiled. He had never been as happy as he was now with Joan so close and knowing that she loved him. "You've been riding," he said.

"Yes, Walsingham wants me to carry on as normal. No one knows you are here and that's how he wants it to stay for the time being. I have to come to see you in secret but I will come as often as I can."

Richard gently prised the comb from her fingers and held both her hands in his and looked into those loving hazel eyes. "Joan, I've never felt the way I feel for you ever before. I never believed I would fall in love so deeply and completely and so suddenly. Thoughts of you fill my every waking moment and I know that I want to spend the rest of my life with you no matter what I have to do to make it so." He raised her hands and kissed her fingers tenderly.

Tears sprang to Joan's eyes as she turned his hands over and kissed his palms in return. "Oh, Richard, my dear love, I had no idea what true love was until I met you. My life is filled with light whenever I think of you, which is always, and I want to be with you forever."

She rested her head on his shoulder and let her arm rest on his waist. He ran his fingers through her hair drinking in the aroma of the perfume she was wearing. After a few heavenly minutes Joan stirred and sat up. "I must go now, my love, the queen will be expecting me. But I will return as soon as I'm able." She kissed him once more before she slipped out of the room.

Richard was daydreaming about how wonderful his life would be with Joan when Sir Francis entered the room. He picked up the stool Joan had left beside Richard's cot. "Good morning, Richard," said Sir Francis. "I'm glad to see you're looking a little better this morning. How do you feel?"

"I feel much better for having something to eat but still as weak as a kitten and very tired," Richard replied.

"You received a very nasty wound and it will be a while before you are up and about again. You must rest until you are stronger. My physician said you had lost a vast amount of blood and that alone would have killed many men. You were fortunate that all the seawater washing over you had kept the wound reasonably clean. You're a lucky man, Richard," said Walsingham. "I assume my agent was killed since he didn't return with you?"

Richard explained what had happened when they had tried to rescue the man. Walsingham nodded grimly but said nothing until he stood up. "I have important work to do now. Thanks to your bravery and the success of your voyage I can make our sovereign more secure on her throne if I move quickly. I will come and see you again soon."

A few minutes after Walsingham had left Will arrived with more medication.

"Oh, God, not more," moaned Richard.

"The doctor said you're to keep taking this until what he left with me is all finished," said Will, and handed the cup to Richard. Richard eyed up the foul-tasting liquid again. "Then let me take it all at once and get it over with."

"If I let you do that, you'd never wake up again," his friend laughed. "Now get on with it! I've got work to do. I don't know what you brought back with you, but I've never seen Phelipps and Walsingham so excited about anything before."

"No good asking me, I was just the messenger boy. I've no idea what was in the pouch."

"Are you going to drink that or do I have to hold your nose?" Will joked.

"Just you try," said Richard. He downed the contents of the cup, grimaced again and handed it back to his friend. Will left and Richard settled down to sleep again.

This was the pattern for the next few days. Joan continued to come and see Richard in secret as often as she could and he carried on taking his medicine, reluctantly and complaining bitterly, much to Will's amusement. But he got a little stronger every day. Eventually he wasn't content to lie in his cot any longer and when Joan came on the sixth day he was dressed and sitting on the stool with his back resting against the wall.

His left arm was no longer strapped to his chest and he was gently exercising his shoulder and his arm.

"Richard, are you sure you should be out of bed?" asked Joan, as she bent to kiss him.

"Don't fuss, woman!" he scolded playfully. "I asked Dr. Lopes, while he was changing the dressing earlier if I could get up for a few hours. He said the wound was healing a lot quicker than he had anticipated and that as long as I didn't do anything to aggravate it I could spend a couple of hours out of bed. So here I am!" He held both arms out to her, ignoring the sudden pain that shot through his shoulder.

"Oh Richard, I'm so pleased," said Joan. She knelt beside him and he wrapped his arms around her. They sat together and talked but as always, the subject of what to do about de Luc came up. Neither of them could come up with a solution for the problem and eventually talked about their future together as if he didn't exist. But he did and he was always in the background like the spectre at the feast.

The time for Joan to go came all too soon and after a long, loving embrace she left him. As usual after she had gone Will appeared, but this time he was emptyhanded.

"Haven't you forgotten something?" asked Richard.

"No," Will said. "You've finished the medicine now."

"Thank God for that!" Richard exclaimed. "What are you going to torment me with now?"

"I'm going to put you back to bed."

Richard would have liked to object, if only to frustrate his friend, but he knew that Will was right. He suddenly felt very tired and weak and allowed himself to be put back into his cot with very little protest.

After a few more days Richard was strong enough to be up all day and now he was bored with just the same four walls to stare at in between Joan's visits. He spoke to Walsingham about it and intimated that he wasn't prepared to be kept like a prisoner any longer when he'd done nothing to deserve it. Sir Francis promised to do what he could but he still didn't want Richard to be seen in public.

The next time Joan came to visit him she was carrying a large key in her hand. "Richard, Walsingham is allowing me to take you to a small private garden at the back of the palace," she said excitedly. "If we do meet anyone on the way, it will only be servants carousing in the shadows. We must wear our cloaks and keep our faces covered until we reach the garden."

Richard was delighted. Fresh air at last!

They made their way through the dark corridors at the back of the palace until they reached the door that opened onto the garden. It was beautiful and surrounded by high walls which hid it away from prying eyes. They found an arbour tucked away in one of the corners and they sat there holding hands together. Richard told her about his life in Topsham and spoke lovingly of his parents and Joan talked about her upbringing at Holyfield Hall and her life at court as a queen's lady. This showed the stark difference between their social standing, but it didn't seem to matter anymore. They loved each other and were comfortable in each other's company and as far as Richard was concerned that was the only thing of importance.

Their time together passed quickly and soon it was time to part. Neither wanted to break the spell but they knew they had to return to the palace. Their daily visit to the garden became an excursion they both lived for. However, on the day that Richard was to tell Joan that he was going home he forgot to cover his face with his hood in his hurry to get to the garden and Joan. As he ran by a couple in the shadows the man, who was ravishing the girl in his arms, looked up and recognized him.

"What the hell is Richard Lovell doing here?" said Geoffrey Marchemont, throwing the startled young girl to one side, "and where is he going in such a hurry I wonder?"

Geoffrey left the half-dressed young woman trying to rearrange her clothes and set off after Richard. He followed at a safe distance, and when Richard entered the garden, he sneaked through the gate in pursuit. Geoffrey then edged his way round the wall under cover of the trees and shrubs towards the arbour. He nearly gave himself away when he realised that the girl who Richard was caressing was his own sister—and that they were obviously more than just friends. What was Joan thinking of? "He's a peasant for God's sake!" thought Geoffrey angrily. He manoeuvred himself to be within earshot.

Richard had just finished telling his love that he would be leaving early following morning for his father's estate in Devon. She was clinging on to him tightly and sobbing into his shoulder. "Richard, please don't leave me," she pleaded. "I'm afraid Lord de Luc will try to force me to marry him very soon."

Richard felt her shudder at the thought, but answered, "I must go, Joan. I need to speak to my father but I promise to be as brief as possible and should be back in your arms within two weeks."

"You must hurry, Richard. I can't marry Lord de Luc, I won't marry Lord de Luc," said Joan with dogged determination.

"I know my love, and I won't let you marry that man. When I return, we will find a way to release you from that betrothal and then you and I will be wed and live far away from here and de Luc," promised Richard.

"Will you indeed, Master Lovell? Over my dead body, Richard, over my dead body," Geoffrey said under his breath, and crept away as silently as he had arrived.

CHAPTER NINE

The Homecoming

Geoffrey was hurrying to his father's town house, seething with rage and already thinking about what he could do to put a stop to Richard's plans, when he almost ran into Lord de Luc rushing in the opposite direction on his way to the palace.

"Ah, Geoffrey, I was just on my way to see if I could find either you or your father and now you've saved me the bother. I've noticed a change in Joan recently, even though she still tries to avoid me at every turn. She has a certain radiance, and if I didn't know better I might think that she had taken a lover," he said, looking directly into Geoffrey's eyes and raising an eyebrow. "She isn't having an affair with some young buck is she? I've no intention of buying damaged goods!"

"No, no of course not, she wouldn't dare do such a thing when she is betrothed to you," stammered Geoffrey in reply, hoping his knowledge of Joan and Richard's intentions wasn't betrayed by his expression.

After scrutinising his face for a few more seconds de Luc seemed to accept Geoffrey's statement.

"I'm rapidly losing patience with your father, Geoffrey. Joan should have become my wife some time ago and I'm tiring of his delaying tactics. Tell him that when my business here is concluded I will expect to wed his daughter immediately, otherwise our agreement will be at an end and I'm sure that you and Lord Thomas are both well aware of what that would mean for both of you. Prison is a very unpleasant place I can assure you," said the vindictive old man. He showed his black rotting teeth as he sneered at the young man, and Geoffrey blanched. He certainly was aware of what it would mean and he'd no desire to go to prison on account of his sister's foolish affection for that upstart Richard Lovell!

"Joan will marry you, my Lord, I give you my word," said Geoffrey. "And Lovell will be in no state to marry anyone when I'm finished with him," he said to himself with a self- satisfied smile.

"Very well. I will send word to your father when the details of the other matter are finalised, and I will expect you both to follow the instructions I give you to the letter and live up to your promises or the consequences you will suffer for reneging will be severe," threatened de Luc, and went on his way leaving Geoffrey to contemplate just what those consequences would be. Something very unpleasant that was for sure! Nothing and nobody must be allowed to stand in the way of de Luc's ambitions and Geoffrey was personally going to see to it that one threat at least was eliminated as soon as possible.

The following morning Richard was waiting in the stables when Joan returned from her daily ride. As she slipped from the saddle into his arms, she told him that she had ridden Caesar only at a gentle canter today. Since Diablo was still stabled in Topsham, he was borrowing Caesar to take him home to the manor in Devon. Joan knew that Richard would take care of her beloved mount. But while she had no doubts about Caesar's stamina, she was very worried about Richard's lack of fitness for such a journey. He was desperate to get home to his parents and was planning on travelling at speed She had tried her best to persuade him to wait until he was stronger but he would have none of it. Richard embraced her tenderly as she relinquished the reins to him and begged him to be careful. Oh, if only he could remain like this forever with his love wrapped safely in his arms, her heart beating next to his and her subtle perfume filling his nostrils but he knew that was impossible. He had to leave her and get home as swiftly as possible and attempt to explain his sudden absence to his parents who must be out of their minds with worry by now. Just the thought of them re-enforced the urgency of his departure. He gave Joan one last lingering kiss and a promise that he would return as quickly as he could.

She pressed into his hand a silk kerchief embroidered with her name and impregnated with her perfume. He sniffed it and lovingly put it inside his jerkin next to his heart, then secured his new saddlebags behind Caesar's saddle and mounted. He was very conscious that he was abandoning Joan when she needed him most for the second time in their short relationship. It tore him in two. "Damn Marchemont and Geoffrey and damn de Luc too," cursed Richard and as he headed for the gate he damned Walsingham too. With a final wave to Joan, quietly sobbing into her kerchief, he galloped off through the palace gate.

"Come back safely soon, my darling," whispered Joan before turning to enter the palace to attend the queen. She would be counting every hour until he returned.

Richard realised soon after he had set out that he wasn't nearly as fit as he'd led Joan to believe. He couldn't keep up the pace he had set himself and had to rest much more often than he had originally planned, much to his frustration, and it was two days later than hoped when he reached Topsham. He'd decided to call at the shipyard before doing anything else in the hope that everything was progressing as planned with his father's ship. Richard was delighted with the progress at the shipyard. The two unfortunate craftsmen had been replaced quickly and the build was still on schedule for the ship to be completed on time. Ralph would love to have known where Richard had been and what he had been doing all the time he had been missing but as he only spoke of matters relating to the ship and Ralph knew it wasn't his place to question his employer and so the shipwright remained silent. After a tour of the new ship a very relieved Richard thanked Ralph and walked the short distance up the quay to his office.

When he found the door open he fully expected to see his father at his desk, but he was both disappointed and surprised to find a young man poring over his papers. "Who are you?" Richard demanded.

The startled man jumped up from the stool. "I'm Hubert, Sir Edmund Lovell's clerk. Can I help you, sir?"

"How long have you been clerk here?" Richard asked him.

"Since Sir Edmund's son, Richard, disappeared. With things being so busy he needed a replacement to take over the office work quickly. He knows my father well from the guild and he kindly gave me this opportunity to work for him," said the clerk.

"Really! And how are you coping with all this?" Richard pointed to the papers on the desk, but Hubert was now becoming wary of this stranger who had walked in off the street unannounced and he didn't like the way he was asking so many questions. "Well enough, sir," he answered. "I've had no complaints from Sir Edmund or anyone else for that matter."

"Have you discovered what's happened to Richard? Where he went and why?" asked Richard, awaiting the young man's reply with interest.

"Look, I mean you no disrespect sir, but if you require to know things personal to Sir Edmund, I suggest you speak to him. It is not my place to disclose anything about my employer or his family," replied the young man.

"My God, Hubert, you'll do!" said Richard. He held out his hand. "I'm Richard Lovell"

"Master Richard, I had no idea you were home, sir." The young man shook Richard's outstretched hand and offered Richard the stool. "Please sit down, sir."

"No, thank you. I just called in to see if there was anything urgently needing my attention before I travel on to my father's manor but I see that you have everything under control here so I'll be on my way."

After saying his farewells to Hubert, Richard left the office. He was somewhat surprised and nonplussed that his father had replaced him so quickly and even more so that Hubert had stepped into his shoes so comfortably. But he understood that his father still had a business to run and since he didn't know when or even if his son was going to return, he would need to make adequate provision to keep the shipping office open. "My God," Richard thought, "what must my parents have gone through not knowing where I was or even if I was still alive." It must have been absolute torture for them. Hopefully they would have received a message from Walsingham by now which would have at least let them know he was still alive.

While he was in Topsham, he had one more call to make before he headed home. He made for the seamen's tavern to make good his promise to his crew and Captain Ashe. He patted the large bag of gold in his pocket. Walsingham had come good when Richard made it plain he'd been forced to promise money he didn't have in order to bribe the crew to battle through the storm and complete the mission they'd signed on for.

As usual the tavern was doing good business and was as rowdy as ever. Richard was delighted to see Tom, One-Eyed Jack and a couple of the other crew members sitting at the table in the corner where his regular crews usually sat when they were in port. When he spoke to the landlord Richard discovered that Tom had promised him that Master Lovell would make good for all the ale that he and the rest of the crew had drunk since they got back to port. Richard thanked the landlord for trusting his word as he paid the hefty bill, believing it was money well spent. He ordered ale for himself and his crew and went over to join them, followed by a barmaid carrying a tray of tankards.

They rose as one when they saw Richard approaching and after much back slapping and greetings they all sat down together when the ale was put on the table. Richard spent a happy hour with the sailors. Having paid their dues plus a handsome bonus to those present, he left money with Tom for the ones who were at sea, to be given to them on their return. Then he bade them all farewell, telling them he was proud to have sailed with each and every one of them. He thanked them once again for what they had achieved against all the odds and for saving his life.

It was later than Richard hoped when he left the tavern but he was so impatient to see his parents he decided to press on to the manor rather than staying at The Bush for the night. He knew it would be almost dark by the time he got home but he knew the road very well and so did Diablo. He would leave Caesar at The Bush's stables to rest after his long trip and ride Diablo for the remainder of his journey. He left money and instructions with the groom for Caesar's care and a little extra for looking after Diablo so well while he'd been away and then at last headed for his father's manor.

It was dusk and Richard was only a few miles from home when he gave Diablo his head. The horse leapt forward and set off at the gallop towards the manor where he knew plenty of oats and his own stable waited for him. However, before he'd travelled very far his front legs were swept from under him by a rope that had been strung across the road between two trees. Richard pitched forward, somersaulted over his horse's head and was knocked unconscious the second he hit the ground. Diablo landed heavily on his knees and lurched forward before painfully getting to his feet again. Fortunately for Richard Diablo had narrowly missed landing on top of him when he had been catapulted out of the saddle.

There had been no movement at all from Richard since he had hit the road so heavily. The terrified horse bolted and galloped on up the road, leaving Richard where he lay. He was found a little while later by a man and woman returning home after a day of working in the fields. As they approached Richard the woman gripped the man's arm. The peasant walked up to the body and searched for signs of life.

"Is he dead?" the young woman asked him.

"I can't tell," he answered. He turned the body over onto its back. "Oh, my Lord!! It's Master Lovell! The man who saved you from that beast Geoffrey Marchemont!" he exclaimed. "What on earth is he doing out here and alone when it's almost dark and where is his horse?"

"Dear God, is he still alive?" asked the distraught woman.

Her husband put his ear to Richard's chest. "Yes, barely, but we can't leave him here in this state," the young man said. "We must get him to the village as quickly as we can and then send for someone who can help him."

"Look, here are some of the others coming," said his wife. She ran towards them and quickly appraised them of the serious situation in the road. After some debate about whether to get him to the manor or carry him to the village it was decided the village was the closer of the two. They managed between them to clumsily carry Richard as far as the first cottage in the village. When they forced their way into the hovel unannounced with the wounded man, the family inside jumped up from the table where they had been sitting eating their meagre meal. The man pushed his wife and child behind him and reached for his pitchfork.

"Please, don't be alarmed. We mean you no harm. It's Master Richard from the manor. He's been badly hurt," gasped the woman who had found him.

Their initial fright at this intrusion gave way to action. The head of the family, who had been staring at Richard open-mouthed, suddenly turned to his terrified wife. "Clear the table, woman," he shouted. "And you go and fetch the old mother," he ordered the child.

The lad pushed his way through the onlookers, who had also tried to enter the small room and sped off to the old woman's hut. Everything was swept off the table and Richard was laid carefully on the top.

"I wouldn't bother," said one of the men who had been helping to carry him. "Looks like he's dead already."

Richard was lying motionless on the table, his face deathly pale.

The old mother was the nearest the peasants had to a doctor. She was well practised in the art of healing using her own ointments potions, herbs and poultices. The more superstitious among them thought she was a witch. No one wanted to touch Richard in case they made things worse. They didn't know what else to do so they all stood around the table staring down at his body muttering amongst themselves. This man was the son of Sir Edmund Lovell, and nobody wanted to be accused of causing more harm to his already badly injured body and incur the wrath of his father.

Soon an old hag of a woman carrying a covered basket was pushed into the room. Word of Richard's unexpected and dramatic arrival had spread quickly throughout the small village and many of its inhabitants were trying to crowd into the room behind the old woman to see him for themselves. With an extraordinary strength for a woman of her age she very pushed them all back outside again and, cursing them loudly, demanded that they stay out until she had finished her ministrations.

She began to examine Richard carefully. When she had unfastened his cloak and loosened his jerkin she could see that his shoulder wound had reopened and was bleeding profusely. She turned his head gently and saw the very large swelling on the back of his head. She could so no other harm and quickly got to work.

She was surprised to discover that the damage to his shoulder had been caused by a bullet which had passed right through his body. She packed the hole with leaves and ointment and held them in place with a piece of cloth soaked in some kind of sticky liquid. When she had arrived the occupant of the cottage and his family had left with everyone else so she had to co-opt the nearest peasant outside the door come and hep her to remove Richard's jerkin and shirt. She wrapped a bandage around his chest to hold everything in place and then they re-dressed him.

Having dismissed the peasant, she made a potion with herbs and other ingredients known only to her and boiled them all together in a pot over the fire. While it was cooling, she looked more closely at the wound on the back of Richard's head, talking to herself quietly all the time. There was no break in the skin, just a huge lump that almost completely covered the back of his skull. The old woman tutted and shook her head. She poured some of the cooled liquid from the pot over the lump and tipped the rest onto a dressing which she attached to the wound with a strip of binding cloth wrapped around his head. She had never seen such a large swelling and had severe doubts that her ministrations would be of any use. She tried to spoon some liquid into his mouth but most of it dribbled back out again.

Richard was cold and grey and there had been no movement from him all the while she had been working on him. The old mother wrapped his cloak around him and took what passed for a blanket off the bed and threw that over him as well. Then she went outside and spoke to the waiting villagers. "I've done all I can for the boy but he's in a very bad way, I doubt if he'll last until the morning," she said. "I'll sit with him through the night or until such time he's no longer in this world."

By now it was too dark to get word to the manor so it was decided to send someone at first light. However, word of a sort had already reached the manor. Eleanor and Thomas were sitting in the private parlour after their meal. Eleanor, by some miracle, had been spared from the plague altogether, much to her relief. Thomas had recovered well from it thanks to his wife's tender care and treatment. He had regained most of his strength although he still tired more quickly than normal. Eleanor's swift and decisive action when Thomas had arrived at the manor already carrying the disease had also prevented anyone else in the house from succumbing to the dreaded sickness.

Thomas had just finished pouring a goblet of wine for himself and for his wife when his steward entered the room. "I'm sorry to disturb you, sir, at this late hour," said the steward, "but a riderless horse galloped into the courtyard a short while ago lathered in sweat and very traumatised. Its knees are badly grazed, probably from hitting the ground with some force and at speed. It looks as if it has tripped or caught its hoof in a hole. The head groom recognised it right away. It's Diablo and he still has saddlebags tied to the saddle. He has calmed the horse and is tending to his damaged legs sir, but there's no sign of your son."

"Can we be sure that it was Richard who was riding the horse?" asked Edmund.

"Although the saddlebags are new, sir, I recognised some of Master Richard's personal things inside."

"Oh, God be praised! My boy has come home at last!" said Eleanor, tears in her eyes. "Why on earth would he be riding at this late hour? It's completely dark now."

"I don't know, but if he's been thrown from his horse he could be lying in the road somewhere badly hurt or worse. We need to find him quickly," said Sir Edmund, rising from his chair.

"Oh my poor Richard!" Eleanor cried, as she visualised in her mind the kind of injury her dear boy might have suffered.

"Go and rouse some of the men, get the dogs ready and plenty of torches. I'll meet you in the courtyard shortly," ordered Sir Edmund.

When the steward had left the room Eleanor's tears began to flow. "Edmund, you will find him, won't you?" she cried.

"Of course, my love. We'll follow the road and search every inch until we do." He gave her a peck on the cheek before picking up his cloak and heading off to meet the others in the courtyard.

The search party left the manor on foot and searched the overgrown verges and parts of the adjacent woodland as well as the road itself. It was a painfully slow task in the dark despite each person carrying a torch or lantern. The dogs had sniffed the saddlebags before leaving the manor but had so far been unable to pick up a scent. There was no trace of Richard or any clue as to what had happened to him.

They had been looking for Richard for hours and they were all tired, especially Sir Edmund, but there was no question of giving up the search before his son was found. Just as dawn was breaking one of the dogs picked up a scent in the middle of the road. It led the search party to the village a mile further on. The villagers, who were keeping a vigil outside the cottage where Richard lay. heard them coming down the road and went out to meet Sir Edmund and his men. The peasants quickly related the story to Sir Edmund of how Richard had been found lying half dead in the road and carried to the village.

Edmund was at a complete loss. Where had Richard appeared from so suddenly and why was he riding at night? He pushed his way through the people still crowding around the door and entered the cottage. It was dark in the small room with only the pale light of dawn creeping through the small opening in the wall that passed as a window and the glow of the embers in the fire. He called for one of his men to bring a lantern. Edmund took the light and held it above the body lying so still and seemingly lifeless on the table. "I'm too late, my beloved son is dead!" he whispered in disbelief.

He didn't notice the old woman, who now got up from the stool beside the fire. "Are you the boy's father?" she asked him.

Sir Edmund started and lifted the lantern. He recoiled slightly when he saw her ugly wart-infested face but soon composed himself again. "I am," he said.

"I've done what I can for him but he's in a bad way. I've dressed the bullet wound in his shoulder that had reopened after his fall. It looks aș if it is a recent wound that had been healing nicely. If you keep it clean and re-dress it regularly it should heal without giving him any more trouble. I've tried to bring down the swelling at the back of his head but I've never seen anything that bad before. He's suffered a really hard blow to the back of his head. It is too swollen for me to tell if his skull's broke or not. It will be a miracle if he survives and if he does, he will have probably lost his wits altogether," croaked the old mother.

"Thank you," said Edmund, as if in a trance, and pressed a coin into her gnarled hand.

She slowly gathered all her medicines together and dropped them into her tattered old basket, then left without another word.

Edmund stood staring down at his son, unable to take his eyes of him. How could this man lying on the table like a corpse be his fun-loving, athletic young son? He was rooted to the spot. None of this seemed real. His brain couldn't grasp the reality. It was like being in a nightmare where you run away as fast as you can from the terror only to stand still in the same part of the horrible dream. He suddenly became aware of his steward, John, standing beside him. John still did not know whether his master's son was dead or alive.

"Is there anything I can do for you, Sir Edmund?" he asked quietly, as he put his hand on the devastated man's arm.

Edmund finally returned to reality.

"Yes, go and find anything you can in this

village that will help us transport Master Richard home," he said with some urgency. "If we get him there alive his mother will know what to do."

With a quick bow the steward left the room. Edmund stared down at Richard's face again, willing it to show some sign of life, but it remained like a death mask. He prayed that Eleanor would know what to do to save their son. He was the most precious thing they possessed. As he watched over his son he wondered where he had been to get himself shot and why? How had such an accomplished rider as his son been thrown from his own equally competent horse? Why had Richard left Topsham so suddenly without leaving any word for his father? So many questions and the only one who could provide the answers was lying unconscious or maybe even dying on the table in front of him.

He collected the stool from the fireside and placed it beside the table. When he had seated himself, he reached for his son's hand under the blanket which was covering his cold body. Surely someone that cold couldn't still be alive. He pressed it against his own cheek as his tears began to flow. "Dear God," he prayed, "You know this is my only child, my only son. Please don't take him from me, I couldn't bear it. He has only done good in the world but someone or something evil has done this to him. If you needed someone to die, why didn't you take me when I had the plague? Don't let him die, send him back to me."

Edmund sat silently with Richard for a few minutes, willing his strength to flow through his hand into his son's body and sustain him until he managed to get him home to his mother. He was still sitting with his head bowed when his steward returned with the news that he had found an old wagon which was now outside the cottage with the only horse the villagers possessed. The young couple who Richard had rescued from Geoffrey Marchemont and his cronies had donated their own thinly stuffed mattress for him to lie on. They were followed by half a dozen more who brought either mattresses or blankets. Sir Edmund thanked them all for their kindness as his men carefully carried Richard out of the cottage and gently laid him into the wagon.

The village horse, called 'Slowly,' was well named. He was an old plodder but that was the perfect pace to move Richard up the road to the manor without causing him any more harm. It took over three long hours to reach the house carefully avoiding as many of the potholes and bigger stones on the way. They were met by Eleanor who had been eagerly watching for their return since dawn broke and who by now was frantic with worry about her son. Her initial relief at her husband's return was almost instantly replaced by a terrible dread when she saw Richard lying in the cart. When she saw his colourless face, she was afraid that her dear son's body had been brought home to be buried. Edmund quickly reassured her that he was still alive, but only just.

As his wife supervised the men, they carefully placed Richard onto a makeshift stretcher and carried him up to his bedchamber. Edmund instructed his steward to send the wagon back to the village together with a barrel of ale and some extra provisions, as well as returning the villagers' bedding and some extra oats for Slowly. By the time he entered the bedchamber Eleanor was already removing the bandage from around Richard's head. The swelling on the back of his head was huge.

"Oh Edmund, I'm so afraid some of that swelling may be caused by fluid. I think perhaps Richard's brain is bleeding," said Eleanor, trying to hold back her tears.

"Good God! What can we do? I'll send for the physician in Exeter right away," said Edmund, unable to bear the thought that he may indeed have just brought his son home to die.

"Even if he came immediately, it would be too late," said his wife. "By the time the messenger found the physician and he gathered what he would need, it would already be getting dark. There is no moon and it would be too dangerous to travel at night."

"But if we use the best mounts he could be here before noon tomorrow," said Edmund.

"If Richard is bleeding he will be gone before first light," Eleanor told him.

"But there must be something that can be done. We can't just watch him die and do nothing, Eleanor," said Edmund, desperately.

"I heard of a new herb a few months ago that was being used to treat badly bruised people with some success," Eleanor said. "If it is just bruising it might help but I've never seen lump that big in my life. If it's bleeding there's nothing we can do but pray for his soul. I acquired some arnica from a travelling apothecary and followed his instructions to make an ointment but I haven't had cause to use it yet and so don't know if the claims are true."

"You must try. You must try, Eleanor, and pray." Edmund reached for her hands and gently kissed her forehead.

While she was away from the room to collect the ointment, Richard began to stir. He was trying to speak, so Edmund put his ear close to his son's mouth. Richard kept repeating the same word over and over again: "Joan, Joan, Joan." He seemed to say something else, but before Edmund could make out what Richard was trying to tell him, Richard slipped back into a coma.

"Who on earth is Joan?" thought Edmund, He'd certainly never heard Richard mention anyone called Joan before. Just what had been going on in his son's life recently? Eleanor returned carrying the ointment, some others of her own home-made healing remedies and fresh bandages. Edmund told her that Richard had been trying to speak before lapsing into unconsciousness again.

"Oh, that's good news. Perhaps he's not as badly hurt as we first thought," said Eleanor. "Now lift his head from the pillow carefully and support him while I use the ointment and re-bandage the wound." When she had finished with his head, she re-dressed his shoulder. "Edmund, why did someone shoot him.? What has happened to him?"

"I don't know but God willing he will live to tell us. He will live won't he, my love?" asked Edmund hopefully.

"I pray he will, but we will know one way or the other by morning," replied Eleanor.

Edmund took both of her hands in his again and kissed them tenderly in turn. "Then I pray God has guided these hands to give us back our son."

CHAPTER TEN

The Miracle

It was six days after Richard had left for Devon that Lord de Luc returned to London following a short trip of his own. The business, which had dominated his life for the last few months, had finally been concluded to his satisfaction after much bullying, brow beating and blackmailing. Now he could turn his full attention to Joan and their betrothal.

He was not a patient man and disliked having to wait for anything. It was now several weeks since he'd made the deal with Lord Marchemont to marry his daughter Joan. He had waited long enough to claim his young, beautiful bride and it was long past time that she was bedded. When de Luc arrived at the palace he went to look for Joan immediately, despite having a number of pressing engagements to attend to. The anticipation of having her completely in his power intoxicated him. She fascinated him, and the more she hated him the better he liked it. He loved to dominate his women. He derived great pleasure from forcing them to submit to his will by using a variety of depraved methods. Joan was going to be a particular challenge and he could hardly wait to compel her to comply to his every wish.

De Luc found her in the Great Hall attending the queen, a woman no man would dare to try to dominate. He was forced to wait in the shadows behind one of the large pillars. It was over an hour before he had the opportunity to catch her alone. During that time he paced up and down, snapping at anybody who tried to start a conversation with him. "This is intolerable," he thought. He'd be damned if she dared to keep him waiting for longer than a minute once they were wed or she would feel the full force of his displeasure.

At last he got his chance, when Her Majesty sent Joan on an errand to the royal apartments. De Luc, irritated at having wasted so much time, quickly followed her through the small side door into the corridor which led to the queen's rooms. He concealed himself in one of the many doorways which led off the passageway and waited for Joan to return. As she hurried back, carrying a tray of Her Majesty's favourite sweetmeats, he caught her arm; he then grabbed her around the waist with one hand and covered her mouth with the other to prevent her from crying out. In her fright Joan dropped the tray, spilling its contents all over the floor.

"Well, my love, what joy to find you alone at last," Lord de Luc hissed into her ear.

Joan began to tremble uncontrollably. She had been so intent on getting back to the queen that she hadn't seen him hiding in the doorway until it was too late. His grip was like a vice, his bony hand as strong as steel. She couldn't move no matter how hard she tried to free herself.

"My dear, you are shaking. You don't feel cold so it must be the excitement of knowing that in a short time we will be wed," he said sarcastically. "Don't fret, my precious, you don't have to wait much longer now before we will be together forever."

Joan couldn't hide her revulsion; the smell of his breath made her heave. De Luc seemed not to notice, as he carried on, "I have some important business to attend to here which I hope to bring to its successful conclusion within three weeks. Your father will then be forced to make good his promise and hand you over to me as my bride or he and his son will find themselves languishing in a debtor's prison for a long, long time. I have already waited far too long. We will be wed and soon, my love. Our bedchamber is already prepared for our wedding night and oh, what transports of delight I have waiting there for you, my lovely," he said, nibbling her ear. "You only have to be patient for just a little longer."

In one swift move he replaced his hand with his mouth and kissed her roughly. Then with his passion roused he threw her against the wall and pinned her there with his body leaning heavily against hers.

"I am not your love nor ever will be!" Joan gasped. Silently she prayed, "Oh, God, let me die now, let me die now!"

Once again the timely arrival of a page in the corridor prevented Lord de Luc from going any further with his intentions. He released her so suddenly that she dropped to the ground. He stood over her, leering down as she struggled to her knees. She slowly climbed to her feet, tears of frustration rising from deep within; but she would not cry before this creature and so the threatened tears quickly turned into a blazing fury. It burst out like the raging flood waters through a dam. "Whatever you or my father do I will never marry you!" she screamed. "You will never, never have me!"

Joan slapped his face. Just as quickly, de Luc slapped her back, hard. Choking back the tears and holding her stinging cheek, Joan declared, "I will marry Richard Lovell or no one at all," without giving a thought to what deadly danger she had just placed Richard into.

"Obviously a man of no consequence since he has neither title nor patron. I promise you, Joan, that I will kill, by fair means or foul, any man who presumes that he can usurp my rightful place as your future husband. You are mine, and don't you ever forget that." De Luc caught hold of her wrist and twisted her arm so that she was forced to her knees at his feet once more. "Don't you ever forget that," he repeated. He then let her go and disappeared into the shadows.

Joan remained on her knees for some minutes rubbing her bruised wrist and burning cheek. She knew she would never marry that man, but she also knew that if Richard didn't return in time her only alternative would be to take her own life and that thought made her feel physically sick. She was still on the floor when one of the other ladies-in-waiting came hurrying down the corridor towards her.

"Joan, what on earth are you doing down there? What has happened to you?" she asked when she saw the sweetmeats and tray strewn about the floor.

"I tripped," answered Joan.

The lady raised her eyebrows and gestured to the ugly bruises now forming on Joan's wrist and her red cheek. "Really? And I suppose you did that when you fell."

Joan didn't reply.

"Come, we must replace the sweetmeats and get back to Her Majesty quickly. She believes you have been philandering with some man on the way and is very cross," said the lady.

Joan shuddered. Philandering? No. But being toyed with and teased like a mouse by a cat before its final execution.

"Richard, my love, please hurry back," she

pleaded to herself. "I need you so much. I don't know what to do. I'm so frightened. The trap is closing on me and I can't see any way to stop it."

Little did Joan realise that at this moment her beloved Richard was fighting for his life. Eleanor had sent a completely exhausted Edmund to his bed, promising that she would wake him if there was any change in their son's condition. Although he had been reluctant to leave his son for even a second, he knew that he needed to rest as he'd been out all night searching for Richard and so had submitted to his wife's wishes. Eleanor then settled herself into a chair at her son's bedside.

His face was grey, his pulse weak and despite being covered with woollen blankets was as cold as death. The fire which had been lit and well fed with logs as soon as Richard had been brought home was now throwing out a good heat into the room. She held his icy hand as she prayed more fervently than she'd ever prayed before. She remembered how disappointed she had been to have only one living child when she had longed, more than anything, for a big family. However, Richard had grown into the kind of son every mother dreamt of. Edmund and Richard were her whole world. Eleanor had thought she was going to lose Edmund to the plague but God had spared him. Was He now going to take Richard in his place? Surely not. He couldn't be so cruel, could He? The tears dropped silently into her lap as she bowed her head in prayer again.

Several hours into her vigil the warmth slowly started to seep back into Richard's corpse-like body, but his pulse remained very weak and there was still no movement at all as he lay in his bed. Eventually, although she fought hard against it, Eleanor fell asleep. She hadn't had any sleep the previous night either as she had been anxiously waiting for Edmund's return or at least some news or her son. She was wakened some hours later by the sensation of her hand being gently squeezed. When she opened her eyes, they were met by Richard's steady gaze. "Hello, Mother," he said weakly. He gripped her hand a little tighter.

"Oh, my son, my son," cried Eleanor, the tears streaming down her cheeks. She leaned forward and gently kissed his forehead. She was delighted to see that some colour had returned to his face and when she checked his pulse, she discovered that it was a little stronger than it had been earlier. It seemed that God had indeed answered her prayers and returned her son to her. She silently thanked Him again and again as she went about the business of checking and redressing Richard's wounds. The lump on his head wasn't any smaller but nor was it any larger which could only be a good sign.

When Eleanor had finished, Richard requested something to eat and drink. His mother was delighted, firstly, because he was talking coherently, which meant his wits were intact, and secondly because she knew that if she could get him to eat it would hasten his recovery. She was now feeling much more confident that he would recover from his almost fatal accident. She sent a servant to the kitchen for some broth while she made her son more comfortable by propping him up on his pillows in readiness for his soup. Then she hurried to Edmund's bedchamber and roused him, telling him that Richard was conscious and lucid. He quickly dressed himself and joined his wife in Richard's room where he found his son sitting up and being fed spoonsful of broth by his mother.

"Hello, Father," whispered Richard.

"Richard! Oh, my boy. Thank God, thank God," said Edmund, tears in his eyes.

"Now don't you go charging at him like a bull," warned Eleanor, as her husband made for Richard's bed. "He's still very weak and needs quiet rest for some days yet before you start pestering him with endless questions."

Edmund sat and held his son's hand and silently gave thanks to God while his wife fed Richard the rest of the broth. When the dish was empty Eleanor gave him a sleeping draught and with Edmund's help gently laid him down again.

They both remained with their son until he drifted off to sleep. Eleanor then went to her own bed, leaving her own maid to sit with him, while

Edmund called for his steward. He wanted to go back to the place where Richard had been found to search for any evidence that might shed some light on what had caused his son to be thrown from his horse so violently.

When they reached the spot, it didn't take them long to discover what had caused Richard's "accident". They found the tell-tale marks on the trunks of the two trees that had been used to anchor the rope that had been strung across the road. There were both hoofprints and footprints beside both trees and they also discovered a length of rope which had been discarded in the undergrowth.

"I knew Richard wouldn't have just fallen from his mount, he's too good a horseman for that," Sir Edmund said angrily to his steward.

"But who would do such a terrible thing to Master Richard and why, sir?" asked John.

"I really don't know. In fact, there's an awful lot I don't know at the moment but I intend to find out just as soon as my son is fit enough to answer my questions," said Edmund. He and his steward remounted and taking the piece of rope with them headed back to the manor.

Richard made remarkably good progress physically over the next few days under his mother's tender care but he was very preoccupied mentally and seemed reluctant to say much at all to his parents. Edmund respected Eleanor's advice and didn't press his son for answers but Eleanor herself was beginning to wonder if the severe blow to Richard's head had caused some kind of memory loss. She had kept treating the swelling on the back of her son's head with the arnica and it was diminishing steadily. The wound in his shoulder was also healing quickly. Eventually he was allowed to get out of bed and to walk about the house. He was eating well and his strength began to build up nicely. Before long walking about the manor wasn't enough for Richard. He was desperate to get back in the saddle. Despite Edmund and Eleanor doing their best to dissuade him he was determined to get his own way. It wasn't like Richard to be so disagreeable. He had changed during his time away from home.

The only concession he made was to his mother's request that he take one of the grooms with him whenever he went out. He insisted on riding every day and for longer each time. He would come home exhausted. When Eleanor asked him to be careful and not overstretch himself, she was told in no uncertain terms to stop fussing and that he wasn't a little boy anymore. This wasn't like Richard at all. Something was driving him to push himself to the limit.

He still hadn't said anything about where he had been or what he had been doing and in his present state of mind his parents were reluctant to press him A few days later when he was sitting with his them beside the fire in their small parlour and the servants had withdrawn, he spoke to Edmund. "Father, do you think you could get Caesar brought here from Topsham?" Richard asked.

"If you wish, but who's Caesar?" asked Edmund, wondering if this was someone who could tell him what had happened to Richard.

"She's Joan's horse and I must get her and me back to Joan as soon as possible, before it's too late. I need to go to London," said Richard.

"No, Richard you mustn't," interjected his mother, alarmed at his sudden statement. "You're not even fit to ride to Exeter let alone London."

"Your mother is right, Richard. I can send John to deliver the horse to the lady, but you must concentrate on getting properly better," Sir Edmund insisted.

"You don't understand," said Richard, now pacing the floor. "I should have been back days ago. I promised her I'd return quickly. She will think I've abandoned her again. Poor Joan! This is the second time I've left her in her time of need. Dear God, what must she think of me?"

Eleanor was astounded. She set down her needlework, went over her agitated son, and put her hand on his shoulder. "Come and sit down and tell us about Joan. I think this belongs to the young lady." His mother took Joan's kerchief from her pocket and handed it to him. "I found it covered in blood and tucked into your belt. It took quite some time to get it clean again too."

Richard took it from her, kissed it lovingly and put it inside his shirt.

Eleanor guided him back to his seat, as she said, "You kept repeating her name when you were so ill. You seem to be very fond of her."

"I'm not just fond of her, Mother, I love her with all my heart, but if I don't get back to London in time, she'll be forced to marry a wicked and debauched man three times her age."

Edmund and Eleanor looked at each other in complete surprise. Their son had never had more than a passing acquaintance with any of the local young ladies and now he was telling them that he was very much in love with someone who he had only just met and who was completely unknown to them and was in London.

"Richard, you're right, we don't understand. We don't understand anything that's been happening to you recently," said Edmund.

Richard looked at his parents for a few seconds. He knew how much he meant to them and could only imagine the anguish they must have suffered when he disappeared and again when he had arrived back half dead. "Have you received any messages from Walsingham recently?" he asked.

"No. Should I have?" replied his father, slightly bewildered. "Although I did get a huge bill for the repair of one of my ships that you had 'borrowed,'" Edmund added.

Richard knew his parents deserved an explanation and so he made his decision. "What I'm about to tell you must remain within these four walls, at least for the time being," he warned.

"Of course," said his father, relieved that at last he might get the answers to the many questions he had been so desperate to ask since Richard came home. At the same time it concerned him that whatever it was had to be kept a secret. The expression on Eleanor's face told him that she felt the same too, but she nodded her acceptance of Richard's instruction.

They both sat in stunned silence as their son related all that had happened to him since he had received his summons from Walsingham. "My God, Richard. I'd no idea," said his father when Richard had finished. "How dare Sir Francis put your life in such peril!" Although he had a healthy respect for Walsingham's love of the queen, Edmund disliked the man—not to mention the thought of Walsingham sending his only son on a mission which had such an uncertain outcome. It infuriated him.

"Father, the queen's life was, and still is, in danger. He had no choice," said Richard.

"Yes, you're right. He would think that Her Majesty's life is far more important than that of my beloved son," smiled Edmund.

"And he'd be right," Richard replied.

Edmund slapped Richard's knee. Then in a more serious tone he said, "Richard you must be careful. That's twice an attempt has been made on your life."

"Twice?" queried Richard.

"Yes. After you were out of danger from your fall from your horse I went back with my steward to the place where it had happened and we found the rope that had been stretched across the road. I knew you were too good a horseman to have just fallen off. Diablo was deliberately tripped and you were left for dead, my son. Who wants you dead and why, Richard?" asked Edmund.

"I can't imagine who would want to murder me. Walsingham already has the information I brought back from France so what good would it do anyone to kill me now."

"Who knew you were coming home that day?" asked his mother.

"No one. I had intended to stay overnight at The Bush and set out first thing the following morning but I was so impatient to see you and father that I decided on the spur of the moment to travel immediately," Richard answered. "No one could have possibly known that I was on that road and at that time."

"Well, someone knew, though God knows how, and whoever it was damn near succeeded with their plan. If those peasants hadn't found you when they did, we'd have lost you," said Edmund.

Richard was more interested in his future than the past and changed the subject again by asking his father if there was any way that they could pay off Marchemont's debts—which would release him from his promise to de Luc, thereby freeing Joan from that despicable betrothal.

"I'm sorry, Richard, everything is tied up in the new ship, but even if we were able, although I think Marchemont might accept, from what you have told us of Lord de Luc I think it highly unlikely that he would let Joan go so easily."

"You're right, of course, Father, which makes it all the more important that I get to London with as little delay as possible and somehow prevent this marriage from happening," said Richard.

"Son, have you considered that it may already be too late?" his mother asked quietly.

"Mother, that is my worst nightmare. It has tormented me day and night since I came home. If my darling Joan has been forced to wed that man she will already be dead. She would kill herself before she would allow him to bed her and if, God forbid, that has happened I will make it my duty to despatch de Luc to hell where he belongs."

Horrified by his son's vehemence, Edmund said, "Richard, you can't! If the marriage is legal you will be guilty of murder and will hang!"

"If Joan is dead my life is nothing to me. I would rather die than see him live," Richard retorted. "Now, Father, will you please send for

Caesar as I intend to leave for London the day after tomorrow."

Knowing further argument would be futile Edmund reluctantly agreed to send the head groom to collect Caesar from Topsham first thing the following morning.

"I will accompany you to London," Edmund told Richard, but Richard shook his head. "No, Father, this is something I must do alone, and Mother needs you here."

"Richard, you are not yet recovered from two very nasty wounds and nor are you fit to travel that distance alone. I fear for you, my son. Will you not reconsider?" pleaded Eleanor.

"Mother, I appreciate your concern but I will leave for London in two days and that's final!" Richard said, and marched out of the room.

His parents couldn't believe the change in their son's demeanour. He'd never been so outspoken with them before or behaved so blatantly counter to their wishes. What on earth had happened to him in London?

Although he had promised his mother that he would make his journey to London by easy stages and not overtire himself, as soon as Richard had left the manor he headed for London as fast as he could go, riding one horse and leading the other. He used the same taverns that he'd used on his previous trip and rode Diablo one day and Joan's horse the next to keep them both fresh. He did, however, have plenty of sleep and proper meals when he travelled this time. Even so he was pretty well exhausted by the time he reached London. After he had stabled the two horses and given the groom a few coins and instructions about their feed, he headed for Walsingham's office. He found Will sitting alone at his desk.

"Richard! How good to see you." Will stood up and walked round the desk to shake his friend's hand. "Are you fully recovered from the wound in your shoulder now? I must say you don't look all that well and you're dead on your feet again."

"Yes, I'm just fine thank you. Don't fuss," Richard replied, impatient to get the niceties out of the way. "Will, what about Joan, is she married to de Luc?" He held his breath, dreading the worst.

"No, not yet, but I believe she will be in a few days' time," Will answered. "Sir Francis will be pleased to see you back, I'm sure."

"I thought he would be here," said Richard absently.

"He was until a few hours ago. Phelipps is in the palace somewhere, but Walsingham went to speak with the queen and then left in one hell of a hurry taking more than half the palace guard with him. There's something big afoot but as usual I'm told nothing and left to get on with all the mundane paperwork," bemoaned Will.

"What do you mean, 'in a few days' time'? Is it

all set then?" demanded Richard, quickly turning the conversation back to Joan.

"Not exactly," Will said. "Lord de Luc is away on some business somewhere, but he has threatened that as soon as he returns, he's going to force her father to arrange the wedding. She's been here every day since to see if we had any news of when you were likely to return. She expected you back some days ago, Richard, and to be honest she seems to be giving up hope of ever seeing you again. She's in a wretched state, my friend, but I fail to see what you, or anyone else for that matter, can do to alter the situation."

"I promise you, Will, that I will do whatever it takes to prevent her from marrying that man, even if it means us both leaving the country."

"There's no way Walsingham would allow that. He'd never grant you a passport," Will said. "The marriage, if it goes ahead, would be entirely legal."

"I wasn't planning on asking his permission," Richard retorted.

"Richard, be careful," warned his friend. "De Luc doesn't take too kindly to being crossed as many have learned to their cost."

"I wasn't planning on asking his permission either! Now I must go and find Joan," said Richard, and turned towards the door.

"She'll be with Her Majesty, Richard. You can't just go barging in!"

"Then I'll wait," Richard called over his

shoulder, and strode off down the corridor.

Joan wasn't with the queen, Richard discovered as he entered the Great Hall. She was standing in a corner having a very animated conversation with Geoffrey's friend, Anthony. She was waving what seemed to be a scrap of paper at him while giving him a severe tongue lashing, until she pushed him with such force that he lost his feet and fell against the wall. Without a backward glance she stormed across the Hall, so intent on her mission that she didn't see Richard until he caught her arm as she sailed passed him.

"Richard! Oh, thank God! Come quickly," she said, and pulled him through a side door into a small anteroom. Once the door closed behind them he wrapped his arms around her, but she pushed him away. He pulled her into his arms again more tightly and kissed her passionately.

When her body stiffened, he loosened his hold slightly. Joan thrust him away so strenuously that he fell against the wall. "No, Richard, no! That's how de Luc treats me!"

"For God's sake, Joan!" he exclaimed. "It's thoughts of you that have kept me alive these past few weeks. As soon as I was fit to ride I came back to you as I promised I would. All the way from Devon I dreamed of this moment and now you won't let me near you!"

"My love, there is no need for you to force yourself upon me. I am yours now and forever but there's no time, Richard. We must go now!" she said urgently.

"Joan, what on earth is the matter? Where have we got to and why so urgent. I've only just arrived and I've no wish to go anywhere until I've eaten and had a good night's sleep."

"You don't understand! Look!" Joan waved that same scrap of paper at him. "This was left for my father and Geoffrey."

Richard took the note from her and tried read it. "This is so ill written I can hardly make out what it says."

"The message is that the assembly point is The Duck and Drake hostelry and that from there they will go together and remove the usurper."

"Joan, this is treason! We must distance ourselves from this as far as we can!"

"No, my love, we must get to them before Walsingham does or they'll both be killed. Hurry, Richard we're wasting precious time," said Joan, now desperately pulling at his arm.

"What is this girl thinking?" Richard thought to himself. "Her father sold her to a philandering reprobate and her brother was is scum of the earth. Those actions alone should prove that neither had any kind of affection for her at all. She should leave them to face their fate." He removed her hands from his arm and put his strong hands on her shoulders and looked into her face. "Joan, be calm, my love, and tell me from the beginning."

"There's no time. We must go now!"

"Joan, please," he returned.

When Joan realised that he wasn't going to release her until she explained, she told him, "Walsingham came to speak to the queen earlier about a plot he had uncovered. Her Majesty was very shocked and retired to her private chamber where she dismissed all her ladies. When I returned to the Great Hall I met Geoffrey's friend, Anthony. He had been looking for Geoffrey at our father's town house but only father was at home. While Anthony was talking to him he noticed the note that father had carelessly discarded on the table and being of the same ilk as my brother he quickly pocketed the piece of paper without him noticing. Anthony came to me once he'd read the contents of the note and started boasting about how grand life would be for the Catholics with Mary on the throne and bragging that father and Geoffrey had ridden off to champion the cause. That's when I took the note from him before he drew any more attention to himself or showed the note to anyone else. I warned him to keep quiet about it unless he wanted to find himself under arrest for treason." Joan paused for a breath before she pleaded, tears in her eyes, "We must get there as soon as we can and warn them, Richard before it's too late. Please hurry."

"Joan, do you realise that if we are caught anywhere near these conspirators we'll be arrested and charged with treason too? Think very carefully before you act," Richard said, but when he saw the fire in her eyes and the determination on her face, he knew he was wasting his time trying to reason with her.

"Fine!" she shouted at him. "If you want to stay here and be safe do so, but I'm going to warn father and Geoffrey and neither you nor anyone else will stop me!"

Richard shrugged and let out a long sigh, knowing she'd utterly defeated him. "Very well, you win. But you can't ride dressed like that," he said, looking down at her court dress.

"You go and saddle the horses while I run and change and by the time you are done, I will be there."

"Joan, our horses have only just completed the journey from Devon. They need to rest as do I," Richard protested.

"They are the best of horses and the inn isn't all that far away."

"Far enough away for a pair of tired horses," he argued.

"Richard, they'll cope, believe me, and so will you," insisted Joan. She gave him a quick peck on his cheek knowing the argument was already hers. "Now please hurry."

"What the hell am I doing?" thought Richard. "It would serve that fool Geoffrey right if he got what he deserves and Marchemont too." But he knew that, despite all his misgivings, he would do all he could to save them for her sake. He would do anything for Joan even if it cost him his life and God knew this escapade could well do just that.

Joan was true to her word and arrived at the stables ready to ride just as he'd finished tacking up the tired horses They mounted, walked quietly passed the guard at the palace gate, hoping not to raise any suspicions, and then galloped into the dusk as fast as they could towards the Duck and Drake.

CHAPTER ELEVEN

The Plot

Joan had ridden out regularly since she had first come to Court and knew the surrounding countryside well enough to allow her and Richard to avoid the roads and any soldiers who might be patrolling them. That, coupled with a full moon shining in a cloudless sky, enabled them to make good time, which was a welcome bonus since Walsingham and his men had left the palace hours before them. Richard was impressed by the way she jumped the hedges and cleared the ditches as they rode full pelt eating up the miles as they went. He trusted Diablo to follow Caesar's lead while he kept watch for any sign of Walsingham or his soldiers. He knew they had absolutely no excuse to be rampaging over the countryside at this time of night and that they'd be arrested for treason.

They approached the Duck and Drake quietly, picking their way through a small tract of woodland on the hill that overlooked the tavern's courtyard. When they reached the end of the treeline they dismounted and tethered their tired horses to a low-hanging branch beside a patch of grass where they would be able to graze and rest for a while. Joan and Richard crept the short distance to the crest of the hill where they concealed themselves behind some gorse bushes. The light from the full moon had been a godsend on their way here but Richard knew that from now on they'd need to keep a very low profile to avoid being seen.

They crawled the rest of the way to the brow of the hill. From their vantage point they could see all of the courtyard, lit by dozens of blazing torches, and what they saw caused Joan's heart to sink. They were too late. The soldiers had arrived before them and were already busy herding the confused and terrified plotters into the middle of the yard where Walsingham watched as they were put in irons in readiness for their long march back to London and the Tower. It looked as though they had walked unknowingly into the trap and had given up without a fight. Weapons were strewn all over the hostelry's yard and there was no sign of any blood. Despite their surrender the soldiers were being none too gentle with their prisoners. Many were sporting bleeding noses and split lips and were being goaded by the pikes of some of their captors. Walsingham looked on impassively.

"Oh, Richard, we're too late! We can't let them take father and Geoffrey to the Tower," sobbed Joan. She pulled on Richard's arm and got to her knees. "We must do something quickly! Go and talk to Walsingham. Tell him it's all a big mistake. Hurry Richard before they leave."

Richard dragged her back down to ground before she was seen and kept her there with his arm across her back. "There's nothing we can do, my love," he said quietly. "If we show ourselves now, we'll be arrested too and that would help no one. We must go back to the palace and speak to Sir Francis privately."

Joan tried to pull away but Richard gently held her down and drew her close. She yielded to his embrace and began to weep into his shoulder. Her sobbing shook him to the core. How much more could this young woman take? What on earth could he do to ease her pain? He felt so helpless and extremely angry that his beautiful Joan had been forced into this position by her foolish family. If he could choose their path they would just walk away and let Geoffrey and Lord Thomas fend for themselves, but he knew that wasn't going to happen as Joan would never give up until there was no hope left.

After Joan had calmed herself, Richard decided that they should make their way back to the horses and return to the palace the same way they had come. As they prepared to leave their hiding place, Joan took one last look back at the tavern trying to identify her father and brother in the bright light of all the torches. "Richard, they're not there!" she whispered, and pointed to a group of prisoners who were now all sitting on the ground, closely guarded by some of the soldiers. "Oh, thank God, they're not there! Look!"

She started to stand up to get a better view. Richard grabbed the bottom of her legs and pulled her to the ground roughly, knocking the breath from her. Before she could berate him, he covered her mouth with his hand; her eyes were blazing as she tried to fight him off. He pinned her down, hissing in her ear, "For God's sake Joan, stop it! You'll get us both killed if we're discovered and what good would that do! Do you understand what I'm saying?"

The fire left her eyes and she nodded her head. He took his hand away and released his grip.

"I'm sorry Richard, I just didn't think," she whispered.

"We must be very careful and very quiet. Sound travels much further at night." Richard checked the faces of the prisoners himself. There was no sign of Lord Marchemont or Geoffrey. "Thank God for that!" thought Richard. "Now we can go home."

They crawled back to where they had left the horses. "They must have escaped," said Joan, her spirits rising by the second.

"Joan, there's something you should know,"

Richard said rather awkwardly. "I think this is why I was sent to France. I believe that the pouch I brought back to Walsingham contained the names of all the conspirators and the date and time of their rendezvous."

As he confessed, he held both her hands in his and looked into her eyes, searching for an answer to his revelation. How would his lovely Joan react to the fact he had, however unwittingly, betrayed her father and brother and undoubtedly led to them both to a traitor's death?

She looked back into his eyes, hers swimming in tears. "Richard, I don't blame you. How could I? Even if you had known what was in the pouch there is no way you could have predicted that the names of my father and brother would be on the list. How could they have let themselves be persuaded to be part of this madness? I know Geoffrey is a young fool and Father sometimes a little misguided, but they are not traitors. I can't understand what got into them. We must find them and help them to escape before Walsingham's men get to them."

All Richard really wanted to do, now he knew that Thomas and Geoffrey had not been arrested, was to go back to London, enjoy a good meal and have a proper night's sleep. "If they are not here then where the hell are they? Where on earth do we start to look?" he asked crossly. "You said they were all to meet here so why weren't they with the rest? Do you still have the note?" He held his hand out impatiently.

"It's here." Joan took it from her pocket and gave it to him. Richard unfolded the note and held it towards the moonlight. "I still can't make this out. It's so badly written," he complained, handing it back to Joan.

She examined the note again. "That's it!" she shouted, jumping up and down, but Richard quickly grabbed her again and put his hand over her mouth once more. "Joan, how many more times? Be quiet!" he said, annoyed.

She glared at him, furious. He slowly took his hand away. "Please be quiet, my love," he whispered, "or we'll be discovered."

She nodded to indicate that she understood. When they were sure they were still undetected Joan carried on in a whisper, "Remember Anthony said Geoffrey wasn't there when he went to the house so it would be father who received the note and his eyesight is so poor he probably misread it as it was so badly written."

"If that's the case, then where on earth are they?" asked Richard, who had just about had enough of this wild goose chase.

"I don't know but we must find them soon before it's too late," she said.

They had just mounted their horses when Joan cried out, "The Lock and Gate! That's where they'll be, I'll wager. It's about five miles further on."

She dug her heels into Caesar's ribs and they

were off. Richard followed close behind as they carefully retraced their steps through the wood. They decided to save time by using the open road this time, hoping that Walsingham's men would be kept busy dealing with their prisoners at the Duck and Drake for a while longer.

When they arrived at the second inn, they saw Lord Thomas sitting on a barrel in the corner of the courtyard nervously mopping his brow with his kerchief. Geoffrey was pacing up and down, shouting at his father for bringing them to the wrong place. Thomas stood up as Joan and Richard reigned in their horses and slid from their saddles. Geoffrey drew his sword but returned it to its scabbard when he recognised them.

"What are you doing here?" Joan's father asked in surprise, limping towards her. She ran to meet him and they embraced for the first time since she was in the nursery.

"We came to warn you. The plot has been discovered, all the others have been arrested at the Duck and Drake and are on their way to the Tower in chains," she said breathlessly. "You must flee before the soldiers find you."

All the colour drained from Geoffrey's face as he stared in disbelief at his sister. Joan walked over to him and took hold of his arm. "Brother, we must leave now. There's no time to waste. Richard and I will help you and father to escape." She looked pleadingly towards Richard who, although he had no idea of how he or Joan could prevent their capture, just smiled and nodded, reassuringly.

Geoffrey, beginning to recover from the shock of Joan's bad tidings, snarled at Richard, "I don't need any help from a protestant upstart like you or from a turncoat of a sister!" He pushed Joan away from him so forcefully that she fell backwards into a pile of empty barrels. Before Richard could reach her Geoffrey had placed himself between them with sword drawn.

"Don't be stupid, Geoffrey!" his father shouted. "This won't help anything!"

"He's been asking for this lesson for a long time. Now I'm going to give it to him and put him back where he belongs with all the other peasants or worse. Say goodbye to your beloved!" Geoffrey yelled at Joan and lunged at Richard.

Richard managed to dodge Geoffrey's thrust but fell over on one of the tumbled barrels. As he tried to get to his feet again, Geoffrey swung his sword at Richard's head. Fortunately for Richard the point missed him and got stuck in the barrel long enough for him to stand up. Lord Marchemont had lifted Joan back onto her feet but was now grappling with her to prevent her from running to Richard. "Geoffrey, stop!" she screamed, still struggling with her father. "Don't do this!"

Her brother ignored her pleas and swung at Richard again after freeing his blade from the barrel.

Richard jumped back but felt the draught from the sword as its point narrowly missed slitting his throat.

"Come on and fight, you coward! I always knew you were afraid of me. You're nothing but a lily-livered peasant." Geoffrey goaded.

This was too much for Richard and he now drew his own weapon.

"No, Richard, no!" screamed Joan, who was by now almost hysterical. Here was the man she loved above all others about to fight for his life against her own brother. She looked on with her father in absolute horror, unable to do anything to prevent the duel which was now about to unfold in front of them.

The fight raged backwards and forwards across the courtyard and the noise of the swords clashing had roused most of the folk who were staying at the tavern. Some were hanging out of their windows while others had actually come into the courtyard and were making bets on which of the young men would be the victor. The two men were well matched and several times both had come close to delivering a fatal blow. They almost fought themselves to a standstill but neither man had any intention of yielding despite being exhausted.

Finally, Geoffrey lowered his guard just long enough for Richard to take his chance. His blow knocked Geoffrey's sword from his hand

and he went down on one knee but as Richard approached him, he threw a handful of dirt into Richard's face and retrieved his sword from where it had fallen. Joan screamed and Lord Thomas shouted at Geoffrey to stop, but he ignored his father's plea and began to swing his weapon backwards and forwards like a man demented. He took another swipe at Richard who ducked and jumped to the side simultaneously while furiously trying to wipe the dirt from his streaming eyes with the back of his hand. Although he still couldn't see clearly, he parried Geoffrey's next lunge and pushed him hard, tripping him with his foot.

Richard made no mistake this time. Before Geoffrey could react the point of Richard's sword was resting against his throat. Joan's anguished voice rang out from the doorway where her father had taken refuge with her when the intensity of the duel had threatened to put their lives in danger too. "Don't kill him, Richard!" she screamed as Lord Thomas released her. She ran across the courtyard to Richard who was still holding Geoffrey at his mercy with the tip of his blade. "Please don't hurt him," she pleaded. "I know he's an arrogant, headstrong young fool but he's my brother."

After a few seconds Richard lowered his sword and took a pace backwards but he kept his eyes firmly fixed on Geoffrey's face. Joan reached for Geoffrey's hand. "Let us help you, Geoffrey," she said. "We can find somewhere where you'll be safe for the time being and then when things have calmed down, we'll get you out of the country."

Still panting for breath, he snatched his hand away. "Joan, what is wrong with you? This peasant is a creature of Walsingham and I know he was sent on a secret mission by him. You little fool, don't you realise that it is probably because of him that the plot was discovered? It is because of him that we are now all under the sentence of death and you and mother will be implicated too!"

Lord Marchemont joined them and put his arm around his daughter's shoulder. She shouted back at Geoffrey, "You condemned yourself when you committed treason! Elizabeth is our lawful queen, and you became part of a plot to murder her and replace her with Mary, Queen of Scots!"

"She's a Protestant usurper!" snapped Geoffrey. "Mary is the rightful queen and she's a good Catholic."

"Since you have no religion, I shouldn't think you'd care who was on the throne," Joan retorted.

"She'll put everything right and our family will be restored to its place of honour again!" Geoffrey raved.

"Geoffrey, we didn't have a place of honour before Elizabeth came to the throne, so how can we be restored to something we're not?"

"All those who help to place her on her rightful

throne will be handsomely rewarded and things will be as they were before that protestant daughter of a whore stole the crown. We'll have power again," he shouted hysterically.

Joan was beginning to fear for her brother's sanity. Richard lifted his sword again and took a step towards Geoffrey. "I think you've said enough, Geoffrey. I'll listen to no more slander against our sovereign lady."

"She's no sovereign of mine!" Geoffrey threw back at him. He then made a move for his sword lying in the dust a few feet in front of him, but Richard was too quick for him and kicked it out of reach.

Joan knelt and took both of Geoffrey's hands in hers and spoke gently to him as she would a frightened child. "Geoffrey, it is finished. Mary will never sit on the throne of England. You and father must save yourselves. Come with us now."

He jumped to his feet. "I'm going nowhere with that peasant," he said, glowering at Richard. "I have friends who will take care of me. I don't need any help from the likes of him or you!" He picked up his weapon from where it had come to rest, closely watched by Richard, replaced in its scabbard and strode across the yard to where his horse was tethered. He mounted, dug his spurs into the beast's flanks and rode out of the gate without a backwards glance, leaving Joan kneeling and sobbing in the dust.

Richard lifted Joan to her feet.

"I tried, Richard, but he wouldn't listen," she wept, leaning into his shoulder.

Richard, who was just glad to see the back of him, said nothing.

They walked over to her father, sitting on one of the smaller upturned barrels, his head in his hands. Now Thomas had lost truly everything. His only son had disappeared into the night going who knows where, his title was no more and his estate would be forfeit to the crown, as would be his life. And Margaret, what about poor Margaret? She'd be left with no husband, no son and no home. She had done nothing to deserve that. She was completely innocent. What would become of her? All this because of a silly spoilt boy didn't know when to stop and a father who didn't have the will to stop him. The only positive thing to come out of the whole sorry situation was that he would no longer have any need for Lord de Luc's promised money because his and Geoffrey's debts would die with them and Joan would once more be free.

Joan sat down beside him and took her father's hand. He looked into her sorrowful eyes and tears welled up in his. He seemed to have aged ten years overnight.

"Why did you let yourself become involved in all this, Father?" she said. "You must have known it would never have succeeded. Walsingham has spies everywhere." Some very unexpected ones, she thought, remembering Richard's role in providing Walsingham with all the information he needed to foil the plot.

"Believe me, Joan, it wasn't by choice," he said.

"You mean you were forced to take part?" said Joan, surprised. "But by whom?"

"That's not important now, the damage has been done. All that matters is that I get home to your mother before the soldiers arrive. She has no idea what Geoffrey and I were about and she'll be frightened if she's alone when Walsingham's men come looking for me. I must go now or I won't get there in time" He turned to Richard, who was standing beside his daughter. "Lovell, you know what will become me."

Richard nodded.

"My daughter will be penniless and my wife cast out and although I have no right at all to ask, I beg you to take care of them when I'm gone," Thomas pleaded.

Joan began to cry and clung to her father.

"You have my word, Lord Marchemont," said Richard. He held out his hand; Thomas grasped it tightly. "Thank you," Joan's father said, "but it's just Thomas now. There's no Lord Marchmont. I will go to my death with one less regret knowing Margaret and Joan will be safe."

"No, Father! We can hide you. You mustn't go, you must come with us. Please father," said Joan, frantically trying to pull him towards the horses.

"No, Joan. I'm too old and tired now to be chasing about the country trying to keep one step ahead of Walsingham. He'll never give up until he's got everyone of us. It's better this way my child, and more honourable. It's time to reclaim some of the honour I threw away when I gave in to your brother instead of standing firm. I must go now," he said as he stood up. Joan refused to let go of his arm and Thomas looked helplessly at Richard. Richard gently prised Joan's fingers from her father's arm and put his own around her shoulders as she wept uncontrollably. Thomas climbed wearily into his saddle and he too trotted away without looking back.

"Richard, we can't let them be taken. We must go and find Geoffrey first and then on to Holyfield Hall to collect mother and father and get them all away to safety," said Joan, in between sobs.

"Joan, my love, our horses are spent," said Richard, pulling her close. "We can't go anywhere until they are rested. Your father and brother have both made their choices and we must respect their decisions. We must let them go. We have no idea where to start to look for Geoffrey and your father needs time to make his peace with your mother before he's taken."

"They're both going to die, aren't they?" said Joan quietly.

"That's the penalty for treason," he gently replied.

"Even if they were forced into it."

"I'm not a judge but I imagine so," Richard said, and steered her into the tavern. The landlord and his wife were sitting at one of the tables with a tankard of ale each, having been wakened by the racket in the courtyard along with the rest of his guests, all of whom had now returned to their rooms, some richer, some poorer. Richard apologised for the intrusion and the disturbance and begged two tankards of ale for himself and Joan. The landlord glared at them and grunted then nodded to his wife who stood up and went into a room at the back of the inn. A few minutes later she reappeared carrying a tray with the two tankards and a plate filled with a loaf and a hunk of cheese. She banged them down on the table in front of Joan and Richard without a word and then returned to her husband.

Richard hadn't realised just how hungry he was until he saw the plate. He cut a share for Joan and persuaded her to eat it before devouring the remainder himself. Richard downed his ale and called for another one which arrived in the same manner as the previous one, without a word being spoken. They sat quietly for half an hour, each with their own thoughts, gently sipping their ale. Richard was done in. He'd only just arrived back in London after the long journey from Devon. Having found Joan, he was about turned and the two of them were back on the road within an hour trying to catch up with her father and brother. Finally, he'd ended up being forced into a duel the young fool Geoffrey. He was exhausted but that seemed to be the story of his life since Walsingham's summons.

They both jumped when the landlord shouted across the room to remind them that he'd got a tavern to run and needed to be up again in just a few hours. Richard apologised once again, paid the man handsomely for his hospitality, and with Joan on his arm, he headed for the horses. "We'll need to take it more slowly this time," Richard said. "Our horses are tired and so are we. We'll keep to road unless we see signs of activity and then we'll take to the country again. There's still a good moon so we'll have no trouble seeing where we're going."

They trotted out of the courtyard and back to the palace. They didn't see any soldiers on the road but they did see lighted torches in the surrounding woodland. Walsingham's men were obviously still looking for the traitors who had slipped the net. "God keep Father and Geoffrey safe," prayed Joan.

They reached the palace safely in the early hours of the morning. Joan led Richard through a side gate as the main gate was awash with soldiers keeping close watch, stopping and questioning everyone who was out on the streets. Richard and Joan kept to the shadows as they made their way to the stables. The grooms were all sleeping in the hayloft, so they attended to the horses themselves quietly and efficiently without disturbing any of the sleepers. When they had finished, they crept to the main building. Once again Richard was glad of Joan's knowledge of the palace as she led them to an inconspicuous side door. They opened the door gently although the click of the latch sounded like a clap of thunder in the silent night.

Richard had just finished closing the door as quietly as he could when they were startled by a voice from the shadows.

"Well, well, well!" said Walsingham. "Master Richard and Mistress Joan. Perhaps you would care to tell me where you have been and what you were doing at this time of night when the only people abroad are traitors or my own soldiers and you are certainly not soldiers."

All the colour drained from Joan's terrified face. She screamed in fright and her knees gave way under her; Richard managed to catch her before she reached the floor. His own blood had run cold when he'd heard Sir Francis's voice. How on earth did that man know when they would arrive when they didn't even know themselves and how did he know which door they would enter by? Richard hadn't even known that door existed until Joan had led him to it. The damned man must be in league with the Devil himself!

"I'm waiting," said Walsingham, his penetrating eyes searching their frightened ones for an explanation.

CHAPTER TWELVE

The Escape

"A word, Richard, in my office," said Walsingham, in a voice that demanded instant obedience. Richard followed Sir Francis through the warren of corridors that would lead to his office, but not before he'd calmed the distraught Joan and sent her on her way to her quarters.

For the second time in as many months Richard found himself in front of Sir Francis, feeling like a schoolboy who had been discovered breaking a cardinal rule. "Sit down," said Walsingham, and offered Richard a stool on the opposite side of his desk. When they were both seated Walsingham sternly addressed him. "I can guess where you have been, Richard, and I can understand why, but nevertheless it was an extremely foolish thing to do. You were lucky not to have been apprehended. My men are very thorough and even now are still scouring the countryside for the traitors who are still at large.

They are under orders to arrest anyone they come across in their search, regardless of who they are or what their excuse is for being outside their homes at this time of night."

Richard knew that every word Walsingham said was true. He'd been an idiot to believe that anything he or Joan did could have done would have made any difference to the final outcome. "Look, I know it was stupid of me to even contemplate doing it, but I couldn't let Joan go alone and certainly not in the state she was in. She was determined to try to intercept her father and brother and warn them that the plot had been discovered."

"And warn all the other conspirators in the process, I suppose. How, pray, did she know that her family was implicated? Could it be because she herself is also involved in this treasonous enterprise?" asked Walsingham, never taking his eyes off Richard's face.

"Of course she isn't part of it!" snapped Richard. "She knew nothing about it until she found the note that had been sent to her father with his instructions to go to the rallying point."

"Or maybe she just told you she had found a note. Maybe she just got cold feet at the last minute and wanted to get herself and her family out of the traitorous situation they had gotten themselves into," suggested Sir Francis.

"You're talking rubbish!" Richard shouted. "You and I both know that Joan's no traitor. She loves her queen."

"Do we, Richard? If such evidence existed a loyal subject would have taken the information directly to the queen or myself immediately," said Sir Francis.

"Oh, for God's sake Walsingham. It's her father and brother we're talking about! After all blood will always be thicker than water and besides that she loves them. What would you have done in her situation?" demanded Richard, angrily.

The blank expression on the man's face made him wonder if Walsingham had ever had parents or siblings of his own.

Walsingham was in fact thinking exactly what Richard had earlier. Why would Joan want to lift a finger to save the very people who had treated her so shamefully? He would have imagined that she would be glad to be rid of them.

"Well, your errand of mercy was all in vain, I'm afraid," he said. "I was brought word not half an hour ago that Lord Thomas had been intercepted on his way back to Devon and had given himself up to the soldiers without a fight. Geoffrey, in the other hand, had been discovered under a pile of straw in an old barn. When my men pulled him from his hiding place, he began to whimper like a baby and pleaded with them, on his knees, not to hurt him. He was not treated gently and they are both now on their way to the Tower to join the rest of the traitorous dogs."

"I was afraid that would happen," said Richard.

"Be honest, Richard, it was a foregone conclusion after you brought the information to foil this plot that everyone involved in it would be arrested and dealt with accordingly," said Walsingham.

"They are done for then," said Richard despondently.

"They'll receive the traitor's death they deserve," said Walsingham, without any trace of compassion.

"Is there nothing we can do, you can do, to help get them released?" asked Richard, although he knew the answer even before he even asked the question.

"No, nothing, and I would be loath to do anything to help traitors even if I could. They were about to attempt to assassinate our Queen, their legal Queen and sovereign. They all deserve to die without exception!" replied Sir Francis, with a vengeance. "Joan must leave the palace before first light. She's no longer safe here."

"Good God, Walsingham. What do you mean, she not safe here?" Richard snapped, losing his temper again. "She's one of the queen's own ladies. Surely, she'd be safer here than anywhere. She wasn't involved in the plot. She didn't know nothing about the plot until yesterday."

"Don't you see, Richard, she's tainted by association. She's part of a family of traitors and that alone could implicate her. She also tried to warn the plotters and you were with her. I could have you both arrested for treason here and now," said Walsingham.

"But she's innocent, and I was just a fool," protested Richard.

"Maybe you were, but in this volatile climate of suspicion and fear if I did arrest you for treason you would both surely be convicted and executed."

This was just the kind of thing his friend Will had told him about when he had first arrived in London. Now he and Joan, both innocent, were in danger of being put to death in the most horrible way for a crime they didn't commit.

"Take her back to her home to Devon," Walsingham said, "and then go on to yours too, Richard, where you must both remain until I have investigated this whole matter thoroughly. I still have loose ends to tie up."

"Does Her Majesty know about Joan?" asked Richard, as the full implication of what could happen to him and Joan sunk in.

"Not yet. I will be speaking to the queen in the morning after you have left, but whatever the outcome, as the daughter of a traitor, Joan will never be allowed to serve her again," replied Sir Francis. "Now go quickly, take care you're not seen, and make your preparations to leave as soon as you can. You don't have much time."

Walsingham stood up and offered Richard his

hand across the desk. Richard shook it. "You do realise," he said, "that on top of everything else that's happened to Joan recently this news will break her heart? Not just being banished from Court but being denied access to her beloved Queen."

"I'm afraid that's just the way things are when treason is involved," Walsingham answered. "It's out of my hands."

Walsingham sat down again and picked up his quill. Richard realised he'd been dismissed and headed for Will's room. He found Will there, sleeping soundly and gently snoring in his cot. "Well at least I don't need to spend any time packing," thought Richard, as he looked at his saddlebags still resting on the stool where they'd been thrown when he'd arrived the previous day. He didn't dare lie down even for a few minutes. He was so tired he knew that as soon as he shut his eyes, he would fall asleep.

He took his boots off, put the saddlebags on the floor, and sat on the stool, stretching his legs in the darkness. What a lot had happened since his arrival! Joan's world had been turned upside down once more and although he'd tried his best to help her divert the disaster that followed, he'd failed. How could her father and brother have been so reckless? Yet again Joan was paying the price for their foolishness.

Richard reached for the boots he'd discarded only minutes before and put them back on. He left Will's room, silently closing the door behind him, and crept along the dark corridors towards the door that led to the secret garden. He hoped that he would find it unlocked and be able to get some much-needed fresh air to clear his head.

He was in luck. The door yielded to a little pressure from his shoulder.

The moon was still providing enough light for him to make out a figure sitting on the seat in the arbour. As he approached, he could hear the sound of a woman sobbing. He trod on a twig; it snapped under his weight, and in the stillness of the night it sounded like a gunshot.

"Who's there?" asked a frightened voice.

"Joan, is that you? It's Richard."

"Oh, Richard, what's to become of us?" Joan stood up and threw herself into his arms. "What does Walsingham plan to do with us? Are we going to be sent to the Tower?"

"Calm yourself, my love," Richard said gently, and led her back to her seat, sitting down beside her. "Walsingham wants us to leave the palace before first light," he said, stroking her perfumed hair. "You are to go to your father's home in Devon and I am to go to my father's manor and we are to remain there until he decides what's to be done."

"Why can't I stay here? I can't go home. We must find Geoffrey first and take him with us and then hide him and father before Walsingham's men get to the Manor," said Joan, the words tumbling out one after the other.

"It's too late for that, Joan," Richard said sadly. "They are both taken and are on their way to the Tower."

"No, Richard, no! There must be some mistake. Father was already on his way home and Geoffrey had gone to his friends!"

"There's no mistake," Richard said. "Walsingham told me himself. They are both prisoners and there's nothing we can do for them now. We need to think of ourselves now and obey Walsingham's orders and leave the palace before we become prisoners ourselves. Remember, Joan, we had gone to warn them that the plot was discovered and we could be called traitors too for doing that and suffer a traitor's death for it."

"But Richard, we're not traitors. We're both loyal to the queen. I'll speak with Her Majesty. She will understand," said Joan confidently, although she was at last beginning to realise where the results of their actions might lead them. The thought of the kind of death she would suffer as a traitor sent a shudder through her body. Oh God, her foolish dash to the tavern might have sentenced Richard to the same fate! "My love, I only wanted to save my father and brother," she told him.

"I'm afraid that's not how the law will see it," Richard said. He explained to her how her situation with the queen had changed and why; he then gave her the time she needed to finish shedding her tears as she clung to him. "Now go and pack just what you can carry in your saddlebags and I'll meet you at the stables," he concluded.

They shared a long embrace and then walked to the garden gate together where Richard gave her a lingering kiss before they parted.

By the time Joan joined him at the stables Richard had their horses saddled and ready to leave. They each secured their saddlebags, mounted, walked out of the stable yard. Richard was fearful they might have trouble getting out of the palace as there were still soldiers everywhere. As they approached the gate the guard stepped forward and ordered them to stop. Richard heard the sharp intake of breath from Joan and his own heart skipped a beat. Had Walsingham changed his mind? If so, they would have to take their chance and make a run for it.

They reined in their mounts. The soldier looked up at their faces. "Ah, Mistress Joan," he said. "I believe you and your companion are going for your morning ride?"

Joan's heart was in her mouth as she replied in the affirmative. The guard stepped back and they walked through the palace gate just as the sun's first rays were cresting the horizon. Walsingham had allowed them to leave.

They set off as quickly as they dared, given that their horses hadn't had enough time to recover from their dash from Devon with Richard. They rode steadily through the morning to put as much distance between themselves and London without overtiring their mounts. When the sun reached its highest point, they stopped at an inn for something to eat and drink as neither of them had eaten since just after Geoffrey's duel with Richard the previous night. They ate a hearty meal and drank a tankard of ale without a word passing between them.

"I don't think I've ever been so hungry but I'm so nervous I just hope I can keep it down," said Joan, as she finished the last morsel. "I think we should leave now. We're still too close to London to be safe and I think travelling together the way we are is attracting too much attention already."

"Yes, you're right." Richard glanced quickly round the room, noting the curious stares of some of other patrons. "I'll ask the landlord to prepare bread and cheese for us to take with us."

They both froze as they heard several horses gallop into the courtyard. Had Elizabeth sent her soldiers to arrest them after all? Richard watched the door but Joan's terrified gaze never left his face. She reached for Richard's hand across the table, fearing the worst, as four young gentlemen noisily entered the room. They were both preparing to flee when they realised from the conversation that the young men had been having a race to the tavern. Now the loser was being forced into buying the ale for them all despite his protestations that the others had cheated.

Richard went to talk to the landlord and returned with a small bundle which contained their bread and cheese. They set off at the again, as fast as their mounts would allow, hoping to reach the next inn before nightfall. It was one of the inns that Richard had used on his previous trips to and from London. The landlord recognized him but eyebrows were raised when he and his wife saw that this time Richard was not only travelling with a young female who was unchaperoned but one that was wearing breeches. When she spoke it was obvious that she was a lady of quality, but why would such a lady be journeying with a man who certainly wasn't her servant, nor was he of the nobility and why was she dressed in men's clothes? Since the lady seemed to be with Richard willingly it seemed unlikely that she was being abducted. The landlord thought it best to say nothing as did his wife since these were dangerous times and it was far safer just to keep the mouth shut. It was rumoured that a plot to replace Queen Elizabeth with Mary, Queen of Scots had been uncovered and that many suspects had already been arrested. Could this man and woman be fugitives? The landlord didn't really want to know. It was better to remain ignorant of such things. He just hoped they would leave at sunrise before anyone who may be pursuing them could arrive and cause any disturbance for his other patrons.

After Richard and Joan had eaten a passable meal, they took rooms for the night. They went upstairs right away and tumbled into their respective cots and fell into a deep asleep almost immediately, such was their exhaustion. They were reasonably refreshed the following morning when they left the inn, after a not too appetising but filling breakfast, just before dawn broke. They were still very wary of other travellers on the road, especially groups of horsemen. Joan was as nervous as a kitten and started at any unexpected noise or sudden movement. Richard kept scanning the woodland and hedges close to the road for any signs of hidden soldiers waiting to ambush them.

Despite all the tension that surrounded them they talked about many things on their journey home. Joan told Richard about how recently she had been reconciled with her mother, Margaret, and how her father had forbidden her mother to have any part in her childhood or adolescence. Richard was appalled. He couldn't imagine growing up without his mother's love and guidance. How much harder it must have been for Joan believing that her mother had no love her. Richard told her about his parents and his upbringing which was so different to hers. He related how, after leaving the grammar school, he had learned everything he could from his father about running the business and that he was now in complete charge of the shipping side of his father's business, and what it entailed. He also told her that being married to him would be a completely different life to that which she had been used to.

The mention of marriage inevitably turned the conversion towards Lord de Luc. "Richard, the thought of that man still fills me with terror!" Joan said.

Richard explained to her that now her father was in the Tower stripped of his title and his estate forfeit, de Luc was no longer obliged to pay his debts and therefore the betrothal would be terminated.

"He still frightens me, Richard," Joan said. "I'm afraid he'll find me wherever I go and force me to marry him regardless. He's determined to have me whatever the circumstances."

"There's no way I would ever let that happen," Richard assured her. "You're safe with me."

She wanted to believe him with all her heart but she knew what kind of a man de Luc was. He wasn't going to let her go without a fight. She also knew that if it came to a duel between de Luc and Richard, de Luc would kill him as he had already threatened to do. If that happened, it would also be the end of her life one way or another.

While Joan was contemplating a forced

marriage to de Luc, Richard was imagining his marriage to her. He knew they couldn't even think about getting wed while things were still so uncertain but Richard allowed himself to believe that Walsingham would get to the bottom of this whole horrid business and exonerate him and Joan, leaving them free to plan for their future together. The very thought of them spending the rest of their lives together filled him with delight. Even with their many differences he was sure that between them they would make the marriage work.

They had caused a stir in every inn or tavern they had stopped at owing to their mode of dress, having no proper luggage and Joan being unchaperoned. It hadn't exactly been an inconspicuous journey, but the closer to home they got the more relaxed they became. When they had almost reached their destination Joan became agitated.

"What's wrong, my love?" Richard asked her. "We've only a few more miles to go and we're home."

"Poor mother. She will still be ignorant of this terrible tragedy," said Joan. "How on earth am I going to tell her that not only has she lost her husband and her son but also her title, the estate and everything that goes with it.? She'll be distraught."

"I'll come with you," offered Richard, even though he was eager to see his own parents who must be thinking he had died on his way to London by now.

"No, Richard, I must see my mother alone. You must go on to your parents. They must be frantic with worry to know that you are safe and well."

"Are you sure, my love?" he asked, torn between wanting to relieve his own parents' anxiety and supporting Joan as she broke the dreadful news to her mother. "It will be a great shock to your mother. Are you sure you don't want me to accompany you?"

"Yes, Richard. You are a stranger to her and your presence would make her feel ill at ease even before I could begin to relate what has happened. I don't want it to be any more difficult than it already is. I promise I will come to see you as soon as I'm able. I would like to meet Sir Edmund and Lady Eleanor. After all its them I have to thank for providing me with the man I'm going to marry!" she said with a smile that melted his heart. He physically ached to take her in his arms and carry her off to some secret place where they could leave this God forsaken world behind forever.

"Very well," said Richard. He drew Diablo up beside Caesar, leaned forward, and kissed Joan briefly before they went their separate ways. He couldn't wait for all this to be over and then they need never be parted again.

He turned Diablo towards his father's manor, touched the horse's flanks with his spurs and galloped home.

Lord Thomas and Lady Eleanor were so relieved to discover that their beloved son was neither murdered nor a murderer. But when Richard quickly brought them up to date with what had happened since he last saw them, his mother was horrified. "Oh Richard, you could be tried for treason. Whatever possessed you?" she asked.

"I couldn't let Joan go alone, Mother. She was trying to save her father and brother. Do you think I would stand by and do nothing if my own father needed help?"

"But treason, Richard!"

"Mother, it is done and now I must take the consequences if Walsingham can't discover the truth," Richard snapped.

"As you say, my son, it is done and now we must wait," his father interjected. He put his arm around Richard's broad shoulders and propelled him towards the parlour before his wife could say any more. "Let's go and eat. You must be hungry after your journey."

When Joan arrived at Holyfield Hall she dismounted and led Caesar towards the stables. Before she reached them her groom, Barnaby, ran across the yard to meet her. "Mistress Joan, a Lord de Luc arrived earlier and demanded to be shown to Lady Margaret immediately," said the groom hurriedly. "He is still here and acting as if he were the lord of the manor, ordering the servants about, and demanding food and drink without so much as a by your leave to her ladyship."

"Dear God! Is he alone?" Joan asked, looking about herself in a panic, her heart pounding in her chest.

Before the man could answer de Luc appeared on the steps leading to the main door. "Well, my lovely, here at last! Come and greet your bridegroom, my precious," he slurred, obviously the worse for drink. He began to make his way unsteadily towards her; while he was still out of earshot Joan whispered urgently to her groom, "Go as fast as you can and fetch Richard Lovell. You'll find him at his father's manor. Tell him de Luc's here and bring him quickly. Travel cross country, you'll make better time that way."

"Now, now my dear, what's this? Secret conversations to stable hands now. What reason could you have to talk to him so urgently I wonder?" asked de Luc. He put his hand on her shoulder to steady himself and glowered at her groom.

"I was giving him his orders about the care of my horse," Joan answered angrily. "We've travelled a long distance and he needs to be well rubbed down and given extra oats."

De Luc cackled like an old hag. "When we are wed you can rub me down well and then I'll give you some extra oats," he said, and laughed again.

"What the hell are you staring at?" he bawled at the groom, who was watching and listening, open-mouthed. "Get about your business before you feel the back of my hand. The lady has given you her orders, now go and carry them out!"

"Right away, sir," said Barnaby. He tugged his forelock and headed towards the stables with Caesar, as Joan and de Luc retreated to the door. "I certainly will carry out my orders just as soon as you are out of sight," he thought to himself.

"Come, Joan," said de Luc, sobering a little in the fresh air. "Your mother will be glad to see you. She has not long received some very distressing news and is in need of your comfort."

"I can only imagine how brutally you imparted that news too and how much you enjoyed it! You despicable creature!" shouted Joan.

As soon as the door closed behind them the groom jumped into Joan's saddle and rode her magnificent horse as fast as he could go towards the Lovell Manor house.

Joan's mother looked like a frightened little mouse sitting on her chair beside the hearth in the parlour. Joan threw her cloak onto the bench under the window and ran across the room to Lady Margaret.

"Oh, Joan, thank God you are here!" said Margaret, her eyes bloodshot from hours of tears. "Lord de Luc has told me that your father and Geoffrey have been arrested for treason. Surely that can't be so."

Joan sat on a stool beside Margaret and held her hands. "Mother, don't upset yourself so. It is true that they are under arrest, but nothing is certain yet," she said although she knew it was probably a false hope that there would be any kind of a reprieve. The names of her father and brother were on a list of traitors and there was nothing that could be done about it now.

"Joan, if they are found guilty, they will be put to death and then what will happen to us?" her mother wept.

"You can shift for yourself," said de Luc cruelly, from his seat at the table "As for your daughter, she will be in my charge. We are to be wed on the morrow and then we leave for France."

He drained yet another goblet of wine, as Joan looked at him in disgust. Not only would she never marry him, she would never leave her mother in such distress and with the prospect of not even a roof over her head. "How dare you speak to my mother in that way! I will not marry you. Our betrothal is at an end!" Joan burst out. "My father is in the Tower and no longer requires your help to pay his debts. You have no hold over him now!"

"Your father promised you to me and by God I intend to have you!" was his thunderous reply.

Her terrified mother wept loudly.

"Stop your blubbering and go to bed before I shut you up myself!" roared de Luc. As her mother scurried across the room and out the door, Joan yelled back at him, "How dare you speak to Lady Margaret in that manner!"

"Not 'Lady' for much longer, my dear. Your family is about to be resigned to oblivion," he sneered. "But you have no need to fear as tomorrow you will become Lady de Luc."

"Never!" stormed Joan.

De Luc leapt from the table to her side with such speed that she had no time to react. He caught hold of her shoulders and held her so tightly that his fingernails cut into her flesh. "Now listen to me, my lady. The priest is arriving in the morning and he will marry us, unless you would like a little accident to befall your mother. In her distressed state no one would be surprised if she took her own life. Do you understand my meaning, my love?"

He gave her shoulders an extra squeeze. Joan winced with pain and slowly nodded her head.

"That's better," he said, and relaxed his grip. "Now you must go and rest because tomorrow is your wedding day, the happiest day of your life." He bent his ugly face close to hers and whispered, "And the happiest night."

She twisted herself out of his grasp and ran for the door. As she slammed it behind her she could hear him roaring with laughter. Joan didn't stop until she reached her bedchamber, where she securely bolted the door. She then threw herself on her bed and wept until she thought her heart would break. "Richard, you must get here before the priest otherwise it will be too late," she sobbed. "I can't let him murder my poor mother and he would even if I killed myself to avoid marrying him. Please hurry!"

CHAPTER THIRTEEN

The Wedding

It was dawn when de Luc finally released the terrified maid who he had forced to share his bed for the night. She retrieved her torn nightdress from the floor beside the bed where de Luc had discarded it after he had ripped it from her body, then picked up a blanket that had fallen from the bed and wrapped it painfully around her battered body. De Luc had also risen from the bed but the frightened girl didn't dare look at him for fear he would make her return to him. While he carefully unwrapped the large package he had brought with him from London, the maid edged her way towards the door. She had just reached for the latch when her tormentor commanded her to stop.

The horror-stricken girl slowly turned to face the devil again. He had the most beautiful dress draped across his arms. "You will deliver this to Mistress Joan and assist her as she prepares herself for her wedding day," said Lord de Luc, transferring the dress from his arms to hers. "If she should refuse to accept the gown you must tell her to remember the conversation we had before she retired for the night."

He had chosen the dress almost as soon as the betrothal details had been settled. This was how he wanted his lovely bride to appear. She was to be presented as someone befitted to marry such a great lord as him. "You can also tell her she will not be allowed to see her mother until after we are wed," he added. "I will not have them conspiring against me."

The gown was exquisite. It was made of blue velvet with white silk sleeves and forepart. The bodice was decorated with expensive gems and richly embroidered with silk threads. The maid's hands trembled as she held it, terrified that she would drop it before she reached Joan's room. She had never touched anything so beautiful in her life. De Luc opened the door for her and gave her a resounding slap across her buttocks when she went past him. With a squeal of pain, she hurried out of his reach and heard him laughing as she ran the rest of way to Joan's room.

It was early in the morning before Joan had finally cried herself to sleep. It had been a terrible shock to find de Luc here in her own home, and to witness the despicable way he had treated her mother. She knew that his promise to kill her mother if she refused him was no idle threat.

She'd spent a long time frantically trying to think of anything, anything at all, that could prevent that perverted animal from forcing her to marry him. The thought of a lifetime of being at that man's mercy filled her with absolute dread but she knew she could never sentence her mother to death by refusing him. She would need to find as many ways as she could to obstruct the wedding until Richard arrived to rescue her.

Eventually she fell into a very disturbed sleep punctuated with horrible visions of that despicable man. She was wakened by a gentle tapping on her door. She raised her head from the pillow, still damp with her tears, and began to panic, imagining that it was de Luc on the other side of her door waiting to be admitted. She was still debating what she could do to put him off when the maid announced herself with little more than a whisper.

Joan opened the door. What she saw first was not the magnificent wedding dress the girl was carrying, but the child's badly bruised face, torn nightclothes and dishevelled state. When the maid almost collapsed against her, Joan threw the dress onto her bed and wrapped the sobbing girl in her arms. In between sobs the maid told Joan what de Luc had done to her and forced her to do to him. "My God," thought Joan. "Is this how it will be for me? Will I be a battered wreck every morning if I don't obey his every whim?" The colour drained from her face and she began to tremble along with the maid. Only then she saw the beautiful dress lying on the bed.

She released the girl and started to back away, never taking her eyes off the wedding dress. "No, no, I cannot marry him! I WILL not marry him!"

The young maid straightened the crumpled dress and laid it tidily on Joan's bed. When her mistress once again claimed that she would never marry that man, the girl relayed de Luc's chilling message, and Joan sank down into the chair, utterly defeated. She was trapped. If she didn't give in to his demands she would sign her mother's death warrant and if she did, she would be signing her own.

All Joan could do was spin out her preparations for as long as she dared. She took so long to bathe that the water was cold long before she had finished, and she had the maid arrange her hair half a dozen different ways before she was satisfied. When she entered the parlour sometime later wearing the magnificent dress, her chestnut hair draped over her bare shoulders in curls, she looked absolutely stunning. Joan felt anything but stunning. For her the walk to the altar would be more like a walk to the gallows.

"Ah, my love, you look even more beautiful than ever," de Luc said, looking her up and down with a lewd grin on his face. Joan was under no illusion that he was seeing the dress, but undressing her with his eyes. She stood straight and proud, keeping her eyes fixed above his head.

She knew that if she looked directly at him, she would break down.

"Just one more little finishing touch and you will be perfect," de Luc said, and reached for the velvet box on the table in front of him. He opened it slowly to reveal a necklace of sapphires and diamonds to match her dress; he stood behind her and put it around her neck, fastening the clasp. He then caressed her bare shoulders and kissed her neck before he released her. "You will soon become accustomed to wearing such rich attire as this as my wife, Joan," he said. "You most certainly won't be allowed to ride about the countryside dressed like an undisciplined hoyden. You will be my lady, my wife, and you will conduct yourself as such. I will insist upon it, and I will be obeyed at all times, or you will be exceedingly sorry."

There was no reaction from Joan. She just sat at the table still as a statue, her eyes never wavering from some point in the background. Her tormentor scrutinised her face, seeking some kind of response, but found none. "I had intended to dismiss your insolent groom," de Luc continued, "but it would appear that he has already left and taken your magnificent beast with him. It's a pity that I don't have the time to go in pursuit and bring the rogue to book. I was going to claim the horse for myself as from now on you will have a mount more befitting a lady, one you will ride as a Lady, not like some young stable lad."

This was too much for Joan. But before she could protest there was a tap on the door and a servant ushered in the priest. Joan's heart sank. Why had Richard not come? Surely now it was too late.

When Joan had arrived the previous evening dusk was falling, and the moon was beginning to rise. Her groom initially made excellent time riding to fetch Richard but then the light from the moon was obscured by thick cloud and he was forced to stop and dismount. It had become so dark that he couldn't even see to walk. He was soon disorientated and had no choice but to wait until there was a break in the clouds before he could continue his journey. He was distraught. If only he'd have thought to lift a lantern from the stable before he left, but there'd been no time. God knows what that odious creature could be doing to his mistress in the meantime.

Barnaby had taught his lady how to ride after she'd received her first pony when she was little more than a toddler, and had ridden out with her most days since then until she left for Queen Elizabeth's court in London. He had a great affection for his lovely young mistress. "If that man has harmed just one hair of our mistress's head, I will tear him limb from limb with my bare hands," Barnaby promised Caesar, while they stood beneath a tree heaven knows where. It would have been an impossible promise to keep as he was no match for Lord de Luc but that didn't stop him making it.

There was no break in the clouds at all and Barnaby was forced to spend the night resting against an old tree trunk in sheer frustration. He had let his lady down when she was depending on him. He was devastated. It was only when the first light of the dawn glimmered in the east that he was able to get his bearings again. He was pleased to discover that they hadn't strayed too far off course while stumbling around in the dark. He jumped into the saddle and Caesar leapt forward, seeming to sense the urgency of their journey. He flew over the uneven ground and barely broke his stride when confronted with an obstacle. Both horse and rider were lathered in sweat by the time they reached the manor house soon after the sun had cleared the horizon and bathed the now unbroken sky in an ethereal pink light.

Richard was still dressing when his father's steward entered his bedchamber and announced the arrival of Joan's groom. Richard grabbed his jerkin and ran down the stairs three at a time; he rushed out of the door into the courtyard where a breathless Barnaby was patting Caesar's foamed neck. Barnaby told Richard as quickly as he could all that had happened at Holyfield Hall and stated his own fears for his mistress.

Richard was dumbstruck. Lord de Luc at Holyfield and his beautiful Joan at that evil man's mercy. He knew why the man had come but how had he got there so quickly? He ran for the stables, Barnaby closely following with Caesar, and shouted for John.

When John appeared, Richard quickly explained the situation to him. "Barnaby and I are returning to Holyfield as soon as Diablo is saddled. Rouse my father and tell him what has happened. I need him to gather some men and to follow us as quickly as he can but bring me my sword and dagger first," Richard ordered, putting his saddle on Diablo.

Barnaby handed a very tired Caesar over to one of the grooms and then saddled one of the other horses. John appeared with Richard's weapons just as they were ready to leave. He was followed by a very bleary-eyed Edmund who had been wakened by all the commotion.

"Follow me as quickly as you can! John will explain!" Richard shouted over his shoulder. He then raced out of the yard, Barnaby directly behind. "Please grant that we will be in time," he silently prayed.

"Welcome, Father Adrian," said de Luc. He gathered Joan on his arm and went forward to greet the short and very rotund priest. "I hope your journey was without incident."

"Yes, thank you, my son. I was well received in the houses you recommended and the people were grateful to receive the sacrament from a priest of the true faith," he replied.

"This is my bride, Joan, daughter of Lord Thomas Marchemont," said de Luc, presenting her to the priest.

"You are a fortunate man, my lord, to have such a beautiful bride," the priest told him, and turned to Joan. "My daughter."

Father Adrian held out his hand for Joan to kiss. Joan stared at him defiantly and didn't move. De Luc put his hand on her shoulder and forced her into a curtsy before the priest. She barely brushed the back of his hand with her lips before she straightened again. Without a word turned her back on both men and went and sat in her mother's chair at the table.

The priest was taken aback by her disrespectful attitude. "A little lacking in manners, my son," he remarked.

"Nothing that won't be quickly rectified once we are man and wife," de Luc said, throwing Joan a threatening look. "You must be hungry after your journey."

"I am indeed, my son."

"Then we will eat before the ceremony," said de Luc and walked to the door. "Food and wine now!" he roared down to the servants, who had already learned that they must obey instantly or be prepared to suffer the painful consequences.

When he took Lord Thomas's chair at the head of the table Joan could contain her anger no longer. "How dare you act as if you were master here!" she cried. "This is still my father's house and in his absence Lady Margaret, my mother, is the head of the household!"

"Your mother is nothing! She is the wife of a traitor and the mother of a traitor, and she is fortunate that I haven't cast her out already which is what she deserves!" de Luc shouted back.

"YOU cast her out?" Joan yelled. "YOU have no rights here! This is her home and what happens to her has nothing to do with you!"

The priest was shocked at Joan's outburst against the man who would shortly be her husband. "My son, are you sure you wish to be married to this hellcat?" he asked. "She doesn't seem fit to be the wife of someone of your standing, my lord."

"Oh, believe me, Father, after we are wed this hellcat will very quickly become an obedient little kitten," said de Luc, smiling at the priest but clenching his fists under the table.

The servants appeared with their meal. As they placed everything on the table Joan quietly asked one of them to take a meal to Lady Margaret in her bedchamber. De Luc would certainly have made no provision for her. She, however, picked at her meal in silence, while the priest rambled on and on in between cramming as much food as he could into his mouth and washing it down with copious amounts of wine. De Luc added his own comments now and again but was beginning to get impatient. He wanted to get to the family's private chapel and have the marriage ceremony before the priest became too drunk to administer the vows.

Eventually de Luc put up his hand to indicate that the meal was at an end and Father Adrian stopped in mid flow, although he did manage to drain his goblet before he got up from the table. He left Joan and de Luc together while he went to change into his vestments before proceeding to the chapel. When the door had closed de Luc said to Joan in a low, menacing tone, "My dear, if you ever raise your voice to me in that manner again, I will use my horsewhip across your back. While it would sadden me greatly to see your lovely skin bleeding and bruised, I will be obeyed!"

"If I am forced to go through with this marriage you will be chastising a dead body," she retorted.

"Not if you want your dear mother to witness another sunrise, my precious," said de Luc with an evil smile.

"Oh my God, I am trapped," thought Joan. "I have no choice but to marry him if I want my mother to live." She had no doubt in her mind that Lord de Luc would carry out his threat without a second thought. "Where is Richard? Why hasn't he come? Barnaby should have reached him hours ago. What if he's had an accident on the way? What if Richard didn't go home and Barnaby can't find him?" Joan could feel the panic rising as her mind span in turmoil. She began to feel faint and took a drink from her goblet, untouched since the servant had poured the wine more than an hour ago.

De Luc was watching her closely, trying to read her face. Was she aware of something he wasn't? The sooner they were wed the better. He was about to go and look for the priest when the steward entered the room to say that Father Adrian was ready for them in the chapel.

Father Adrian stood in front of a crucifix wearing his papist vestments. The wafers and chalice were resting on the altar in readiness for the Eucharist which would be administered immediately following the marriage ceremony. Joan and Lord de Luc knelt together at the altar and the priest began the service. Joan's heart felt like a little bird battering itself against the bars of its cage in its desperation to be free. It was only when de Luc squeezed her hand hard that she realised that Father Adrian was waiting for her response to his question. She looked at him in a daze and he repeated the question. "Joan, will you accept this man as your lawful husband?"

The answer stuck in her throat.

"Joan, answer!" said de Luc angrily, squeezing her hand until she winced.

"The answer is no!" said a voice behind them.

De Luc spun round, still on his knees. "You!" he said, hardly able to believe his eyes when he saw Richard standing in the doorway. He jumped to his feet in a panic when he realised that Richard was armed whereas he was not.

Richard smiled at the man's discomfort. "Don't worry, de Luc," he said. "I may not have a title, but I am a man of honour. I would never kill an unarmed man and certainly not in a place of God, even a Catholic one. I'll wait in the courtyard while you arm yourself."

"You had best make your peace with your God then while you wait," de Luc snapped, incensed. "When I have despatched you to your maker Father Adrian can complete the ceremony." He glanced over at Joan, whose face betrayed a mixture of emotions. He pushed Richard out of his way and stormed off down the corridor to his bedchamber to collect his weapon.

Joan rushed to Richard and flung her arms around his neck. "I thought you weren't coming. I was so frightened, Richard. He said that if I didn't marry him he would kill my mother!"

"Don't cry, my love. Everything will be alright now. Barnaby is on his way back to my father's manor with your mother. She will be safe there." Richard said, holding her close.

"But, Richard, de Luc is an expert with the sword," Joan said. "In the past he has killed many men who have challenged him. Don't fight with him. Now that mother is safe, we can run away. There is a secret way out of the chapel. Father created it when Edward was on the throne as an escape route for the priest if the king's men came hunting for him."

Richard put his hands on her shoulders and looked into her face. "No, Joan. I run from no man and especially one like de Luc. If we run now, we'll never stop running for de Luc would pursue us relentlessly wherever we flee and so would Walsingham. It would just be a matter of which of them would find us first and both would want to take our lives."

"Walsingham?" queried Joan.

"Of course, my love. If we take flight now, he will assume it's an admission of our guilt regarding the plot against the queen."

"Of course. I hadn't thought of that," said Joan quietly.

"I will meet de Luc in the courtyard and put my faith in God to protect me. Pray for me, my darling. I love you." He embraced her tenderly and kissed her briefly before he left her to go and face de Luc, although he would have given anything to have remained folded within her arms forever.

The priest had watched the whole exchange open-mouthed. He couldn't work out what was happening. Just when he'd been in the process of marrying Joan to Lord de Luc, she had flung herself into the arms of another man, and now the two men were trying to kill each other. Maybe God would guide him. He turned back to the altar and knelt to pray.

Joan ran from the chapel to follow Richard.

Lord de Luc was already waiting in the courtyard and had swapped his wedding garb for a plain shirt and breeches. Richard gave his jerkin to Joan who now was stood beside him.

"Be careful, my love. I love you so much. I couldn't bear it if anything happened to you," she whispered, before retreating to the steps at the main door.

"Well, Lovell, I hope you are prepared for your death because I promise you, you will be dead very shortly and then your beloved will belong to me forever," threatened de Luc.

"And I promise you, de Luc, that the only way you will get to her is over my dead body and I've no intentions of dying," Richard replied, never taking his eyes off de Luc's evil face.

They stood facing each other with swords drawn for a few seconds. The dual then began, both men knowing that it was a fight to the death.

Richard was forced backwards time and again. Only his natural agility and quick reactions saved him from being skewered. The expression on de Luc's face was demonic and his strength almost supernatural as he came at Richard relentlessly. Even if he hadn't still been recovering from all that had happened to him recently, Richard knew he was no match for de Luc's skill. The sweat was running from both men and Richard was visibly tiring as he tried to parry de Luc's strokes. More than once, Joan covered her eyes, expecting de Luc's lunge to hit home. She wanted to turn her face away, but she was mesmerized. She had already decided that since her mother had been taken to safety, if de Luc was the victor she would run to her bedchamber and take her own life before he could claim her.

Richard was really struggling now. De Luc was deliberately forcing him backwards towards Joan, with a view to killing him at her feet. When Richard's heel hit the step, he toppled over, landing on his back. De Luc prepared to deliver the coup de grace. With a glance at Joan he brought his sword down with enough force to decapitate Richard, but although weary, Richard managed to roll out of the way of the weapon; it smashed into the step with such force that it broke in half. Before de Luc could recover himself, Richard managed to kick the legs from under him, scrambled to his own feet and rested the point of his sword above the man's evil heart. Just as he began to exert pressure on the sword to administer the fatal blow a group of horsemen galloped into the yard.

Walsingham jumped from the saddle. "Hold, Richard! He's mine!"

Richard stepped back in surprise.

"That would be too quick a death for this dog," said Walsingham. He motioned two soldiers to take hold of de Luc. They roughly dragged him to his feet, bound his hands behind him and led him away.

Richard and Joan were embracing on the steps when Walsingham reached them. "Good day, Mistress Joan."

"Welcome, Sir Francis," replied Joan.

Walsingham made a slight bow and turned to Richard. "Is there somewhere we can talk, Richard?"

"You may use the small parlour," Joan said. "You will not be disturbed there and then I will have food and drink prepared for your men."

"Thank you, you are very kind," Walsingham replied, and followed her and Richard into the house. He waited until Joan had left them to tell Richard, "I think you had already guessed that the package you brought back from France contained the names of the traitors."

Richard nodded.

"There was one name missing from that list and it was the most important one. I still didn't know the name of the person who had organised and financed the plot. However, a little time on the rack soon loosened the tongues of the more prominent persons and it wasn't long before I had the missing piece to the puzzle."

"De Luc?" asked Richard.

"Yes. When I arrived at his house to arrest him, I discovered that the bird had flown but with a little bit of 'friendly' persuasion one of his servants gave me his whereabouts."

"But I thought de Luc was a staunch

Protestant," said Richard.

"So did everyone else. He kept his true colours well-hidden which made it all the more difficult to root him out," Walsingham replied. "I also discovered that Marchemont was blackmailed into taking part. I don't think that his worthless son would need much persuasion, but the father was certainly coerced into going along with the plot. I have related all this information to Her Majesty and because you risked your life for her safety, your love for Joan and the loyal service she received from Joan, she is prepared to be lenient."

There was a tap on the door and Joan entered carrying a tray of food and wine. She placed it on the table between them. "Your father has arrived, Richard. He is waiting outside."

"Send him in," Walsingham answered. "Our discussion involves him too."

Richard gave him a quizzical look but said nothing. He noticed that Joan had anticipated the answer and had put three goblets on the tray. He poured the wine and set out the tray of sweetmeats. When Sir Edmund appeared, and they had dispensed with the usual greetings, Walsingham bade Sir Edmund to join them at the table.

"Sir Edmund, is your ship ready to sail yet?" he asked.

"All seems to be in order for her maiden voyage in four weeks' time, although I am still waiting for written authorisation from your office," said Sir Edmund, raising an eyebrow.

Walsingham smiled. "It will be forthcoming in plenty of time, my friend. What I need to know is if you would be prepared to allow two passengers sail on her."

"What passengers?" asked Edmund.

"Lord Thomas Marchemont and his son Geoffrey."

Now it was Richard who raised his eyebrows.

"The queen, in her mercy, has offered to commute their death sentences to lifelong banishment and exile," Walsingham said. "They are to go to the New World and stay there for the rest of their lives. The Lady Margaret may travel with them if she so wishes. If your ship encounters any other on the way or docks at any other port before reaching her final destination, they are to be locked in the hold out of sight."

"I see," Edmund answered. "But she's a cargo ship with no facilities for passengers."

"They will be better facilities than those in the dungeons of the Tower and infinitely better than the grave and far better than they deserve in my opinion," Walsingham coldly replied.

"Very well then, I have no objection," said Edmund.

"Good. It is settled then. I'll return to London with my prisoner and perhaps you could follow me later when you have finished your business here, Richard."

Walsingham left the room before Richard could reply. He had assumed as usual that Richard would comply with his wishes regardless.

When Walsingham reached the courtyard, he discovered that he had another prisoner. De Luc was already secured to his horse, but the soldiers were tying the priest onto a mule. "We found him in the chapel, sir, still wearing his vestments with the altar set out for the papist Eucharist," the sergeant at arms told Walsingham. "He was tearing the place apart trying to find a way out. Put up quite a fight he did too, for a fat friar. Took three of us to hold him."

"Did you search the rest of the house?" asked Walsingham.

"We did, sir, but there was just the servants and Mistress Joan. We also searched the stables and outbuildings but we found nothing."

"Very well. Let us leave," said Walsingham.

Another of the soldiers brought his horse to him. He climbed into the saddle and the party galloped away with their prisoners in tow.

CHAPTER FOURTEEN

The Subterfuge

Richard, his father, and Joan returned to the parlour after Walsingham and the soldiers had gone. "So de Luc was the mastermind!" said Richard. "I can't help wishing that Walsingham had arrived a little later and then I could have already rid the world of that evil man's presence."

"Don't worry, son, the world will soon be rid of him," Edmund answered. "I think it would be best if Joan came to join her mother at the manor. She can't stay here alone with just the servants."

Richard gave his father a look of surprise.

"We met Barnaby with Lady Margaret and a badly beaten servant on the road as we were coming here," said Edmund, in answer to his son's tacit question.

"Oh, heavens!" Joan exclaimed. "What will I do about the few servants that are left here? I can't turn them out with nothing. Most of them will have nowhere else to go. There isn't any money left to pay them what they are owed and all they're guilty of is faithful service and loyalty to this family throughout the most difficult of times. I have no idea when they were last paid or how much. I suppose my mother could sell some of what little is left of father's assets, or do they already belong to The Crown?" Joan's eyes filled with tears. "Richard, I don't know what to do. I have nothing I can give them."

Edmund was full of admiration for this young girl who had been through the most horrendous ordeal and whose first thought was the fate of her unfortunate servants. "Don't worry about that now, my dear," he said. "They can remain here until we know what is to be done with Holyfield Hall and I'll see that they are paid what they are due if they have to leave."

"Oh, thank you. You are very kind, Sir Edmund," said Joan. When Edmund saw the relief on the young girl's face and the gratitude in her eyes, he understood why his son had fallen so deeply in love with her. "Richard, stay with Joan while she packs what she needs and then escort her and her maid to the manor," he told his son. "I will go on ahead and let your mother know that we are about to receive another most welcome guest." He gave Joan a quick peck on her cheek and nodded his acceptance of her to his son. Richard smiled lovingly at both of them before Edmund left.

Joan's heart leapt. She was going to be living in close proximity with Richard and the threat of having to marry de Luc was gone forever. As she thought of her new life with her mother, Richard, and his family, she hoped that Walsingham would soon have them both exonerated from the treason charge. Then her life would be perfect.

In the Tower, Geoffrey was delighted to receive a letter and a basket of food and drink from his friend Anthony. He had mostly recovered from the beating he had received from the soldiers when they had found him hiding in the barn, but he and his father had recently been separated from the other prisoners and put in a different cell together without any explanation. When he had demanded to know why, he'd been rewarded with a smack across the mouth and told that it was none of his damn business.

The conditions in their new accommodation were still as filthy and damp and the food the same as before. All very far removed from the decadent lifestyle they were used to. Geoffrey quickly rubbed his dirty hands down the side of his leggings and scanned the contents of the letter, while his father carefully removed everything from the basket and laid it out on top of the cleanest straw he could find in their squalid chamber.

Geoffrey, this has been brought to you by Jane,

the daughter of the Constable of the Tower, the letter began. *When I finally discovered where you and your father were being held I renewed my relationship of some time ago with Jane. She's a very 'friendly' lass (if you know what I mean!). It didn't take me long to get her between the sheets again and with the promise of more to come I soon persuaded her to act as a messenger between us. Her talents don't end in bed either. She's not averse to listening at keyholes amongst other things. I set her to spying on her mother and father and last night she got the information we were looking for when she overheard them talking in their bedchamber. Great news, Geoffrey! God knows why, but both you and your father have been spared execution and are to be exiled. All the other members of the plot are to be executed in the next few days. You will leave on Sir Edmund Lovell's ship in four weeks' time when she makes her maiden voyage to the New World.*

"Like hell I will," said Geoffrey angrily.

"What's wrong, son?" asked Thomas, as he swallowed a mouthful of bread and cheese.

"Nothing to bother you," Geoffrey replied impatiently, and continued to read the letter. *Let Jane know if there's anything else you require, and she'll tell me. She'll come to visit you again in a couple of days' time. Anthony.*

Geoffrey looked at Jane. She was a pleasant faced, buxom lass and he wouldn't mind having a roll in the hay with her himself. "When you come again bring me quill, ink and paper," he said. "I need to write to Anthony and tell him to send a bigger basket next time. The swill they feed in here isn't fit for pig."

Jane took an instant dislike to him. She didn't like the way his eyes were undressing her, either. "I'll tell him," she said, and collected her basket from Thomas, who smiled at her gratefully. It was good to taste fresh food and to have a good wine to wash it down with. Thomas and Geoffrey had nothing with which to bribe their jailers in order for them to bring something more palatable than the disgusting prison food they were being fed.

Geoffrey caught Jane's arm as she passed him. "Perhaps a friendly little kiss before you leave. I'm sure Anthony won't begrudge me one kiss," he teased.

"I'm not a whore," she spat.

Geoffrey grabbed her tightly and brought his lips down hard on hers. It was too long since he'd had a woman and this one would be as good as any other. He was already tearing at her bodice, trying to rip it from her breast, when she kicked him hard on his shin and stamped on his foot.

"You bitch!" he shouted, rubbing his leg. "I'll make you pay for that!"

"Geoffrey, for God's sake leave her be!" his father shouted. "She's our only contact with the outside world!"

Jane pushed Geoffrey away from her and ran to the safety on the other side of the door. "You ungrateful cur!" she shouted. "You're nothing but an animal! If you want me to come again, you'd better find some manners or I'll leave you to starve in your own filth!"

Geoffrey turned to his father. "You shut up, old man!" He then limped over to where Thomas was sitting and dropped down beside him. "There'd better plenty of that food and wine left for me or you'll be sorry."

It was a far happier gathering at the Lovell manor. By the time everyone sat down to eat they were already relaxed and chatting together very comfortably. There was no class distinction here. Lady Margaret was grateful to have been rescued out of the clutches of that evil man and Joan was in seventh heaven at being so close to her beloved Richard. There was nothing standing in the way of them getting married now and the thought of spending the rest of her life with him filled her with delight. Lady Eleanor had taken to Joan almost as soon as she'd met her and was pleased that her son had settled on such a lovely girl.

When the meal was finished, and the servants had withdrawn, Edmund said, "My dears, I think Richard and I have some news that will cheer you all. When Walsingham came to arrest Lord de Luc, he also brought news concerning Lord Thomas and Geoffrey."

"Please tell me they're still alive," pleaded Lady Margaret, suddenly losing the colour she had only recently regained.

"Not only are they alive but they are going to remain so," said Edmund.

"But how can that be?" Eleanor asked. "They've been charged with treason and that always results in death."

Joan looked at Richard, not knowing what to think. Did that mean that she and Richard were safe too?

Richard took up the story. "Because of Joan's loyal service to Her Majesty and the fact that Lord Marchemont was blackmailed into taking part in the plot, the queen has mercifully commuted their death sentence to banishment."

"It was also in gratitude to my son for risking his life to bring Walsingham the vital information he needed to put an end to the treachery," added his father, proudly.

Lady Margaret turned to Richard. "So it's you I have to thank for my dear husband and son being prisoners in the Tower!"

"No, Mother, it is not his fault that father and Geoffrey's names were on a list of traitors," Joan said, jumping to his defence. "They have only themselves to blame, or at least partly, as father seems to have been an unwilling participant. Richard was only doing his duty as a loyal subject of the queen."

Richard's eyes met her eyes across the table, and he was overwhelmed with the love he saw there.

"If they are banished what will become of me?" asked Lady Margaret. "I can't stay at Holyfield Hall now it has been claimed by the crown and nor can I impose on your hospitality indefinitely."

"If you wish you will be allowed to travel with them," said Sir Edmund. "It won't be an easy life though. The new colonies are barely beginning to establish themselves and there's much work to do. I am hoping to set up a trading post there very soon and will need someone to run it. I thought that perhaps Lord Marchemont would give it some thought."

Although Lady Margaret had no idea what Edmund was talking about, she nevertheless replied, "I would much rather be working alongside my husband, however hard, than remaining here alone."

"You wouldn't be alone, Mother," Joan said. "You will have Richard and me if you wish to stay behind. You could live with us."

"No, my child. You and Richard have your own lives now and my place is at my husband's side just as yours must be beside Richard," her mother answered, smiling at both of them in turn. "I know you will be very happy together and I am more than happy to give you my blessing. However, knowing my daughter as well as I do I have no doubt that she would marry you with or without my blessing."

"Yes, I would but I would much prefer it with

your blessing than without," Joan said, flashing a loving smile at her mother. Margaret hugged Joan affectionately.

"Well said!" Edmund declared. "Let us drink to the happiness of Richard and Joan."

They all raised their goblets and took a drink.

"I promise you, Lady Margaret that I will love Joan with all my heart and protect her with my life for as long as I live," said Richard, and raised his goblet again. "Now let us drink to Lord Thomas and Lady Margaret and their new life together in the New World."

It was only then Margaret realised that the place where Thomas and Geoffrey were to be exiled to may well have been on the moon, for all she knew of the New World. But as long as they were going to be together and alive, she didn't care where it was. "When do we leave?" she asked.

"You will be sailing on my ship which leaves in about three weeks' time. I will escort you to Topsham where we must await our final instructions from Walsingham. I hope you will accompany us, my dear, and travel with us to London as companion to Lady Margaret," said Edmund, smiling at Eleanor.

"Of course. I will look forward to it, but before then we must return to Holyfield Hall. No doubt Lady Margaret will have a good deal of packing to do before she leaves," replied Eleanor, knowing that such a 'minor' detail would not have occurred to her husband.

"Mother, Richard has to leave for London soon and I would like to travel with him," Joan said. "I could meet you on board ship when you arrive and be there to say goodbye to you and Father and Geoffrey. You won't need me if Lady Eleanor is travelling with you."

Before Lady Margaret could reply, Richard said, "Joan, my love, I will be riding hard and with little luxury."

"You know that I can ride every bit as well as you and you've never afforded me any luxuries on our previous travels," she said with a wicked twinkle in her eyes.

"Very well, you win!" laughed Richard. "But only with your mother's permission."

"Mother?" asked Joan.

"Would anything I say make any difference?" ventured Lady Margaret, smiling.

"No," Joan replied with a mischievous grin.

"Then go but take heed and be guided by Richard," her mother warned.

Richard looked at Joan and raised an eyebrow while she dropped him a mock curtsy. "Well, I suppose I'd better prepare myself to offend the gentle folk's sensibilities again by having an unruly wench in breeches in tow once more."

He winked at his father, and everyone laughed. They carried on with their genial conversation until it was time to retire for the night.

True to his word, Anthony sent Jane to visit Geoffrey two days later. This time she was carrying two baskets of food and drink as well as the paper and ink that Geoffrey had requested. There was also another note from Anthony complaining that he had had to borrow some money off Robert to pay for the contents of the baskets and bribes for a couple of the guards. Geoffrey laughed as he screwed up the note and threw it into a corner. Lord Marchemont was already busy examining the contents of the baskets while Jane stood well out of Geoffrey's reach.

"What have we this time, Father?" Geoffrey asked. "Something a bit more decent, I hope."

"There are fowl and pies, bread and cheese, some sweetmeats and wine," answered Thomas. He picked up a pie and began to eat hungrily.

"Good, that's better. You can tell Anthony to send me some fresh clothes next time. These are nothing more than stinking rags now," Geoffrey said to Jane.

She looked on him in disgust.

"What's the matter, my dear? Do I offend you?" he asked, leering at her.

Jane edged towards the door. Why was Anthony trying to help this creature? If it was up to her, he could rot in hell.

"Come back tomorrow and I'll have a letter ready for Anthony." Geoffrey pointed to the baskets that his father had emptied, as he added, "You can fill these again too. The slop they give us in here will poison us. And don't forget the clothes."

Jane quickly gathered her baskets and was gone before Geoffrey could molest her again.

She returned two days later with just one basket and a small parcel.

"Where the hell have you been? I told you to come yesterday!" stormed Geoffrey.

"I had errands to run for my father and you're lucky I come at all! If you yell at me again, I certainly won't come back," Jane returned.

Geoffrey withstood the urge to strike her and in a more conciliatory tone asked if she'd brought the clothes. She handed him the parcel and Lord Marchemont took the basket from her with a smile.

Geoffrey unwrapped the package. "Dear God in Heaven! These aren't even fit for a peasant!" he roared, holding up the breeches and jerkin. "What the hell is Anthony thinking? I'm the son of a lord for God's sake! I don't wear the likes of these!"

"My son, I am no longer a lord, and I would advise you to be grateful for what Anthony has sent," said Thomas.

"Shut up, Father. I don't need your advice!" Geoffrey shouted.

Jane had heard enough. "These are all Anthony could afford. You are costing him dear, and he is already in debt thanks to you. You're nothing but an ungrateful wretch and if I were you I'd start giving some serious thought to the situation I was in and what would happen to me if Anthony stopped helping me."

Geoffrey was about to answer her with his fist but thought the better of it. He didn't want to do anything that would cause Jane to stop coming to collect or deliver letters as well as delivering the extra food. She was his only link to Anthony, and he needed to preserve it.

"Will you bring me Anthony's reply as soon as you have it?" he requested in a more polite tone.

Jane nodded, knowing that, for the time being at least, she had him at her mercy.

Geoffrey knew it too and he didn't like it. He promised himself that if he got the opportunity, he'd make her pay dearly for putting him in this position. Very dearly indeed, and he would enjoy every last minute of it!

On the day that Sir Edmund took Eleanor and Lady Margaret back to Holyfield Hall, Richard and Joan left for London. They arrived five days later after an uneventful journey, although Joan's travelling attire had raised more than a few eyebrows again. No one had been brave enough to ask for any explanations, however. They were far more relaxed on this journey than the last, relieved that this time they did not have to keep looking over their shoulders for any sign that they were being pursued. Joan found it strange to be going to London for other than to take up her duties as the queen's lady again as she usually did when she returned from visiting her parents. She was still very upset that she was no longer allowed to attend Her Majesty and wondered if Elizabeth would find it in her heart to forgive her.

They made their way to Walsingham's office as soon as they had settled their horses at the stables. Just as they reached his door Sir Francis walked up behind them. He had been so light on his feet they hadn't realised that he was following them along the corridor, until he greeted them. Jane nearly jumped out of her skin. It reminded her of that dreadful night when he had caught them returning to the palace after the failed plot.

Phelipps and Will were busy at their desks when Walsingham ushered Richard and Joan into the room. They both rose from their stools. "Please, Mistress Joan," said Will, offering his stool to her.

"Thank you, Will," she said, and sat down.

Sir Francis sat down behind his desk. "I've had Will take rooms for you both at a decent inn close to the palace. You can stay there until you have a chance to make other arrangements. I've also taken the liberty of having all Joan's belongings transferred there from her room here."

"You are very kind, Sir Francis. Will I be

allowed to speak to Her Majesty?" Joan asked hopefully.

"I'm sorry, Joan, but the queen will no longer grant you an audience. She is still very shaken by the plot to overthrow her and as your family were party to that plot she can no longer allow you into her presence again, however harsh that may seem."

"I see," said Joan, disappointed that she would not be able to thank the queen in person for her mercy towards her father and brother. "Would she accept a letter, perhaps?"

"I can deliver a letter to her, but I can't guarantee that she will read it."

"I will write to her," Joan said. "Will I be able to visit my father and Geoffrey while I am here?"

"No," Walsingham answered. "You will not be able see them until they are released into Richard's care before they are transported to the New World."

This was news to Richard, now leaning against the back of the door since there was nowhere for him to sit. "Me!" he said in surprise as he stood up straight. To himself he thought, "Dear God, Walsingham's doing it again. He's getting me into things I know nothing about without any consultation whatsoever."

"Yes Richard. It is a delicate operation," Walsingham told him. "There are many who will see the release of Marchemont and his son from the Tower as an escape from proper justice and there's a danger that they will take the law into their own hands. If I send them to your father's ship with an escort of soldiers they will be observed by those who always lurk in the shadows. It must all be done in secret and as quietly as possible. I still have a few of the final details to put in place before we can go ahead but your father has already received his instructions and his ship will be in place at the appointed time."

He knew the boy was less than happy and likely to fly into a rage again. He turned to Joan and offered her pen, ink and paper and suggested she go to the enclosed garden to compose her letter to the queen while he and Richard concluded their business. After thanking him Joan left the room, closing the door behind her.

"And just how much danger are you putting me into this time?" said Richard, annoyed that once again Sir Francis had assumed, without a by your leave, that he would comply with his wishes. The man was insufferable.

"If all goes well there will be no danger at all and the plans are being meticulously made to prevent anyone knowing about the venture until Joan's father and brother have left England," Walsingham replied.

"Just like the last time and that damn near got me and a ship's crew killed!" Richard planted his hands on Walsingham's desk and stared into those soul-searching eyes as Walsingham's expressionless face looked back at him. "You don't give a damn do you or care who gets hurt as long as the job gets done? You're despicable!" He turned and headed for the door.

"Richard, wait!" commanded Walsingham. "I am Her Majesty's spymaster and it is my duty to keep her alive by any means and if that puts people in danger or even costs them their lives then so be it. That's the way of it and if that makes me despicable, I'll live with it willingly if it means my queen is safe."

Richard let go of the door latch and turned back to face Walsingham.

"Would you like to know why Joan's father took part in the plot?" Walsingham asked him.

Richard nodded.

"He was blackmailed into it by de Luc who had threatened not only to withdraw his offer of financial help but also to harm both Joan and Lady Margaret if he refused."

"Merciful Heaven, is there no end to that man's evil?" Richard exclaimed.

"There will soon be a permanent end to him and his evil. Within days he is due to be hanged, drawn and quartered which is still too good for him in my opinion," Walsingham replied.

"I'm glad, as I don't think I could ever be totally at ease knowing that he was still in this world," Richard said. "I don't think he'd ever give up trying to take Joan. He's like a man possessed."

Meanwhile Joan was in the garden, composing her letter to her Queen. As she tried to put her thoughts onto the paper she began to cry and her tears fell onto the words, making them illegible. She got a little further on her second, and last, piece of paper, but when she thought about never seeing her beloved sovereign again her tears began once more and ran down her cheeks and onto her letter.

"Oh no!" she cried. "Now how will I ever tell her how much I love her and how sorry I am for what my father and my stupid brother have done?"

"Perhaps it would be better if you told her face to face rather than in a letter," said a voice behind her.

Joan dropped from the bench where she had been sitting onto her knees and bowed her head. "Your Majesty."

"Come, Joan, we'll be more comfortable here," said Elizabeth. She lowered herself onto the bench where Joan had been sitting seconds before, indicating for Joan to join her.

Joan obeyed, still weeping. "How did you know I was here?"

"I had commanded Walsingham to let me know immediately when you returned, which of course he did. While he was with me, I made it quite plain that he was to persuade you to come to the garden." The queen took hold of Joan's trembling hands in her own. "Come, let's make things right between us before we part for good."

They talked together until Elizabeth left to return to her private apartments. Joan had no sooner returned to Walsingham's office when Sir Francis was dismissing them. "Now, you must leave us to continue our work here and when everything is in place," he said. "I will send word. I will send Will with you now to show you to the inn and introduce you to the landlord."

Richard and Joan took their leave and left with Will for the inn. Will was desperate to know what was afoot and very disappointed when Richard refused to reveal anything, but they all parted amicably enough.

Joan could hardly wait for him to leave so that she could tell Richard about her meeting with Her Majesty in the garden. He was pleased they'd made their peace as it was another burden lifted from his love's shoulders.

Geoffrey and Lord Thomas received regular visits from Jane during the next two weeks. She brought more food and letters from Anthony, and at the end of the second week she came for the last time with the news that his father and he were to be released the following day into the hands of Richard Lovell.

"Lovell! How wonderful!" Geoffrey said, hardly able to contain his excitement.

Jane had no idea why he should be so elated

and was glad that this was the last time she would have to be in his company.

"How many soldiers?" he asked Jane, his eyes full of curiosity.

"No soldiers," she answered, "just Richard Lovell and your sister I believe."

"Did you say Joan? This is more than I'd dared hope for," said Thomas, who had come over to join them.

"And me," Geoffrey said to himself. "Jane, I need to write a short note to Anthony. Will you wait until I'm finished and then deliver it immediately?" He was now even more pleased that he had made the effort to stay on the right side of her.

"If you wish," replied. "I will be going to meet him when I leave here."

"Excellent!" said Geoffrey. He quickly scribbled a note for Anthony and gave it to her.

When she had left Thomas quizzed his son about the note, anxious to know if it contained anything that would jeopardise their release.

"What kind of fool do you think I am, old man?" Geoffrey snapped.

Thomas shrugged and went to sit by the wall where he quietly ate some of the fare Jane had left, contemplating the morrow when he would see Joan and Richard again. Geoffrey rubbed his hands together; he had a very smug smile on his face as he leaned against the cell door.

After two glorious weeks together, Richard and Joan finally received the summons from Sir Francis. Once everyone was seated in his small office Walsingham unveiled his plan. Thomas and Geoffrey were to be released from the Tower by 'traitor's gate' and rowed three miles downriver by Walsingham's own men to where Joan and Richard would be waiting with horses. They would travel together as an ordinary family group without too much haste to avoid raising any suspicion. They were to continue in this way until the road veered away from the river some miles away from the cove where Sir Edmund's ship would be waiting for them sheltered from any prying eyes.

There they would take to the boat that had been left tied to the bank in readiness for them. This would also throw off anyone who might be following them. Although it would be getting dark by now Sir Francis couldn't risk them being seen from the lookout post that sat on a bend in the river two miles upstream from the creek. They were to leave the boat, hidden in the overhanging branches that reached into the river, out of sight from the observation post. They would travel the rest of the way on foot.

"You will be able to remember all these instructions?" said Sir Francis to Richard, more of a statement than a question.

"I suppose I'll have to. When do we leave?"

Richard asked.

"You'll need to leave within the hour in order to rendezvous with the boat. You will find that two horses have been left at the stables for Thomas and Geoffrey. I presume you'll be taking your own mounts."

"Yes, but what do you propose we do with them when we take to the boat?" Joan asked him.

"It is very concealed where the boat has been left. They will be quite safe there until you return," answered Walsingham.

"I don't suppose it has occurred to you that there will only be two of us returning. Surely you don't expect Joan to row a boat upstream, possibly against the tide by then, do you?" asked Richard, at risk of losing his temper again at Walsingham's seemingly high-handed methods.

"No, I don't, Richard." Walsingham smiled at Joan. "Sir Edmund took on two extra hands specifically, to return with you and Joan."

"Oh, I see," said Richard, the wind somewhat taken out of his sails. Joan tried to disguise the smile that was creeping across her face.

"It's time to begin your preparations," said Walsingham. "Good luck to both of you."

"Thank you, and I sincerely hope that this will be the last time that I'll be called upon to do a service of any kind for you. I have my own life to lead and don't have time for running about the countryside at your behest," Richard informed him.

Walsingham made no reply but stood and opened the door for Joan.

"Goodbye, Sir Francis," she said.

Richard followed her into the corridor, mentally reviewing his instructions to make sure he'd remembered everything. Typical Walsingham, nothing written down! He'd never met such a conniving, devious man in his life. Nor did he ever want to meet him again.

Now to get Geoffrey and Thomas safely despatched from the realm and then return home to some semblance of order. Geoffrey was another man he had no wish to meet again once he'd left England for the colonies—even if he was Joan's brother.

CHAPTER FIFTEEN

The Reckoning

Joan and Richard stood nervously on the riverbank waiting for the boat that would be carrying Thomas and Geoffrey to appear upriver. Joan couldn't stand still. She was terrified that something would happen to prevent them being released at the last minute. Surely Elizabeth wouldn't have had second thoughts about exiling them, especially not after the intimate conversation they'd had in the garden. However, she knew she would not believe that they were really safe until she could see them for herself. "Richard, where are they? Surely, they should be here by now."

"Patience, Joan. The Thames isn't the easiest river to negotiate even for those who know it well," he answered confidently, although he was beginning to feel uneasy himself. He had expected them to be here by now too. Walsingham had made no secret of the fact that he disapproved of the queen's decision and that in his opinion Thomas and Geoffrey they should be executed with the rest of the traitors. Surely, he wouldn't disobey Elizabeth and have them killed anyway. He would have the perfect opportunity now to have them thrown into the river and then accuse them of trying to escape! Although Richard had no liking for the man, he had to trust that Walsingham would keep his word. Yet if they didn't arrive soon there wouldn't be time to keep to the tight schedule he had been given. His prisoners needed to be aboard the ship on time for the tide to carry them away into exile. There was no margin for errors.

Finally, they saw a boat round the sweeping bend in the river.

"Oh, at last!" cried Joan, squeezing Richard's arm, unable to contain her excitement.

It seemed to take the little boat forever to finally reach the bank, because the boatmen were fighting the incoming tide which was trying to carry them back towards the Tower. After shouting to verify that Richard was the person to whom they were to relinquish their passengers, Walsingham's men put Thomas and Geoffrey ashore beside Joan and Richard; both prisoners had their hands tied in front of them. Without another word the boatmen pushed off from the bank and left as silently as they had arrived, thankful that they would now be rowing with the tide

Joan embraced her father tightly, but Geoffrey glared at Richard. "I hope you're not expecting me to grovel in gratitude, peasant," he sneered.

"Hardly," said Richard, returning his stare.

Geoffrey hadn't suffered too badly during his time in the Tower; he'd made sure that he got the most and the best of any food that arrived with Jane. On the other hand, the cold, damp conditions and the lack of any real sustenance had left his father ill and very weak. He had lost weight, had a very sickly pallor and his eyes were sunken.

Richard drew his knife and sliced through Thomas's bonds. "Thank you, Richard," he said, grasping Richard's hand. "I don't know how, but I'm sure you had something to do with our release from that hellhole."

"Not just me, sir," said Richard, nodding towards Joan. "It's time we were leaving here if we are going to reach the ship before the high tide."

Geoffrey walked over to Richard and held out his hands.

"You really don't think I'm that stupid, do you?" laughed Richard.

"You released my father," growled Geoffrey. "Why not me?"

"I trust Thomas," Richard replied, and helped the poor man into his saddle before mounting Diablo. Geoffrey stood his ground and glowered at Richard.

"Are you going to get into your saddle or must I throw you over it and tie you to your horse?" Richard asked him. "It makes no difference to me which way you ride, but ride you will."

Geoffrey managed to drag himself up onto his horse's back, cursing and swearing throughout.

"You'll ride alongside me," said Richard. "I want you in my sight at all times."

"What's the matter, peasant, are you afraid someone will come and spirit me away?" sneered Geoffrey.

"Unless you want to be gagged as well as bound, you'd better keep your mouth shut! I've no intention of listening to you mouthing off all night," said Richard angrily.

Geoffrey opened his mouth to make a comment but then thought better of it as he knew Richard meant what he said about the gag.

Joan rode alongside her father who was now wrapped in the warm cloak that she had brought for him. Geoffrey rode in sullen silence, occasionally casting a murderous look at Richard, who continued to scan their surroundings. The longer they rode, the more concerned Joan became about her father. Although he had rallied when he met Joan, he was now slumped over his saddle, unable to remain upright. She prayed that he would be able to complete the journey to the boat. He seemed to be getting weaker with each mile.

Finally, they reached the spot where the road

turned away from the river and found the boat exactly where they were told it would be. Walsingham was right about their horses, too; it would be difficult for anyone to see them from the road, especially in the gathering gloom. Everything had been planned meticulously.

Joan and Richard carefully helped Thomas climb down from his horse and made him as comfortable as possible in the bow of the boat. Geoffrey was still mounted. "Well, aren't you going to help me down?" he grumbled.

"I'm damn sure I won't," answered Richard. "You're a big boy now, you can get down yourself!" He turned to the boat again and heard the thump behind him as Geoffrey slid out of his saddle and landed flat on his back. After much muttering and swearing Geoffrey scrambled to his feet and walked to the boat. Joan guided him to the mid-section and helped him to sit down before he capsized it.

Richard tethered the horses before returning to the boat and sitting down beside Geoffrey. He finally cut the ties from Geoffrey's wrists, but promised to bury the knife between his shoulder blades if he tried to escape. Joan sat in the stern and took control of the tiller, while Richard motioned to Geoffrey take hold of one of the oars. "Surely you don't expect your father or Joan to row, do you?" said Richard, when Geoffrey made no attempt to reach for the oar.

"Why should I row? You're the peasant,"

Geoffrey snarled.

"For God's sake, Geoffrey!" Joan exclaimed. "You might think Richard's a peasant but you are a traitor and if we are found by anyone at all they will kill you on sight! Stop being so damned pig-headed and row!"

Richard turned to Joan and quietly reminded her that they needed to keep any noise to a minimum. She gave him a chastened look and nodded to show she understood.

Shocked by his sister's words Geoffrey begrudgingly took up his oar and on Richard's count they began to row. It was hard going as the tide was coming in and at times, they didn't seem to be making any headway at all. Geoffrey never stopped complaining and at one point stopped rowing altogether which sent them backwards and they lost many of the precious yards they'd worked so hard to gain. It was only after Richard threatened to take him back to the Tower where he would be hung, drawn and quartered that he started pulling on the oar again, muttering threats of his own through clenched teeth. Although Geoffrey didn't care a fig for his father's life, he was very fond of his own and he had no intention of going back into captivity or to the New World either if he had his way.

After what seemed an eternity Joan alerted them to the lights on the watchtower. They rowed to the shore and secured the boat ready for Joan and Richard to retrieve on their return journey. Richard's left shoulder was painful; the hard rowing had aggravated his recent wound. He also had more than a few blisters on his hands, as did Geoffrey, much to his disgust. Thomas, on the other hand, had slept for most of his time in the boat and the rest had done him good. He seemed a little stronger and more alert.

"My father's ship is moored in the cove on the other side of the headland," said Richard. "The lookouts on the tower face the river so we will make our way behind it and through the forest to reach the ship."

There didn't appear to be any clearly defined path that they could see and they didn't dare use a light to search for one for fear of alerting the guards on the watch tower. They had to navigate as best they could by the intermittent light of a nearly full moon as it peeped in and out of the clouds that were being lazily blown across it by the light breeze. Although the guards usually just watched the sea for signs of invaders or smugglers, it would be just their luck for one to look inland if they used a lamp.

They headed off towards the meeting point as the crow flies in the hope of coming across a trail of some sort. Even an animal trail would be better than nothing. To begin with Thomas managed to keep up well with the others as they scrambled through the undergrowth. Joan supported him as best she could as they clambered over fallen trees and forced their way through thickets of brambles. She did this without a word of complaint, just a dogged determination to get him to the ship and safety. Geoffrey, on the other hand, was in a rage and kicked out at anything that got in his way and let go a torrent of oaths when some thorns on a bramble scratched his face.

"Dear God, how much further is it?" Geoffrey loudly demanded, aiming a kick at an unfortunate hedgehog that wasn't quite quick enough to avoid being tossed into a mound of bracken.

"How the hell do I know! I've never been here before either." hissed Richard, rapidly losing patience with Geoffrey and his grievances. "If you don't make less noise, it won't matter anyway because we'll have been captured by the guards from the watchtower and on our way back to London. Sound travels much further at night when everything else is quiet and you sound like a herd of wild horses charging through the undergrowth. If you don't stop your incessant complaints, I'll bind your hands again and tie a gag around that big mouth of yours," he added.

Geoffrey glowered at him but kept silent.

"I hope it's not too much further, Richard, Father is tiring again and finding it difficult to keep to his feet," said Joan.

Richard had already noticed that Joan was

struggling with her father. "Let me take him for a while," Richard said. He slipped his arm around Thomas's waist and took his weight off Joan. "We'll look for somewhere to rest a while. We can't have too much further to go now I hope but it's difficult to know exactly where we are when the moon keeps disappearing."

They stumbled through a seemingly unending patch of bracken. Richard had kept Geoffrey within touching distance in case he made a run for it. Thomas was barely conscious when suddenly the bracken ended and they found themselves standing in a clearing.

"We'll rest there for a few minutes before we press on. I can hear the river again so we must be close to the ship now."

Richard eased Thomas down to rest against a tree trunk. As he straightened himself to look for Joan, he was caught completely off guard by Anthony, who had stepped out from the bushes on the other side of the clearing, brandishing a pistol. Before he could react, Richard was hit on the head from behind with something hard and his legs gave way under him. The weapon was a cudgel ably wielded by Geoffrey's other friend, Robert.

Joan screamed, not caring if it was heard by the watch tower soldiers or anybody else. She ran at Robert and slapped his face hard, then dropped to her knees beside Richard.

"About damn time too! I expected you hours

ago," Geoffrey complained. "You've no idea what that bastard of a peasant has put me through."

"We had no idea where to find you!" Robert answered. "Your directions weren't exactly explicit, Geoffrey! We just had to follow the racket you were making. Once you stopped, we had to approach unseen or all would be lost."

"Well, it's a damn good job for you that you weren't seen! Is the other half of the plan in place?" asked Geoffrey.

"Set and ready to go," Anthony said with a grin.

"What's going on, Geoffrey?" Thomas asked. He painfully pulled himself to his feet and leaned against the tree where he had been resting. He staggered a little closer towards Geoffrey but sat down on a fallen tree trunk, exhausted, before he reached his son.

Joan tried to rouse Richard without success. "Robert, what have you done?" she cried. "You've killed him!"

"No such luck. These weak-willed fools haven't got the guts for that," said Geoffrey.

Anthony offered the pistol to Geoffrey. "If you want him dead, you kill him."

"Don't be so damned stupid, Anthony!" Geoffrey returned. "A shot would be heard for miles around and in case you hadn't noticed we're very close to one of the queen's watch towers. The soldiers would be on us in no time. Are you sure everything is ready?"

"Everything just as you ordered and you'd better make sure we get paid. This has cost us a small fortune. Anthony and I have had to borrow a tidy sum to pay for this venture," said Robert.

"Pay for what venture? Geoffrey, what are you doing?" demanded Lord Thomas.

"Father, you didn't really believe that I would allow myself to be carted off to the New World or that I would be prepared to allow my sister to marry this peasant, did you?" Geoffrey snapped. "For God's sake man, she's the daughter of a lord and he's a nobody. Where's your pride?"

"I keep telling you, I am no longer a lord! Richard is the son of a knight and no doubt will soon be a knight himself. He's already more of a gentleman than you'll ever be," said Thomas angrily. "He loves Joan and she loves him."

"You didn't have any qualms about giving her to Lord de Luc even though she hated him," taunted Geoffrey. "At least *he* was a lord."

"I made the worst mistake of my life when I did that and I'll spend the rest of what life I've got left regretting it. For God's sake, Geoffrey, stop whatever you're doing or we'll both end up back in the Tower," pleaded Thomas.

Joan was kneeling beside Richard, his head cradled in her arms. She now looked at her brother, her eyes blazing. "Don't you dare tell me who I will or will not marry, Geoffrey! It has nothing at all to do with you. I've already been given mother's and father's blessings to marry

Richard and there's an end to it!"

"That can soon be amended, sister dear," drawled Geoffrey, a sardonic smile on his face.

Before Joan could speak again Richard began to stir. He put his hand to the back of his head and winced.

"Richard, my love, are you badly hurt?" Joan asked, stroking his forehead.

"I don't think so." He tried to get to his feet, but Joan gently pushed him back to the ground. "No, Richard, don't try to get up," she said. "You need to rest for a while before we go on."

Geoffrey smirked. "Oh, how very touching."

"Geoffrey, we must leave now," Anthony said. "The ship is waiting off the point and we must hurry or we'll miss the tide."

"What ship, Geoffrey? Our ship is moored in the cove, not off the point," said Thomas in some confusion.

"As I said, Father, I have no intention of letting myself be shipped to the New World. I'm for the continent where I have friends. You may come with us if you wish, but you'll need to make up your mind now." Geoffrey turned to Joan. "*You* can say goodbye to your peasant."

"I'm going nowhere with you now or at any other time," snapped Joan.

"Oh, but you are," Geoffrey answered, and raised his hand. Two sailors carrying a sack ran from the bushes where they had been waiting for Geoffrey's signal. They grabbed Joan and threw the sack over her head, securing it at the bottom before she had any time to react. One of them heaved her over his shoulder and both he and his companion vanished into the darkness.

"Geoffrey, what are you doing? This is madness!" shouted his father.

Richard tried to get up but Geoffrey put his foot on his chest and pinned him to the ground. "There's nothing you can do now, peasant," Geoffrey said. "You've lost her forever. I have someone in mind who will make a fine husband for her. Someone of her own status." He smirked at Richard. "Oh, by the way did you ever wonder who tripped Diablo when you were returning home from Topsham? What a pity you didn't break your neck as planned. You nearly caught us napping. We'd been watching for you in Topsham and once we'd seen you arrive, we knew it wouldn't be too long before you would head for home. We left to prepare the trap, ready for the following day, but then you surprised us by galloping along the road in the evening just minutes after we'd stretched the rope to test it. I was sure you were dead when you hit the ground so heavily and then lay so still. You've no idea how disappointed I felt when I heard that you'd survived. However, it's of no matter now. I have won and you have lost."

"How could you do such a despicable thing and how dare you do this to your own sister?" Thomas exclaimed. He used the last of his strength to launch himself at his son, but Geoffrey was too quick for him and stepped out of his father's path, causing Thomas to fall headlong into the bushes behind him.

Richard tried to get to his feet again while Geoffrey's attention was temporarily diverted, but he had only managed to get to his knees when Geoffrey turned and kicked him on the side of the head. "Goodbye, peasant," Geoffrey said. "Here's a little something else to remember me by."

He kicked Richard in the ribs. Richard moaned and fell to the ground yet again while Geoffrey, Anthony and Robert ran off in the same direction as the sailors who had taken Joan.

Thomas managed to extricate himself from the bushes and make his way over to where Richard lay, clutching his side. "Richard, I am so, so sorry," he said.

"It is not your fault, Lord Thomas." Still gasping for breath, Richard once again painfully attempted to get to his feet, but this time Thomas helped him to stand. The two of them were holding each other up and wondering what to do next when they heard voices coming towards them.

"Where the hell can they be?" said one of them. "Surely, they haven't got lost. They should have got here by this time."

Recognising Edmund's voice, Richard groaned, "Father, we're here."

Four men walked into the clearing, but as the moon was completely covered in cloud it was hard to make out who the other three men were. Even though he was still seeing double, Richard recognised Tom Ashe and One-Eyed-Jack. The other sailor was a stranger to him.

"Dear God, what happened to you?" asked Edmund, when he was close enough to make out Richard's bruised face.

"Geoffrey Marchemont happened to me, and he's taken Joan. We have to go after them and stop them before they reach the ship," said Richard, desperately trying to focus his eyes.

"What ship?" asked his father.

"The one that's waiting for them off the point," Thomas answered him.

Richard wiped his bleeding cheek on his sleeve. "We were ambushed by two of Geoffrey's friends and they had two sailors with them who put Joan in a sack and carried her off."

"I thought I caught a glimpse of another ship as we turned into the cove and I'd bet money on whose it is. This is just his kind of work. He'd top his own mother if he was paid enough!" snarled Jack.

"Look we're wasting time," Richard said impatiently. "We must get after them now before it's too late. If they catch the tide, we've lost them."

"You're not fit, my son. Go back to the boat with Lord Thomas and we'll go after Geoffrey and Joan," said Sir Edmund.

"Please don't argue with me, Father," Richard answered. "I'm going to bring Joan back or die trying."

"Very well," said his father, knowing he was defeated.

"You take Lord Thomas to the boat and wait for us there," Captain Ashe told the sailor who was with them.

"I'm afraid you might not catch them," Thomas fretted. "They've got quite a start on you."

"We'll take the smugglers route," said One-Eyed-Jack. "Keep close behind me and watch your footing. There's a long drop off the cliff if you slip. Are you sure you can cope?" he asked Richard, weighing up his injuries.

"Yes. Let's get going, we're wasting time!" Richard staggered off after Jack, holding his ribs, determined to get his hands on Geoffrey. Every step was agony but he would never give up. He would reach his beloved Joan before it was too late.

They slithered and slipped their way down to the shore, hanging on to whatever undergrowth they could to prevent themselves from falling to the beach below. After what seemed an age they finally arrived at the foot of the cliff. Richard's head felt ready to explode and every breath almost unbearable. He knew it was a miracle he hadn't fallen off the cliff on his way down in his condition, but despite their frantic effort to overtake Geoffrey and the others they were too late. Just as they scrambled over the shingle, they could see a small light bobbing up and down on the little boat that was midway between them and another light showing on the ship.

"Damn, damn, damn!" shouted Richard in frustration. "How the hell are we going to get to them now?" He paced backwards and forwards, muttering numerous oaths as he went. "Father, is there any way your ship could catch them?"

"By the time we got back to the ship and headed after them they would be long gone, my son," Edmund said sadly.

"Maybe there's another boat close by," Tom put in.

"Even if there was, we'd never see it in this light," Jack told them. He walked down to the water's edge. "Hawkins, is that you?" he bellowed.

"What if it is?" came the reply.

"Do you know who this is?"

"Aye! One-Eyed Jack!" Hawkins yelled. "I'd recognise that voice in Hell itself!"

"You have something in your boat that I want!" Jack shouted back.

"I've been well paid to take this cargo and I'm damned if I'm going to hand it over to you!" Hawkins returned.

"I'm not interested in the money—I just want the merchandise. If I don't get it you know you'll never rest easy again. I'll follow you until I find you and then I'll slit your throat from ear to ear," promised Jack.

Sir Edmund silently crossed himself while Richard held his breath for what seemed an eternity, waiting for the pirate's answer. After a few moments of silence, Hawkins replied, "Do you promise that neither me nor my men will be harmed?"

"I just want your cargo and nothing else," answered Jack.

There was a heart stopping delay before the little light finally began to retrace its journey and return to the shore. As soon as the boat beached, Jack and Tom took hold of an indignant Geoffrey. Richard lifted Joan, still tied in the sack, out of the boat and onto dry land. Anthony and Robert, in the meantime, took off into the night as fast as their legs would carry them.

"I'll take the lantern," said Jack, lifting it from the bow of the boat. "You won't need it to find your way back to your ship."

There was no objection from Hawkins, who pushed off again and was soon on his way with his crew to his own ship.

"We'll need to go back up the way we came or we'll not catch the tide," said Jack.

Richard finally managed to free Joan from the sack; she ran to Geoffrey and gave him a resounding slap across his face, but he was unable to retaliate as he was being held fast by

Tom. "What about the lady, sir, will she manage the climb?" Tom asked Richard, already mightily impressed by this feisty lady.

"Oh, don't you worry about the lady, Tom, she will cope very well," said Richard. Despite his discomfort, he smiled at the look of shock on Geoffrey's face.

"I thought I was lost, Richard, when they put me in the boat," Joan said breathlessly. "I'm not sure what happened but I could hear two men arguing and I think one was Geoffrey, but it was hard to hear anything clearly because the sack muffled the sound somewhat."

"We heard the argument, too. It was Captain Hawkins and Geoffrey. We didn't know who had won until we saw the boat return to the shore," said Richard.

They gave each other a quick kiss and again they set off to climb up the cliff as quickly as they dared.

Geoffrey, walking between Jack and Tom, almost lost his footing more than once. He became even more terrified than he already was when Jack threatened to throw him off if he didn't move more quickly.

They eventually reached their boat on the other side of the bluff. Thomas was delighted to see Joan was safe; he didn't even look at his son. Jack and another sailor bound Geoffrey's hands to prevent him causing any more trouble on the way to the ship and manhandled him into the boat, ignoring his loud protests. When Edmund and Richard were carefully settled and Joan had been helped aboard, they shoved off.

Jack and the other sailor made short work of the trip to the ship and they were soon alongside. It took a little while to get Richard and Thomas on board, as they both needed help to climb the ladder. Geoffrey was almost thrown up the ladder by Jack and yanked up by the scruff of the neck by Captain Ashe.

When they were all finally on the deck, Eleanor and Margaret rushed to meet them. Margaret flung herself into her husband's arms, almost knocking him off his feet. She was shocked to see the state he was in and sat him down on one of the crates that were still waiting to be stowed in the hold.

Eleanor gave Edmund a quick peck on the cheek before going to her battered son. "Oh, Richard, what has happened to you?" she said, examining his head. "This is just too much! You've not long recovered from one serious head injury!"

Richard moved her hand away from his face. "I shall be absolutely fine, Mother, please don't fuss."

Once everyone was on board and had greeted each other, Jack dragged Geoffrey across the deck. "What the hell do you think you're doing?" Geoffrey raged, now fully recovered from his ordeal on the cliff. "Don't you know who I am?

I'm the son of a lord! Get your hands off me, you scum!"

Jack spun him around and landed his fist right in the middle of Geoffrey's face. "Now shut your mouth," he spat. "I've heard enough of your prattling to last me a lifetime."

Geoffrey's lip was split and his nose bled. He was crying like a baby, his tears mingling with the blood that fell from his nose and now dripped onto his chest. Jack punched him in the ribs for good measure before he dropped him none too gently into the hold and secured the hatch.

"What will happen to him now?" Joan asked Captain Ashe.

"He'll be left to cool his heels living on water and ship's biscuit for a few days and then he'll be put to work with the crew until we reach our destination," he replied.

Richard smiled to himself. He knew the kind of treatment Geoffrey would receive from the sailors. It was going to be a long, hard and painful voyage for young Marchemont.

Edmund walked over to join his son. "How are you feeling?"

"As if I've been kicked by a mule and hit over the head with a mountain," Richard replied. "I must say, Father, that I was surprised to see One-Eyed-Jack with you when you found us."

"He came aboard just before we set sail. He said he needed to get out of the country for a while to let things settle down again,"

"What things?" asked Richard.

"I don't know and I don't want to know. Whatever it is it will likely be something very unsavoury. The only reason I allowed him to sign on was because Tom told me how he had stood by you when you were in danger and had a hand in saving your life. I'm not happy about it but since Tom is prepared to have him as a member of the crew I decided to give him the chance."

Joan appeared at Richard's side. She slipped her arm through his and looked up lovingly into his battered face. "Oh, Richard, I was so afraid that you wouldn't reach me in time to save me from being taken away to France!"

"Did you really think I'd ever let you get away from me now or ever?" he said, thanking his stars for that roughest of diamonds, One-Eyed-Jack.

"There has been so much going on I almost forgot to tell you that we were asked to take on one extra passenger at the last minute by order of the queen herself," said Edmund.

"Who is it?" Richard returned. "I thought this was supposed to be a secret mission."

"He's a Protestant minister being sent out to establish a church in the colony by Royal command," his father answered.

"Oh, I see," said Richard, rather disinterestedly.

"No, I don't think you do, son. Ministers can officiate at weddings and I wondered since we have the bride and groom and both sets of parents present whether you and Joan might like to take advantage of the situation," suggested Edmund, his eyes twinkling.

Richard stared at him like a beached fish; when he looked at Joan her expression was very similar. However, she recovered herself more quickly and squeezed his arm. Richard searched her face for a reaction. The smile she bestowed on him gave him courage. "Will you marry me, Joan?" he asked her. "Now?"

She raised her eyebrows.

"Oh God, have I read that smile wrong!" he thought, his heart landing in his stomach.

"I think, sir, that when a gentleman asks a lady to marry him, he goes down on one knee or she might not believe he's serious," replied Joan with a mischievous smile.

Richard painfully got down on one knee and took her hand in his. "My dearest love, will you please say you'll marry me before I topple over and fall flat on my face?"

Joan nearly collapsed in a heap of laughter as she tried to get him up on two feet again. "Of course I'll marry you, you goose. Now hurry and go and find the minister before we end up going to the New World," she said, and pushed him off down the deck towards the captain's cabin.

He soon returned followed by the minister, who was clutching a plain cross and a bible. Thomas and Edmund had found a table and

Margaret covered it with a pretty cloth. Richard and Joan held each other's hands and looked at each other. The love in their eyes said it all.

Then Richard began to laugh.

"What's so funny?" asked Joan.

"We are about to get married and I look like a wounded soldier with ripped leggings and doublet and my face all covered in blood and bruises as well as having a couple of broken ribs. Whereas you, my beautiful bride, are wearing riding boots caked in mud, torn breeches, a filthy ripped shirt and the most unruly hair I've ever seen!

They were still laughing when the minister called everyone to order and so the ceremony began. Everything went well until the exchange of the rings. Nobody had given a thought to the lack of rings. Joan's mother quickly removed her own wedding ring with a smile of approval from Thomas and gave it to Richard. Edmund gave his ring to his future daughter-in-law with a nod from Eleanor. At last, they were pronounced man and wife. They embraced and kissed each other hungrily.

Everyone on board cheered and clapped and their respective parents rushed to congratulate them, but their celebrations were short lived. "We should be setting sail sir or we'll miss the tide," Captain Ashe told Sir Edmund.

"Very well. Time to say your goodbyes, everyone," said Edmund.

Joan embraced her father. Tears in his eyes, he asked her, "Joan, can you ever forgive me for what I tried to force you to do?"

"I forgave you long ago," she said, and kissed his cheek. When she turned to her mother, Lady Margaret was already crying. "I love you, Mother," Joan said, and hugged her.

"I have always loved you so much, my dear," Margaret wept, returning her daughter's embrace. "Even though an ocean will separate us I will always be thinking of you."

"And I you," said Joan.

Richard shook hands with Lord Thomas and wished him well. "Who knows what the future holds? Hopefully one day we'll meet again," he said. Richard then took both of Lady Margaret's hands in his. "I will take great care of Joan and always keep her safe," he promised.

"Thank you, Richard," she whispered. "I know you will."

"Richard," his father said, "it's time."

Richard let go of Lady Margaret's hands and went to his father. "Don't tell me you and Mother are off to the New World too," he joked.

Edmund laughed. "No son, not this time. Once we've cleared the river and are out to sea, we will be transferred to one of our other ships which will take us back to Topsham. From there we will return to the manor."

Eleanor hugged Joan and kissed both of her cheeks. "You are the daughter I always longed for and you will be the perfect wife for my son," she said.

"After we've reported to Walsingham, Joan and I will leave London and meet you there," Richard told them.

"Richard, we must go," Edmund said.

"I know," Richard answered. He followed his father's gaze to where Joan was still talking to Eleanor, and walked to Joan's side. "Now then, wench, give this peasant upstart a kiss," Richard demanded playfully, his heart bursting with the love he felt for her. "And if you treat me well, I might even be good to you."

Joan left her parents with a last embrace and kissed Richard tenderly on his lips. "And if you don't treat me well, you'll be sorry," she said with a wicked twinkle in her eye.

Despite the terrible pain in his ribs, Richard gathered Joan into his arms and handed her gently to the four men waiting for them in the boat, and then joined them. As the sailors hauled on the boat's oars, the sailors on the ship began to raise the anchor and hoist the mainsail. When Joan and Richard reached the bank all that could be seen of the ship now beginning its maiden voyage was a single light on its stern. Lord and Lady Marchemont were on their way to freedom and a very different way of life, as was their worthless son.

Richard and Joan were also beginning their own voyage. They were embarking on their new life together as husband and wife, against all the odds.

.

ABOUT THE AUTHOR

Lil Niven

Lil lives in a small Ayrshire town in Scotland, with husband Pete. Lil is the mother of three grown-up children, Loraine, Elizabeth and Heather and enjoys walking, gardening, reading and crafting when not writing books. This is the first of four books in this series.

Printed in Great Britain
by Amazon

80811655R00200